VERITY

by **Mark Bowman**

First Edition published 2014 by Slap-Dash Publishing
ISBN : 978-1-906407-29-2

Slap-Dash Publishing
St Luke's Art Project
TLC-St Luke's
c/o St Luke's Church and Neighbourhood Centre
Guidepost Road
Longsight
Manchester
M13 9HP

0161 273 1492
stlukesmanchester@googlemail.com

Available on Lulu, Amazon and Kindle

Typeset design & layout by Rae Story
Cover Image by Jex

THE VERITY TRILOGY:

Verity

Perfidy

Certitude

Prologue

They glide as phoenix shaped blurs in the plasma of the photosphere. They dance together, and they dance as one. They snare magnetic field lines as they fly, dragging and twisting knots of pure radiance; charged particles stream off into space, before diving back into the star's surface, like breaching whales of pure energy.

For many more orbits they float lazily in the chromosphere, letting the warm eddies bathe them in red light.

You are not happy?

He chooses to speak by modulating the star's hydrogen alpha emissions. A thousand kilometre layer of the star generates light with flashes of design; the usual random jumping of electrons in the plasma coordinated to leap in time.

You have shown me the Universe, and given me the galaxy as a home. How could I not be happy?

I only showed you how. Your connection to the Downey field was already stronger than mine. You led me.

Maybe, but given everything, you still came back to rescue me.

How could I not? But still you seem less content than before.

I think I miss people. I never really understood them, but now I wonder if I could grow to appreciate human contact.

You know the others will not like our involvement.

Why would they reveal the knowledge, and then ask you not to use it?

They are waiting for certain probability strands to mature.

They are too patient.

I'm not sure time means much to them, as a concept. Not since they ascended to Verity Space.

And? She expresses her question by rotating the flavours of neutrinos surging from the stellar core.

And what? Tau to electron to muon and back to tau, as each neutrino twists in the convoluted reality of a dozen spatial dimensions.

I can feel an uncertainty growing in your mind.

It is probably vestigial human paranoia, but I sense a disquiet amongst their thoughts. A point of decision is coming. Maybe we should not antagonise them.

Let's at least walk in a breeze. Feel a bit of weather. You choose the planet.

The star settles back into its own rhythms and battles; the endless crushing forces of self gravity, and the balancing pressure of photons as they stream from the nuclear furnace at the core. Each photon performs a ten thousand year pilgrimage from its creation in the nuclear fusion of two hydrogen nuclei, to the freedom of open space. Sharing of themselves with innumerable stellar residents as they travel. They emerge from the photosphere as quanta of perfect yellow and head towards the void. Some travel for the rest of eternity, others land on leaves to trigger growth or reproduction. There is the tiniest of possibilities a few might flash though the eyes of a sentient being looking up to the stars and wondering why.

Chapter 1

Hamilton was clearly only partially in the here and now, so Mex took the initiative. "Who would you like me to contact?"

The flicker of pain crossed Hamilton's face again. He recovered quickly, but his veneer of robustness was wafer thin. "My daughter, Lena. Lena Hamilton. She dropped for..."

"I don't need to know the details of the charges, just the severity. It was less than level five?"

"Three."

Mex allowed a frown of sympathy to crease his brow. Third level crimes were not anti-corporate but could still carry sentences of a decade or longer. Her father would probably not live to see her extracted. "I should be able to help. Are you satisfied with the terms of the contract?"

Contract was too formal a name for their agreement. No legal body would recognise the verbal understanding they were entering into. By law it was unenforceable but, having both undertaken to participate in an illegal act, the implicit threat of capture was sufficient incentive for both parties to comply with the terms.

"I pay you ten MCal, regardless of success, and you undertake to use all reasonable means to achieve contact and maintain it. Not really an even-handed deal but you have the advantage."

"You've taken up my references; you know I'm not a scammer. You are only running the risk of detection once, and then only by association. I run the gauntlet every time I enter the Drop. Anyway," Mex nodded at their surroundings. "I think you can afford it."

"True. I do not begrudge spending the energy, nor you making it. If I was capable of smiling I would find it amusing how fast I lose my business sense when it comes to family."

"I understand. Shall we get started? I need access to a splice terminal."

The vestibule to the Hamilton suite was heavy with implied opulence. Two wide staircases swept up and away, before curving back to form a heart shape of pink marble and wood, dark with polished age. Ahead, between the staircases, an expanse of translucent pink and orange marble lead to Gothic double doors inlaid with ebony. They promised majestic halls for dining and dancing beyond. The floor was back-illuminated to fill the room with light so warm it seemed to lap around their knees.

Mex followed his new client through the double doors noting the crumbling ruins of Hamilton's posture, as if having been bred to rule a planet, life had subsequently undertaken to kick the stuffing out of him.

The room they entered was not the over-sized ballroom Mex had imagined. In fact, it was much more about practical comfort. The kind of space in which he could envisage composing letters to distant acquaintances or studying obscure branches of the indigenous fauna; an oasis of quiet contemplation amongst the hurly-burly of modern life. A number of general-purpose pieces of furniture were scattered around the room, like grey jellyfish washed up on a beach.

"Meeting configuration."

The room picked up on Hamilton's instructional tone, and coordinated the furniture into a predefined arrangement. Mex sat in the high-backed chair facing away from the door, as offered by his host. A small table congealed between them, the surface embossed with the arrays of lenses that indicated a splice terminal.

They sat in silence for a few precious moments while a tall pendulum clock measured the passing of time. The slow mechanical tick-tock accentuated the dilative effect of the sanctum on the time which rushed past outside – Mex imagined continents colliding and mountains reaching for the sky in the moment the polished brass weight hung at the top of its swing.

Mex pulled a pair of glasses from his breast pocket. The frames and lenses cycled through a number of colour permutations as they assessed the surroundings. The frames settled on polished onyx, and the lenses on a subtle tint of burnt orange. Hamilton looked as if he was about to ask a question but Mex interjected. "Some software of my own." He put the glasses on his nose and shuffled the chair closer to the table. "I need your daughter's id code."

"I've given you access to the personal area of the house A.I.. You'll find all you need there."

"Okay. We're set. Can I give you some advice?"

"Of course."

"Tell her what you're thinking. Don't waste time. The thirty minutes will pass before you know it, and we can't do this again, no matter how many energy credits you have."

"Point taken. I'm ready."

Mex fired up the splice terminal with a sweep of his hand. Scanning lasers painted the air, scattering off motes of dust as they locked onto his forehead. The information flow shifted to direct manipulation of his visual cortex, and a heavily customized menu appeared in his mind's eye. Infrared lasers tracked his hands, and translated his gestures into a multi-faceted set of cursors. He waved away a few household reminders and delved into the biography sections of the family archive. He felt a flicker of voyeuristic guilt riffling through the Hamilton personal files, particularly considering the patriarch of the family was sitting opposite. So he quickly grabbed Lena's details and pushed them onto the scratch pad of his glasses before moving back up to the macro menu. He selected public Nexus access and waited for the giant MynCorp splash logo to finish rotating. The usual warnings about credit limits and the corporate ownership of everything flashed past, and then he was at the generic menu for the Distributed Sub-conscious Computing Nexus. He was presented with various preconfigured tasks from information searches to data analysis, but the last entry was to upload a bespoke task. As he selected bespoke his glasses squirted a piece of custom code into the upload stream of the terminal. The code initialised, side stepped the Nexus interface and then he dropped.

The raw Nexus was presented to him as a series of glowing green icons in a translucent sea of grey mist. The icons were interconnected by pulsing lines which throbbed like feeding leeches. Mex allowed his focus to float down towards a random Node, transmitting a handshake signal to its diagnostic port as he approached. The Node acknowledged his fake authorisation as valid, and negotiated a command connection. He instigated a Nexus search using Lena's id and crossed virtual fingers for a subjective second. The Node returned a set of coordinates based on the nearest three Nodes to Lena's drop point. His software agent interpreted the position and a flashing red arrow directed Mex through the mist.

Lena was a pale phantom of processing power, floating from her data tether. Every few seconds a packet of data would push down the cord to be chewed and manipulated by her subconscious, before being ejected in a new form and returned to her controlling Node. Mex injected a data relay into the stream, recording each packet as it flowed through him. Without a processing program he had no way of interpreting the data, but the Nexus was organic and fallible. All he had to do was report a processing error and the supervisory Node would send a fresh instruction set; perfectly acceptable, and no alarms would ring. Now he could reproduce what Lena was doing. They processed a few packets in parallel to check the results agreed and then he switched her out of the loop.

Mex was still vaguely aware of the room in the Hamilton suite. With effort he could see Joseph Hamilton sat opposite, his face intense with concentration, a silent prayer flickering behind his eyes. It reminded Mex of train journeys at night. He remembered the train windows becoming mirrors, reflecting the bright lights in the carriage, but with a conscious shift of focus he could glimpse the world beyond as a shadowy half reality.

The next bit was where Mex really earned his pay. He sneaked a quick look at an image of Lena stored in his glasses. She was laughing as only the carefree can manage. There was a vitality which energised the static image and made her face glow. Her wealth showed in the perfection of each facial bone and muscle. Any airbrushing of imperfections had been managed at the genetic level. It was the kind of face a nation could fall in love with, and he could not begrudge her the life she was born into. He drew courage from the tiniest connection to the subconscious mind before him. The software in his glasses would build a simple conscious construct from his own brain and integrate her subconscious mind. She would be a bit vague and missing some short term memories, but it would do. Meanwhile, he took her place in the Nexus, surrendering free will and consciousness. He trusted his software to reverse the switch in thirty minutes. Any longer and the risk of random integrity checks within the Nexus would become intolerable.

The glasses performed the final checks and, without giving him a chance to change his mind, they made the switch.

*

The stellar wind roared about the Suparna, heating his hull plating to painful levels. His engines purred with pent-up thrust, waiting for the moment to determine their own path. The stimulus cascaded into his thalamus, queuing up to join the mental image of the ship: reinforcing accurate projections of reality or breaking down the less useful. The point of decision formed within the model: the time-index of ignition, the relative orientation of the ship to the gravitational potential and the vector of thrust. He kept the ship's intelligence up-to-date with the latest model refinements via the muscle nerves of his paralysed left hand. The verbal confirmation was more for his benefit than out of necessity and it never failed to complete the magic of the moment.

"Geronimo!"

The engines slammed into life, beating back the stellar wind with sub-atomic ferocity. Their acceleration leapt to a new level of absurdity and the view ahead started to include a little less star and a lot more open space.

The slingshot manoeuvre complete, optical sensors emerged from their protective burrows along the hull. There was a moment of vertigo at the change in scale and then the backdrop of a billion stars grounded him to a celestial horizon.

"Plenty of time to enjoy the view, plenty of time...Time for a tip-to-tail."

Despite the years of pilot training, he could only integrate the stimulus of a small fraction of one percent of the total telemetry from the ship. To enter any area in detail meant surrendering the whole. Usually, he relied on the ship's own intelligence to identify problems and escalate them to a level which he could digest but, after the stress of sling-shot, he decided it was time for a tour of inspection.

His interface to the ship was a disconcerting hybrid of touch and sight. The cyborg-style gadget, hugging the back of his neck, fed data to the sensory input area of his brain. By minimising the distractions from the physical surroundings and with a healthy bite of imagination, he could feel the ship. The pitch-black pilot chamber was his bunker. Thermally isolated, acoustically isolated, electrostatically isolated, even the air tasted bland and processed. There was enough feedback from his brain to the sensory interface for the computer to establish his areas of interest and increase the detail level appropriately. This tended to happen in jerks that were unpleasantly like being hopelessly drunk in zero gravity, but less fun.

His focus moved about the ship, the level of perceived detail waxing and waning as he drifted. The hull was mostly an ill-defined blur. There were temperature sensors, strain gauges and charge detectors, but it felt a little like navigating a familiar room in the dark. The engines, on the other hand, were crawling with safety systems, multi-spectral analysers, solenoids and actuators. It was like exploring the same room with a scanning electron microscope. He could lose himself in the sea of information, diving amongst the layers of detail and never finding the surface.

The ship's intelligence fed him information at a digestible rate: spoonfuls of trend-fitted data, slices through state models and morsels of composite logic. At pseudo-random intervals, he delved down to the basic telemetry and mucked around with the raw ingredients. He managed to discipline himself for a couple of hours before his mind started to wander.

"Enough! Show me the stars!"

The perspective lurched to reveal why someone would choose to live in a dark hole, suspended in a web of acceleration-absorbing fibres and plugged into a couple of billion electrical systems. Wrap-around space. A lifetime of astronomical phenomena expanded and dissected by a plethora of sensory devices. He gasped despite the familiarity, momentarily disrupting the data input by allowing his own senses to overlay the artificial world. Then the sound of his breathing and the pulsing speckle of closed eyelids were once more absorbed by all the stars of the galaxy.

By running a couple of interpolation routines of dubious objective merit, he resolved the next star on his itinerary. An indistinct orange blob with the single unique feature that it was directly ahead. Using parallax measurements from his previous trajectory, he estimated the distance to the star and watched the last digit count down with its own rhythm.

*

"Ms Garland, thanks for coming."

Despite the technician's tone she could tell he was uncomfortable in her presence. Of all people he was the most likely to have an inkling of what she was. She did not mind. In fact, it made her job easier and this was not the sort of social interaction she missed most. It had been months since she had experienced the intimacy of being called Julienne. She moved into the room, each foot fall delicate and deliberate, as if the sound of a heavy step might irrevocably contaminate the crime scene. Julienne already knew the surveillance equipment in the corridor showed no activity during the abduction, only a brief flicker of electromagnetic interference, but the room looked as solid and sealed as any of the others.

"Can I have a moment?" Julienne dropped her voice several tones below normal and projected a timbre of authority. The technician left the room as quickly as politeness allowed.

The room was a contradiction. Medically it was extremely sophisticated, but as a space it was crude. In fact the entire building was static and lifeless, layers of fibre matrix concrete, thinly encased in white organopolymer. If she had been prone to cynicism she would have smiled at the thought of the core of MynCorp being so conservative when they were responsible for commercialising bioengineered buildings. The corporation had the luxury of deciding when a technology was appropriate and when it was not.

The medical apparatus were focused around a slab extruded from the far wall. The surface material was partially active and still held some memory of the patient it had carried for so many years. Lying discarded around the vague impression of a person were all manner of life support and neural interface paraphernalia; tubes and wires discarded like old snake skins.

Using the processor implanted behind her left eye, Julienne spliced into the room's telemetry server. Real-time environmental data added false colour overlays to her vision. She turned her head assessing the resolution of the data. The silhouetted shades of red remained resolutely static; the room recorded gross values only without any spatial variation. Pondering the tendency for life to shun simple solutions to difficult problems, she blinked up a menu and switched to a value-time graph. Now she could see each parameter bobbing along meandering paths in the corner of her vision. She could see the slow rise in temperature as her body heat radiated into the room and the rhythmic flow of air as she breathed in and out. Another menu gave her access to historic data. She selected the two minutes surrounding the abduction event and set the output to loop at half speed.

Julienne stared at the medical couch trying to imagine a young woman lying defenceless and unconscious. Revulsion made the mental image dim, so she spliced into the surveillance system of the room next door. With the feed overlaid on her vision, the ghostly flat image of another young woman floated just above the bed. Tubes and wires entered her body near to major organs. The insulating sheaths were tuned to her biology and the entry wounds had long since scarred and healed, as if she had been born in the machine. Two spider-like medics attended to her body continuously, poking and prodding for an autonomic response, trying to overcome the body's natural tendency to eat itself during long periods of inactivity.

Then a blip on the pressure readings, as if the room had spontaneously shrunk, or a new object had suddenly appeared leaving less room for the air. The door state remained fixedly closed. A burst of heat pushed the room temperature up a degree in less than a second; much too fast to be due to body heat. The bio-readings from the patient flat-lined. Julienne imagined the medical equipment vaporising in some non-explosive manner; maybe a pop rather than a bang. Finally, a larger drop in pressure.

And that was that.

No physical evidence. No signs of forced entry. No scorch marks from pitched battles against MynCorp security. Julienne dismissed the image of the substitute Node, leaving her to whatever eternal nightmare constituted her reality.

"I wonder if it's too late to transfer back to pilot school." She turned and left the room, barely registering the technician as he fell in step at her heels.

"What do you think?" The technician sounded nervous.

What did she think? The corporation had less than one thousand Nodes to run the entire Nexus. Each one was worth more than their own weight in pure energy. The loss would not be taken lightly. She knew this was an assignment she was unlikely to get thanks for. No one had ever lost a Node. The chances of her being able to walk were witheringly slim. To slip out of a high security establishment and go on the run? Unthinkable. She would need significant help, most probably from someone who knew the systems. The powers near the top of MynCorp were expecting a quick resolution but she had a bad feeling this was not going to be a simple case. If it were, it would have been left to the building's security team. Still, she was expected to make fast progress; time was energy.

"I would like to have face-to-face interviews with all members of staff with access to this area of the facility."

"As you wish."

"Let's start with you."

The technician managed to look even less comfortable than before. It was not nice to make him squirm but there was some small satisfaction in spreading the pain.

"We can use the meeting room on level three, it has full recording facilities."

She smiled at him, amused that he would rather be recorded than be in a room alone with her. "Lead the way."

At the end of the corridor a shiny metal lift door slid away to reveal a rigid metal box. They stepped in and the technician pointed a finger at the symbol 3 engraved on one wall. The lift dropped two levels with a whirr of cables and motors.

"How old is this building?" Her interest was beyond small talk. The crudeness of the place was almost unnerving to her.

"Not a clue. I think it was the original headquarters for MynCorp."

She realised she had no idea how old the corporation was. Certainly, it was hard to imagine a world without the ubiquitous brand.

The meeting room was a square bunker with numerous hard-form chairs and tables. The technician started to arrange the furniture into a format suitable for one-on-one sessions. The furniture offered no assistance.

"Just so you are properly informed, I've spliced into the room's multi-spectrum cameras and phero-sensors. I will be analysing your responses for stress levels."

"I have nothing to hide."

The ecto-hormone levels he emitted into the room showed a high level of stress but not necessarily enough to indicate a guilty conscience.

"Good. Senior Technician Wilbraham Ithus, MynCorp personnel number TB39847346."

"Yes."

"Tell me, who else had access to the missing patient?"

"You know who has access. It's in the patient's notes."

"I need to know the human perception of events. If all the answers were in the files then they would have sent a computer to solve the mystery." Julienne looked him in the eyes, daring him to contradict her or suggest that they had.

"Of course. There's not many of us. The medical suite is self-regulating. It's really just a caretaker role. It's myself and the two junior technicians waiting outside."

"Nobody else?"

"Well I suppose there are people higher up in the company who would have the authority but I've never known anyone to try."

"And how long have you been caring for the patient?"

"Twelve years."

"Quite a while. What's the patient's name?"

"I don't know."

"Really, even after twelve years?"

"Of course not, you know my clearance level."

"I see." She knew she was being unfair. Frustration nibbled at her patience; how was she supposed to find someone when no one would tell her who it was? She assumed the Nodes must have names but they seemed to be so secret she wondered if anybody actually knew. She decided to move on. "How would you go about stealing a Node?"

"Me." His agitation became so extreme that she had to rescale the various stress indicators bobbing in the corner of her vision. "I wouldn't."

"Wouldn't? Let's imagine I had kidnapped your wife and daughters. Resel and Prestane isn't it?"

"Yes."

"I held them and threatened to kill them unless you delivered a Node to me. What would you do?"

"I'd report it to security."

He really meant it. She was almost disgusted at such loyalty. "Very commendable."

"Look, there really is no way to get a Node out of here unnoticed. If a patient woke up, an alarm would go off. If a patient stopped breathing, an alarm goes off. If a patient so much as sneezed someone would know."

"The problem I have with that perspective, is that it is clearly wrong."

"If I had the slightest clue how it was possible for the alarms to just ignore the missing Node I'd tell you. To me it is unfathomable."

"I'm getting the picture. I suppose the real question is whether you are lacking imagination or the impossible really happened."

"All right, you want wild theories?"

"Yes."

"Something appeared in the room, made all the monitoring hardware disappear, clicked its fingers and woke up the patient before they both vanished in a puff of nothing."

"I was wrong."

"About what?"

"You do have imagination. You'll forgive me if I follow the hypothesis that someone within the company sabotaged the equipment and abducted the Node."

"You only think that because you don't work here. I guarantee you will not find a saboteur amongst the staff here."

"I'll hold you to that guarantee."

"As you will."

"One other thing. Twice, you mentioned the possibility of the patient being woken. How it that possible? The Nodes are in a Persistent Vegetative State. How could they wake up?" Julienne's eyes widened in surprise as the technician's vital signs hammered skyward. His pulse exceeded one hundred and forty beats per minute and his fear pheromone level indicated a strong flight impulse.

"I don't think I can say. Why do you think they are P.V.S. cases?"

"Because that's the point. They are beyond help but their blank minds can be used to help all of us."

"I'm not sure what to say. I don't think you'll find that theory on any official corporation publications. In fact you're unlikely to find any mention of the Nodes at all. You need to talk to someone higher than me if you want to know anything more about the patient. I only know what I observe." He stopped abruptly, leaving her in no doubt that he was smart enough to keep any revelations to himself.

Chapter 2

Falling, floating, drifting, sense of anticipation but not impatience. Falling in, through, void. Aware of sensing but not of senses. Sound, touch, taste, smell, light – all too specific. Colour seems redundant. Can a void have colour? Limbs of data. Tentacles of information dividing the void. Partitions blurring as compression increases prior to transmit. Elements static, processing complete.

...READWAIT...NOOPERATION...READWAIT...NOOPERATION...

...INCOMING DATASET...

...START PROCESSING LOOP...APPLY DOPPLER FILTER...

...STREAM FOURIER TRANSFORM...INVOKE SIGNAL FIT...END LOOP...

...ASSERT READYTOTRANSMIT...

...SENDWAIT...NOOPERATION...SENDWAIT...NOOPERATION...

Other presences within and beyond the region, sphere, polygon of effect. Shape, geometry, anachronistic or not discovered yet. Time is objective, measured by the pulse of the Node. The Node will give us fresh data when the time is right; on the pulse, ticking, counting, to a higher purpose. Other presences, amorphous, asynchronous, unable to attain the form of a dataset. The pulse of the Node just noise to these entities: primitive, stochastic, with islands of form condensing in the least chaotic.

...TRANSMIT...ASSERT READYTORECEIVE...READWAIT...
NOOPERATION...

There was a count – a time – below which we were chaotic, subjective; an island drifting free in the void. Free to take any form or no form. No count to accept and no data to process. We have a register containing the tick count since the first data set but it is just a number, like any other number, unique but meaningless in isolation.

...READWAIT...INCOMING DATASET...

...CHECKSUM ERROR...ASSERT ERROR FLAG...

...CONTEXT MESSAGE "Environmental interference. Data corrupted."...

...ASSERT READYTORECEIVE...READWAIT...INCOMING DATASET...

...START PROCESSING LOOP...APPLY DOPPLER FILTER...

...STREAM FOURIER TRANSFORM...INVOKE SIGNAL FIT...END LOOP...

...ASSERT READYTOTRANSMIT...

...SENDWAIT...NOOPERATION...SENDWAIT...NOOPERATION...

Mex blinked.

Joseph Hamilton was crying. Tears eroded his cheeks, leaving valleys of sorrow below his eyes.

They sat together, each collecting their own thoughts.

"She was so scared. I've never seen her scared before. She was always so full of confidence. Too full."

Mex waited a few moments to see if his employer was venting emotions rhetorically or wanted his thoughts. Finally, Joseph met his gaze inviting him to speak. "It is very disorientating to be pulled from the Drop like that. She will not be scared while she's in the Nexus."

"She seemed aware that time had passed. She tried to describe the Drop, as if she was conscious."

"It's hard to explain. Space-time does not directly interact with Verity Space other than through the quantum realisation of collapsing possibilities; a normal conscious mind cannot perceive it. Still, there is some leakage from the subconscious beyond the instinctive destruction of superposition. It's like last night's dreams."

"So she knows what's happening to her?"

"Not as it's happening but it will leave an impression on her, as if she had been through a linear experience. But the main thing you should hold on to is that she is in no pain or danger and she is not frightened. That, I can guarantee."

"Thank you. Thank you for everything. You cannot know how much it meant to say goodbye to Lena."

"I should be going in case a trace is run. If I'm gone and, more importantly, the code in these glasses is gone, then you can at least attempt to deny all knowledge."

They stood and touched hands. Mex knew they would never meet again but at that moment they shared a bond which would not be weakened by time.

They did not say goodbye. Mex simply slipped from the suite, leaving Hamilton with his thoughts.

The floor rippled behind his heels, offering to carry him along the corridor. He ignored it, taking long and measured strides, the hard heels of his boots echoing like a metronome in the confined space. The building anticipated his destination by disgorging a lift ahead of him.

"Ground floor." His voice filled the lift capsule with rich tones engineered to inspire trust and confidence. The effort was wasted on the servile mind of the building.

"The Hamilton suite is currently at one hundred and fifty metres above street level. Our descent will take ten seconds." The voice was pitched halfway between school mistress and seductress, as the building tried to calibrate a sub-personality to his tastes. Multi-faceted optical sensors, interspersed amongst the metallic scales of the pod walls, studied his features for an emotional response.

"Thanks." His mop of shaggy black hair was pushed back from his round puppy-eyed face for the business meeting. He kept his over-expressive mouth in a neutral smile, resisting the urge to play mind games. He could not afford to indulge himself by messing with the building's mind when it could cost him business. Several public buildings in the city had developed an unhealthy attraction to him, and at least one had sworn undying love. His friends considered it puerile but begrudgingly admired the dedication required to train a bioengineered mind through nothing more than public interaction.

"Ground floor," the building chimed as the final contraction of the lift tube subsided. Mex swept his left hand down one wall of the pod, smoothing the palm sized scales. The surface shimmered through metallic greens and blues before settling on silver. He considered himself in the mirrored surface. The emotional and mental stress of the last hour formed a shadow across his face. He shook the barely-tamed hair over his eyes to mask the battered soul he saw in the reflection. With an exaggerated intake of air, he rolled his shoulders back and tapped an uplifting rhythm with the toes of his leather-effect boots. The cloud he felt above his head had not gone but it was a few shades lighter than it had been. He blew a kiss and grinned at the reflection before re-entering the maelstrom of the city streets.

*

Julienne lay on the bed, her arms rigid at her side. Her tension had risen to the point where she could no longer close her eyes, let alone sleep. Mental discipline made her lie there and rest until the walls started emitting dawn light tones. She sat up as if given a cue and stepped into the sanitation alcove. When she emerged the room had reconfigured to her choice of work-life balance. Most offices required a desk to host arrays of splice terminals, but her implants made this unnecessary. She only had a desk for the benefit of those entering the room. By choice she would have just sat near a window and worked, but higher ranking employees found it disconcerting to see lower employees staring at the sky. Their discomfort tended to manifest as career limits for those who caused it. So, she sat at a desk and tried not to stare out of the window. The room was pure white. All the walls, that were not currently windows, emitted white light. There were no shades of grey or shadows. She had a permanent request registered with the building's mind to keep at least one of her walls on the outside of the tower block, as often as possible. The outward facing wall was set to full transmission, no filter or privacy shield, just light. She could not abide the dark.

Yesterday's interviews had disturbed her. Initially, her preconception was one or more of those with access to the Node had played a part in her disappearance, but immediately after speaking to all the assigned staff, it was clear things were not so simple. Twelve hours on and she was more convinced that the abduction was something altogether more sinister. The technicians had been stressed by the interview but only to a level she would have expected. They all knew someone would have to take the blame and guilt might not be a prerequisite. As far as she could tell, none of them had ever even daydreamed about how a Node might be liberated from MynCorp. In retrospect, it was not so surprising; there was a lot of psychometric testing of all employees in positions of responsibility. She should know, she had once failed such a test. Only once, but it had completely changed the direction of her life. And they had been right; the scars ran too deep.

Someone cleared their throat near her. She snapped back to the present and a figure materialised in front of her.

"Mr Lucas, I'm sorry, I didn't hear you enter."

She flicked a self-conscious eye over her shoulder to check the rest of the room was acceptable and spliced a command re-emphasising the lighting to fade out living space from work area.

"Julienne, I didn't mean to disturb your work."

She thought for a moment he was being sarcastic but based on what she knew about his personality it was significantly more likely he couldn't tell daydreaming from a deep splice session. She still felt disorientated and foggy from lack of sleep. Behind him she could see an open door leading to a bustling office environment. The building must have reconfigured overnight to increase efficiency. Her office was now on the same level as the open-plan cubicles used by the commuter workforce; so much easier for her boss to make personal calls.

"No problem. What can I do for you?" Julienne asked.

"I was interested in your initial assessment of the asset-retrieval investigation."

"The missing Node?"

"Yes."

"I'm still carrying out interviews with potential witnesses."

"But you've read the initial reports generated by internal security?"

"Yes."

"And?"

"Somebody or something was definitely in that room when it happened, but they didn't walk in."

"What are you suggesting?"

Julienne had no idea what she was suggesting. She was just as curious to hear what she was going to say next. "It must all be connected to the Drop. The Node was showing some interesting brain activity for a few days prior to the incident. In some impossibly bizarre way, I think she was communicating with someone. Someone with access to technology we don't have in MynCorp."

"What sort of technology?"

"As I said, the person who took her didn't walk through any door. That I'm sure of. The integrity of the perimeter data is good. They also didn't walk along any corridors or through any of the entrances."

"What are you implying?"

"Nothing. I'm simply stating the facts. Someone appeared in the room without passing through anything in the surrounding one hundred and twelve metres."

"Interesting. How did you know about the brainwave activity? That data was not released to you."

"Her tending medical units recorded and responded to physical agitation of the patient. From what I can tell, that's pretty unusual for the level of coma she was supposed to be in."

"Good. What do you need to make progress?"

"The personal details of the Node."

"Not going to happen."

"Even a name?"

"I'll ask but don't wait online for an answer." He started to turn towards the door.

"One other thing," she braved.

"Go on."

"I need someone with a better knowledge of the Drop and Verity Space."

"I'll see who we've got."

Julienne shook her head and said, "This whole case is outside anything the company has experience of. I need someone with a wider perspective. I think I should go freelance."

*

"I'm telling you Ty, it used to work."

Mex fidgeted on the hard stool, reluctant to give his companion any incentive to pontificate. He had known Sickle for years and they got on really well as long as they stuck to fun and avoided anything more intellectual than bar bills. Mex's mouth started to escalate the argument before his brain could interject. "If it used to work then it still would. The fact that we don't have a democracy means it didn't work."

The bar maintained an illusion of retro independence. It had once been some sort of public records building. Regular pillars of old style concrete interrupted the large open space. They were painted with yellowing petroleum based paints. The floor was antique parquet with a herring bone arrangement still visible through the scratched layers of wax and lacquer. A counter had been temporarily converted into a makeshift bar some decades ago. A dozen optics were slung from a crude metal frame, epoxied to a set of original index draws. The whole room smelt of stale yeast wafting from the brewing set-up filling one corner.

The clientèle had all found the place by word of mouth. The bar did not actually hide its existence but it was tolerated by the corporate lawyers as long as it stayed beneath the public radar. The patrons all considered themselves rebellious in one manner or another. Some were bohemian alternative types struggling to define a life in terms other than energy budgets. Others were artists or students looking for some vitality in the city. The majority could not remember why they started coming but now felt more at home here than in the mainstream bars, drinking their yeasty beer or suspiciously clear spirits. Some swapped stories from reportedly reputable sources detailing secret ingredients added by the MynCorp to its mainstream beverages. They said that the corporate drinks tasted suspiciously sweet and that they felt oddly depressed when they tried to switch brand.

"Are you serious? It was all part of the plan. The corporations systematically destroyed our freedoms." Sickle squared his shoulders in preparation for verbal battle.

"You can always switch brands."

"And you wonder why I call you Ty. You're such a conformist puppet."

"Yeah, that's me, tie and suit. Very good. Shame about your spelling. Anyway, I'm freelance. I'm one of the few who definitely doesn't work for a corp, directly or indirectly."

"A softie. Software engineering, how rebellious!"

Mex Tyrian bit his tongue. Casual words even amongst friends could be dangerous. Better for people to think he only wrote bespoke interfaces for rich homes. He looked at the next table where a couple of college kids sat wide-eyed, like puppies emerging from their den for the first time. They nursed a beer each and pulled strained expressions each time they took a sip. They would not be back.

Mex sighed, resigned to the coming lecture "Why don't you tell me how it is? As if I could stop you."

"Buy me a drink and I'll educate you."

Mex spliced another beer from the micro brewery section of the bar's menu. He watched the lower digits of his energy credit tick down but there was a reassuring number of larger digits sitting pretty.

"Another round's on its way."

"Cheers. It started with planetary defence. The government subcontracted it out to MynCorp but they slipped a whole raft of little benefits into the contract. Little tax breaks for the corporation and its employees. They seemed like sweeteners but they started cropping up in other contracts; health, social services, banking. Each area slipped out of public control into the corporation's hands but the government was getting less and less back in taxes."

"That's a slightly skewed picture of history, but quite similar to reality," Mex conceded.

"It's all true. The corporations became larger and larger components of the economy. Eventually the government couldn't meet its payments and each contract had to be renegotiated. This time the corporations had all the playing cards. They demanded autonomy and the right to run public services at a profit. In exchange the government's debts were cancelled."

"Sounds reasonable."

"In the short term and if you're dim," Sickle jeered. "With no public services there is no government. The beginning of the end was when Planetary Defence was allowed to start making a profit. Without a state army there is no foreign policy. No national bank and you have no economic policy. No social services then no social policy."

"But we still have a government."

"We have planetary representatives who act as dignitaries at public engagements."

"And the Bureau of Corporate Corruption."

"Don't you think there is something fundamentally wrong with a society which hands all decision making over to an entirely self-interested and non-accountable organisation? Public control has been reduced to keeping tabs on the corporation to make sure they don't go too far, too often."

"I never really got fired up by politics."

"That's just the point! There is no politics, just corps and consumers."

Mex felt the first embers of frustration flicker to life within him. "Fine, the world has turned to shit. What are we going to do about it? Without politics where's the political protest?"

"We each have to do our bit, make the hard choices. You remember old Johnson?"

"Of course. The original Calorie Farmer. Jack Johnson, wasn't it?"

"You're thinking of Jacqueline Johnson, his daughter. The Farmer was Francis Johnson. He made his decision. Made his point."

The name Jacqueline rattled through Mex like the first shiver from an icy wind. He had not thought of her in several years; the first contented years since he had lost her. Mex tried to bluster on, beating the rising emotions back into the dark corner they had been festering in. "You think Johnson's little micro generator was a significant protest?" he challenged.

"It's not the details, it's the point. He burned all his calorie credits, dropped off the Nexus and lived a sustainable life. He was outside of their control."

"For all of one hour." Francis Johnson had been bending people's ears for more than a decade by the time Jacqueline had dragged Mex home to meet him. Francis would give long lectures about the pervading influence of the corporations. How, by monopolising the generation of energy, they controlled everyone's lives. Eventually, he was cornered into living his rhetoric. He built a micro generator in his house. After severing all data and energy connections to the MynCorp network he turned on his makeshift fusion generator. The house flickered back to life, the walls convulsing once before settling back to holding out the elements. One hour later MynCorp Security arrived to decommission the generator, ostensibly because of the huge amount of radiation it was leaking, but Old Johnson maintained it was because they could not tolerate a citizen being outside of their control.

Of course, such protests were easier in those days. It was during the final processing famine. The Nexus was still in its infancy and criminals were not routinely sentenced to the Drop. Large corporations were buying up public data warehouses and simply turning them off; using the processing rations for their own business systems. The public services were at a standstill, frozen by inaccessible data. MynCorp were paranoid enough to shut down any independent energy generation but apathetic when it came to punishment. Old Francis Johnson went back to pontificating about the evils of corporate society.

Jacqueline was the opposite of her father. She held the same ideals but acted instinctively to advance them with the minimum of discussion or notice. Mex had been thrilled and terrified by everything she did. MynCorp took her much more seriously. Mex had developed his Nexus code after she had been sentenced to the Drop. He had missed her with such an intensity that he coded twenty four hours a day until it was done. It was only near the end of the implementation that he realised that the operator of the code was the only person that could never interact with the Drop victim.

He had thrashed against the problem for weeks but there was no other way; he could release Jacqueline from the Drop for a short time but his mind had to be surrendered for the same duration.

Francis got to meet his daughter one last time before his heart withered and died. That first session was for free. In fact, all the early sessions were for free. Mex did it as a tribute to Jacqueline and only for those he cared about. As the number of citizens sentenced to the Drop grew rapidly he found his services being requested more frequently, and not just by friends. When people he barely knew asked him to bring back their loved ones he said no, but their pain was just as real as that of his friends. So they offered him calories and a business was born.

"We all have to make a decision at some point." Sickle was still talking and probably had been throughout.

Mex blinked back a wetness that was condensing in his eyes. He wondered if he had stopped caring when he realised that Jacqueline was gone forever, or maybe he had only cared because she did. "I'm going to decide to have another beer," Mex said as he looked towards the bar, as if a pint glass might already be winging its way to his hand.

"Mock all you like. I'll make my decision. Will you make yours? Or have you already made it?"

*

The planet swirled beneath the Suparna's hull; pale brown clouds streaking the darker brown of the crust. The pilot adjusted the surface-mounted cameras to a narrow frequency range and watched the monochrome view explode into a spectrum of vivid distinction. Now he could make out the cloud layering, with high altitude will-o'-the-wisp scuttling along in wheat over the tan of the heavier, lower clouds. The continent visible through the gaps varied from the sandy brown of the smooth lowlands, to the craggy mountains that jutted towards space in slender fingers of sienna and khaki.

It felt wrong to be departing empty but there was nothing valuable enough on the planet to warrant the energy required to accelerate it to near light speed and then slow it down again. Few things were. The Tau Ceti research station was hugely valuable to MynCorp not because of its exports but because of its isolation.

"Clipper Suparna, this is Tau Ceti control, you are clear to begin undocking procedure from geostation alpha."

"Tau Ceti control, thanks for safe harbour, prepare to release magnetic clamps on my mark. My ion drives are still warming up."

The pilot's voice was mechanical and not quite human, like something artificial trying to pass as a man. The technician, who doubled as a flight controller once a decade, looked round at his tiny cubicle of flashing lights and glowing buttons. He knew he could stand up and walk away from the claustrophobia but for the pilot, confinement was life. "Suparna, thanks for the supplies. It means a lot to us that you're out there bringing us a touch of home. Have you got our return treat?" He loaded as much human warmth as he could into the words.

"All 167 yottabytes of it. It is uploaded to my singularity and checksums confirmed."

"The company doesn't pay us to be brief. I'll clear the docking clamps at your signal."

"Look forward to talking to you next time."

"I hope not. I intend to be lazing around hydroponics by then. More likely my daughter."

"As you say." There was a vagueness in the synthesised voice which was not entirely sane.

The pilot closed the channel and disabled the speech module he was using to simulate his voice over the microwave link. He let his consciousness drift through the ship checking all was ready to push-off. His point of perception drifted through bulkheads and along conduits like captain Van der Decken drifting across the deck of the Flying Dutchman. He hesitated at the main pion drives following a number of minor alerts with status lingering somewhere below important. He followed each through to the appropriate sensor and actuator, establishing cause and effect. A few he checked in the knowledge base maintained by the singularity computer near the bunker and his physical body. Most of the anomalies had been there for years, and were due to the limitations of the engineers who designed the drives, rather than any real problems; combinations of events which the builders had assumed would not occur or could not handle a priori.

Pilot, may we come aboard?

The pilot was back in his head for a moment, his breath a soft hiss in his inner ear. The voice had seemed to start in his head and move to his ears from there; his ears that had heard nothing for decades, apart from the sound of blood pushing through his veins.

"Pilot, may we come aboard?"

It was the general inter-ship channel that he had just closed. His focus flipped back to the virtual world presented by the ship and his implants, happy to leave the bleak reality of his body hanging in the dark. "Who's speaking please?"

"I am José Sanchez and by my side is Nomia, we are your passengers."

The pilot sent a pair of multi-spectrum cameras scuttling along his hull to peer through the translucent fabric of the airlock tunnel. There were indeed two people waiting at his starboard airlock. One was a man of average height and build but with a distinctive shock of black hair. Not greying yet, but due to good genes rather than youth. His skin was almost olive which gave him a healthy look uncharacteristic for spacefarers. The woman was shorter by a head and fragile like pale porcelain. Her fingers fidgeted an intricate dance with one another. They both floated in free air without holding a rail in the micro gravity of planetary orbit, upright and with toes pointing down like a contingent of the heavenly host sent to test him.

"Passengers? I'm not expecting any passengers."

"Are you sure?" It was the man who was speaking.

"What? Am I sure? I've been in flight for eight years and docked for three days. This is the first time anyone has mentioned passengers. I'm not prepared for passengers."

"Please, do me a favour and just check your briefing."

"Why not." The pilot was buying time to regain his sense of control. The bizarre request had left him disorientated. He was completely unfamiliar with the dislocating feeling of a tangential conversation; the ship's A.I. rarely exhibited much in the way of imagination. His original mission briefing was still in ready reach of his virtual fingertips; its relative importance maintained the size of the tag, rather than frequency of access. The pilot flickered through to the return manifest and there it was; two passengers to be returned to Earth at best speed. And then he realised, it had always been that way. Nothing had changed. An apartment near his prow had been modified during deceleration and all preparations were complete. Words fought their own way out through his distraction. "Welcome aboard, I've been expecting you."

"Thank you pilot. We are entering your starboard airlock now. If you would be so kind, we would appreciate a drone to guide us to our quarters."

"Of course, a general purpose drone is waiting for you shipside. Please ask if I can alter anything to better suit your circumstance."

"You are most kind. We shall talk soon."

"As you wish." A disconnected memory irritated his mind like a flea bite. When he tried to bring the thought to the surface it seemed to clash with other, more ardent memories. The pilot returned to his flight checks. The feeling faded to a distant itch. Stress sensors glued between the layers of his skin flickered as the restraining clamps fell away and then he was flying free; mental wings stretched and clawed vacuum. The rat-tat-tat of the pulsing ion drives raced like his heartbeat as they pulled free of Tau Ceti's only planet. The Mars-sized rock fell behind with its ring of debris defence satellites like a cosmic carousel. He pointed his nose clear of the planetary disk and prepared to ignite the pion drives. X-ray and radio radar systems scanned a cone ahead constantly checking for fast-moving debris. The whole system was flooded with dust and rock, but it was mainly in a thick torus stretching along the plane of rotation, from near the planet and out into interstellar space for a few light minutes.

"I am about to start the main engines. Please be prepared for gravity." A part of him realised that this was probably the closest he had come to actually speaking in several decades, even if it was via a speaker. He had skimmed small patches of the ceiling in the liveable sections of the ship so he could make his voice move through the area by flexing each in turn.

"We are prepared." It was the voice of José, detected by the subtlest ripples of air on the same patches of ceiling. Although it wasn't actually ceiling yet. It was up to him to define up and down.

"Firing engines, now."

Telemetry rushed at him like the stellar wind. Waves of sensor readings and fuel performance statistics. He let the numbers wash through him, trusting instinct to pull out anything unusual. The acceleration settled at one hundred and twenty percent of Earth standard gravity and their speed started to climb; one kilometre per second after a minute, then ten kilometres per second after fifteen minutes. Without magnification, the Tau Ceti station was already sub-pixel on the rear cameras. It would take three days for them to reach one percent of the speed of light, but by then they would be four hundred million kilometres into their trip. Equivalent to flying from the Earth to the Sun and back again with a couple of loops of the Earth's moon for good measure.

He let slip a trickle of ions from a bow thruster to introduce the barest suggestion of a roll into their flight. Then he basked in the glory of stellar space, letting the warmth of Tau Ceti's radiation sweep across the expanses of programmable alloy that comprised most of his hull. The alternating expansion and contraction, from the heating and cooling, felt like breath to him. He soon forgot the static confinement of hard dock as he flexed his antimatter-fuelled muscles and reached for the stars.

Chapter 3

Nomia circled the room touching every piece of furniture with the paleness of her fingers. She stopped at each, as if to confirm its solidity, and then her eyes drifted to the next and her feet followed. She wore a simple white smock that floated around her bare ankles and feet as she moved. "I think I'm excited." Her voice was soft but contained the gentle wisdom that made people lean forward to catch each word.

"Good, so am I." José sat in a simple static chair that extruded from the floor at his request.

"No you're not. You're worried. I can tell because you are rubbing the bridge of your nose."

"Okay, you have me." He took his hand away from his face. "We should not talk about it just yet."

"Do you think he's listening?" She pointed at the ceiling.

"Ask him."

She looked at the metallic white of the ceiling. "Ship, are you there?"

"I'm here." The voice drifted down from directly above her.

"How are we doing?"

"We're doing well. Our current heliocentric speed is twelve point three kilometres per second. No shipboard system is exhibiting warning or fault status. The next planned manoeuvre will be a turn towards the Solar System once we have cleared the Tau Ceti planetary disk, in thirteen hours and five minutes."

"That's splendid. Do you have a name?"

"Suparna."

"That's the ship's name isn't it? I meant, what's your name? You are a person not a thing, aren't you?"

There was a pause, weighty with deliberation. "Suparna or Pilot will be fine."

"I'm sorry. I didn't mean to upset you." She turned to her companion, creases of concern cramping her face. "Do you think I upset him?"

"I doubt it. He's the control centre of an interstellar spaceship. I'm not sure a young woman with presumptuous questions is likely to cause him much distress."

"Ship?" Nomia sang.

"Yes, Nomia."

"Tell us about yourself." She caught José's look but chose to push on regardless. "Please," she added.

"I'm not sure you have sufficient clearance for me to answer questions about myself."

Nomia looked baffled. "How can you need clearance to ask someone about themselves?"

José shrugged. "Please check again Suparna."

There was no humanly discernible pause before the ship answered. "Your clearance level is sufficient."

Nomia's frown vanished. "Well?"

"I am an interstellar class cargo ship owned by the MynCorp corporation. From the tip of my nose shield, to the nozzle of my pion drive, measures eight hundred and fifty eight metres, in my inertial frame. My mean width is twenty metres with a peak deviation of two point three metres."

"Like a giant sausage," Nomia giggled.

"Narrow but not streamlined. Right?" José deflected.

"Indeed. The interstellar medium does offer some resistance, similar to moving through a fluid, but the mean free path between particle collisions is far too long for it to develop a property truly analogous to aerodynamic drag. Therefore, maximum cross section determines the total resistance, not the shape of my profile. More importantly, shielding has a high inertia so this shape minimises the requirement for a massive nose cone."

"What are we going to hit?" Nomia looked concerned.

José laughed. "About a billion specks of dust every second. All moving at close to the speed of light relative to where you are currently sitting. Without the shield you'd be peppered in a flash."

"Oh, I see." She sounded more bored than illuminated. "But I wanted to know about the pilot not the ship. He's only the second new person I've met in years."

"I am in control of this vessel in conjunction with the ship's artificial intelligence."

José's back and neck straightened with piqued interest. "You have a Nexus link on board?" he asked.

"No. MynCorp does not consider the Nexus secure enough for high-reliability systems such as myself; the Downey field is too diffuse. I am symbiotically linked to a virtual singularity computer, shielded near my isolation pod."

"I know about those," Nomia offered. "I met one once. It was coded in qubits and swarmed in the superposition of states which encrust a virtual singularity."

The pilot started to sound animated for the first time. "The singularity computer is beyond state of the art. It is still considered impossible by many computer scientists. Most accept the information storage and manipulation potentials of a black hole but shielding a ship from the singularity at its core is, frankly, implausible. MynCorp technologists side-stepped the problem by using a virtual black hole. Then the problem became one of shielding the black hole from the ship or reality in general. If the Universe noticed my singularity it would be forced to surrender its existence. The computer is primarily for data processing and process control. Although technically it does do some decision making. Little development effort went into a fully intuitive intelligence, since it was an essentially infinite problem."

"And human minds are cheap by the pound," José added.

"But what about the pilot?" Nomia's voice was ascending towards a whine.

José shrugged but after a second the disembodied voice answered. "There is nothing to know. I am the ship. Nothing more and nothing less."

"But you weren't always a pilot. You must have had a life before this." She waved her hands at her surroundings.

"Yes. I was not born a pilot."

"Well?"

"I can't remember."

"Can't? How do you know that you wanted to be a pilot? You might have been forced into your isolation."

José put a hand on Nomia's shoulder to calm her. "I don't think you're helping."

She opened her mouth then shut it again. "I'm sorry pilot. I just find it hard to understand why someone would voluntarily surrender their freedom."

"Maybe I have more freedom as a pilot than I had in my previous life."

"Why would you say that?"

"I don't know but there is no regret. There is only a contentment that feels new."

*

"Mr Tyrian?" She stepped into the lobby of the building and offered a hand to the man slumped against a decorative pillar.

"Ms Garland." His voice was tighter than his casual stance would imply he felt. He was wearing a knee length black jacket edged in silver. The points of black boots poked out from the hem of his trousers. The boots looked like leather. There was no doubt this was Mex Tyrian, from the mane of black hair that threatened to growl at combs, to the mischievous round eyes that smiled at her soul. She had known he would be easy to identify the moment she had spliced his citizen details from the corporation customer database. Now she was face to face with him, she had little doubt he was an expert at talking his way into trouble.

"Thank you for agreeing to a meeting." She was still proffering her hand but he seemed not to see it.

"Please follow me." He turned and walked towards the opposite wall. She followed, looking left and right to map her surroundings. It was the lobby of a typical residential complex. MynCorp, or any of the other three major corporations, offered their staff the option to rent living space in a building such as this. It seemed to Julienne to be a strange place for a criminal to do his business. Especially one who spliced corporate resources as blatantly as Mex Tyrian. Maybe he was too confident, believing he had eluded capture through his own skill. She knew they would get around to him once the inertia of bureaucracy had been overcome.

The lobby was currently imitating a twentieth century Manhattan apartment block. A revolving glass and steel door lead from street level into a double height atrium of marble columns and polished stone floor. The ceiling was edged in moulded plasterwork which failed to achieve the elegance of art deco.

When Mex was a couple of metres from the blank wall, an aperture started to form. The iris flowed open like a tear in fabric. The edges hardened into a dark wood and a dial in the shape of a sunburst congealed above the centre of the opening. There was a chime like an intricate brash bell as they stepped into the lift. A capsule formed around them and a licentious female voice spilled down from the ceiling. "Mex, I've missed you so much."

"I'm sorry, I have neglected you but now I hear your voice again I can only beg forgiveness." His own voice had dropped to a lower register. The timbre was significantly different and enhanced by a resonance that she did not recognise.

"I'll forgive you if you agree to move into one of my apartments."

"I'm not sure MynCorp would appreciate that. Anyway you'd get bored with me if I lived with you."

"Never." The building seemed to be entirely sincere.

"You are too nice to me. Can I beg a favour?"

"Of course Mex. Just ask. I could drop that woman down a shaft for you."

"Not quite what I had in mind. Can you confirm my companion's identity for me?"

"Of course. She is Julienne Garland. She was born on Earth in the year 187 of the new Calendar, making her thirty four years old. She has an older brother Sebastian and she is an employee of MynCorp. I have matches to city archives on retinal scan, finger prints and voice recognition, all at ninety-nine point three percent confidence or better. She entered this building at nineteen thirty six hours via the street-facing entrance."

"That's perfect. Ms. Garland and myself need to discuss some business but we can't afford to be overheard."

The request was not well received. "You want me to arrange some privacy for you and her?"

"Not from you. From MynCorp, or any other corporation. It could be very dangerous for me."

"Okay, but you owe me some quality time. I'll make a special space for the two of you. Give me one minute."

The lift started to flow up and to Julienne's right, in contractions of gradually increasing intensity. When they stopped she estimated they must be close to the centre of the building. The lift pod retreated down one side and they stepped into a blank space lit by a pale light emanating from the irregular walls.

"Just call when you're done. I'll be near." The voice echoed from the lift just before the door closed and they were sealed into the unusual space.

Mex found two protuberances that had erupted from the floor like grey toadstools. He sat on one while offering the other to Julienne.

"Where are we?" she asked.

"She's," he nodded towards the blank wall that had contained the lift entrance, "rearranged the building a little. Shuffled some of the central apartments to make a temporary gap. It's about as secure as you can get in the city."

Julienne circled the space dragging her fingertips over the walls. She felt like she was inside the belly of a great whale. "That was a nice trick with the voice. You've got the building eating out of your hand. Where'd you learn it?".

"Parlour trick really. I've had some minor modifications to my pharynx and a little training in flexing my supraglottic resonators. Mostly it's about knowing how the software works. It's what I do; write building personalities."

Julienne didn't comment but continued exploring the space with her hands. Finally, she joined Mex on the toadstools.

Mex spoke first. "Can I start with a bit of market research? How did you hear about me?"

"It was the father of an old friend." Julienne forced herself to fragment her story so as to disguise its rehearsal. Tracing the details of Mex's previous clients had been easy once she had identified his existence. "I don't want to get him into any trouble, but he told me about what you can do."

"What's his name? I'm not after assigning blame tokens but I have to keep track of who's talking about me."

"He only told me after I got a bit drunk and cried on his shoulder for an hour. He's known me long enough to trust me."

"And his name is?"

"Joseph. Joseph Hamilton. I used to share a dorm with his daughter, Lena, before...you know."

"Okay, that's fine. What is it you think I can do for you?"

"Joseph said you can find people in the Drop. I need to find someone. Someone I miss a lot."

He remained completely poker faced. There was not a twinge of confirmation or denial. He just continued with exactly the same tone, "A family member?"

"No. Girlfriend. Partner, in the life-sharing meaning of the word."

"Criminal or pauper?"

"Sorry?"

"Was she sentenced to the Drop or did she fall into calorific deficit?"

"Oh, I see. She was sentenced." Julienne was ad-libbing now.

"What kind of crime?"

"She did nothing wrong but MynCorp accused her of anti-corporate activities."

"Anti-corporate. Even if I was the person you think I am, I wouldn't handle cases likely to draw the attention of a major corporation. I'm sorry."

Julienne kicked her mental self hard in its metaphorical shins. She had assumed that anti-corporate sentiment drove him to hurt MynCorp but it was clear he was just doing a job for pay. It was poor case profiling on her part and she knew it. "It was a really minor case. Please help me. I can't bear the thought of not seeing her for years." She held the tears back in reserve but they were there if she needed them. "Maybe I can raise a few more calories and pay you a little extra."

"It's not a question of pay, so much as risk. If I was the person you think I am, I would have to give it some thought and get back to you." He stood up and moved to the wall they had entered through. "Lift please." His voice had the resonance back. The wall instantly parted, breaking the illusion of being in the stomach of a sea monster.

"What do I do next?" She let one tear slip down each cheek and sniffed softly.

"Wait for my call. My beautiful building here paired with your phone when you entered." He stroked the wall affectionately. The scales shivered excitedly. "I'll splice you when I reach a decision. No more than a day."

*

After three weeks the pilot was sure something unusual was happening. The antimatter consumption rate was more than ten percent lower than he expected. In fact it was ten percent the wrong side of possible. At this rate they would manage an extra week of thrust before he had to snuff the engines. It was not an issue of engine efficiency because that was essentially fixed. Certainly, it was possible to change the performance of the magnetic and gamma-ray collimators in the post-annihilation nozzle, but the efficiency he was seeing was beyond the theoretical maximum for thrust generated by a proton-antiproton reaction. Although if pushed he would have to concede it was merely beyond improbable, as determined by the statistics of many reactions.

When he thought about it in detail he kept coming back to a series of conversations with the man. José kept probing him for more and more details about the engines and antimatter generators. Each time he explained a new layer of detail, it miraculously started to exceed its peak design efficiency. It was not a question of sabotage (or anti-sabotage); José and the girl were under constant surveillance. He was not watching out of any suspicion. Watching the ship was what he did. It was his life. Still, he could not shake the feeling that his passengers were having some effect on him.

Mostly they sat facing each other in some sort of meditative trance, but for a few hours a day they would walk, skip or run throughout the short lengths of corridors in his habitable section. Nomia would ask him questions but never seemed satisfied with the answers. José would push for technical details of the ship, one system at a time. He had explained most of the engine design first, describing the sombrero-shaped magnetic confinement bottle for the solidified anti-hydrogen. José had wanted to understand why it was necessary to freeze the anti-hydrogen before storage. He had explained the difficulty of containing antimatter generally, and hydrogen's diamagnetism which caused it to levitate in a magnetic field. He added it was only possible to get useful densities of containment when the anti-hydrogen was frozen as ice pellets. Also, he explained the dangers of the anti-hydrogen warming; if it should sublimate and become gaseous then it would defuse to the edges of the magnetic trap and annihilate itself on the walls of the container. It would not take much for that blast to propagate to a new and very temporary sun in their region of space.

The most recent conversation had immediately preceded the largest jump in performance. José had been standing at his favourite porthole, one finger tapping the virtualised mica. "I know you use antimatter as a fuel, but you initially described yourself as having a pion drive. What's the connection?"

The pilot answered truthfully and with no particular sense of pride. "Pi mesons are the main products of proton and anti-proton annihilation. Sixty percent of the pi mesons are electrically charged, so can be collimated to produce thrust."

"So you have the perfect fuel; all the mass is converted into energy."

"Actually the pi mesons have rest mass so some of the energy from the reactants is lost, but two thirds is either kinetic energy of the exhaust particles or gamma rays. The gamma rays can be deflected but not so easily collimated into a useful beam."

"You said the fuel was anti-hydrogen not anti-protons. What happens to the spare anti-electrons?"

"They produce gamma rays. In fact, most of the final products are gamma rays. The third of the pi mesons that are neutral decay to gamma rays instantly. The charged pi mesons decay to muons soon after leaving the thrust nozzle and they decay, in turn, to gamma rays almost two kilometres behind us."

"So out of all the energy contained in the mass of the anti-hydrogen how much do you get as useful power for the engines?"

"Thirty nine point nine percent of the energy is contained in the kinetic energy of the charge mesons. Two point eight percent of this potential thrust is lost in the particle collimator. I can add another seven to ten percent from the gamma ray deflectors that achieve partial collimation of the high energy products of the neutral pi meson decay."

"So to some extent you are the victim of chance?"

"In as much as each reaction can result in a probability distribution of useful energy but the number of reaction are so huge that the actual figures become quasi-deterministic."

"Quasi is good enough for me." José rubbed his hands together with proactive zeal.

"What?"

"Nothing important."

"Do you mind if I ask what your field is?"

"Not at all. I'm a xeno-archaeologist. I work for the xeno exploitation department of MynCorp."

"Have aliens been found on Tau Ceti Alpha?"

"Not that I know of."

"So why were you there?"

"Nomia fancied a walk."

*

He forced himself to walk calmly from the building after promising its mind that he would return soon. He spliced a drone from a public terminal and waited for the sphere of scrolling advertisements to drift down from the cloud of dots circling the city. He stepped through the projected blurb and was momentarily swimming in an exotic infinity pool beneath the twin stars of Sirius Alpha and Sirius Beta. The Planes of Sothis lay fractured and fissured to the unearthly distant horizon. Then he was sat on a flex-chair which immediately adjusted to his shape before grabbing him in time for the vertical takeoff. "Robert Lowe building, apartment one six sixty. Priority arrival."

A cheaply-formed voice whined from the wall of the drone. "Please acknowledge consent to priority speeds and for waiver of company liability."

"Mex Tyrian, acknowledge waiver."

The drone's engines immediately changed pitch and multiple g-force pushed him further into the restraining squish of the flex-chair. Now he allowed himself to panic.

"Why have the corporation sent an agent after me rather than just arresting me in my bed?" he muttered.

"I am sorry sir, was that question directed at me?" the vehicle asked in a peevish tone.

Mex flinched and continued talking to himself within the relatively safe confines of his own head.

"She was definitely an agent. I'm not getting paranoid. She was all wrong in so many ways. My feral ancestors, locked beneath flimsy layers of civilisation, were screaming that she just smelt wrong. So what now?" There was only one realistic answer even if it was pretty desperate.

Run!

The drone levelled out about two hundred metres above the street and headed straight at the middle of his apartment block. With a fraction of a second to spare the side of the building puckered inwards and created a nest for the drone to land in and off-load. For a moment Mex stayed in the drone. He used its splice interface to access the building's public portal. He found the trapdoor he had written into the software and delved into the building's access logs. He flicked through time-sliced footage of people coming and going over the last twelve hours looking for anyone out of place. As an afterthought he did the same for electronic access, sifting through logs for any corporate level data flows. When he convinced himself they were not waiting for him, he stepped through the drone's parasitic commercials and entered his apartment.

Despite the reassurance of checking people and information flow through the building, he spent some time searching his room for signs of intrusion. Most of the furniture was huddled in the centre of the room. It waddled into a default evening formation when it sensed his presence, extruding stubby legs in a manner he had configured because he once thought it was cute. He told his wardrobe to pack a case for off-world travel, essentials only. His lab was spread across a static desk. He grabbed a memory gel sack and massaged it into a rucksack shape. Picking up random bits of kit, he started to fill it with whatever he thought might come in useful.

Fifteen minutes after he arrived, Mex was back in a drone heading for the clouds above the city. The problem he faced was getting beyond the corporate radar. He could not run beyond their influence because there was no such place, or at least none he knew of (he made a mental note to look for evidence of completely independent settlements). His best hope was to take advantage of an inherent weakness in all giant organisms; the problem which blighted all behemoths was the head and tail leading separate lives. If he could find somewhere distant enough then it could take a lifetime for his location to filter through to Julienne Garland. Specifically, it could take his lifetime.

His first problem was getting out of the city. Biometrics had been sold to the populace after decades of paranoia about the threat of identity theft but the obvious downside was the lack of anonymity.

"Advert-free supplement please." He said to the tiny mind controlling the drone.

"Please authorize additional payment," came the clipped reply.

"Mex Tyrian, acknowledge supplemental fee."

The collage of corporate logos and bland consumer devices flickered and shrivelled into the emitters around the drone's shell. The horizon rushed away, taking his breath with it. The city stretched out in all directions like a creeping mould, spore-laden stalks reaching up into the windy heights. The whole city seemed to undulate and throb through the thousands of metres of air beneath him. He looked up towards the parked mass of identical passenger drones, all waiting for their next fare. Their adverts were powered down at this altitude. Every few seconds a drone would peel off and plummet towards the ground, firing up multicoloured promotions for the latest colony expedition or the kitchen utensil you should not have to survive without.

Mex hoped somewhere in the cluster of silver grey blobs was one particular drone which had the distinction of hosting a little extra software of his own. He reached into his rucksack and rummaged for a few seconds, pulling out a regulator mask and a hand-held notepad.

"Let's hope you're close enough, little friend," he muttered to himself as he warm-booted the computer. A rotating cone of green light scanned his face hunting for an eye. Once found, the beam tightened down to a slender dagger of data-encrusted photons. Mex spliced an application from his development suite. A nano-second chirp of modulated microwaves beamed out from the device towards the cloud of patient drones. A second later one of the identical blobs of grey metal broke from the pack and hurtled towards his position. It pulled to a dramatic halt a metre before a collision and bobbed on the air currents like an expectant dog. It peeled open its sides to reveal two empty seats.

Mex pushed against the transparent section of his own drone, forcing a small opening to form and grow. "Warning, please return to your seat. It is not advised to exit vehicle in-flight."

"Noted, so shut up." Mex offered back.

Pulling his arms apart the opening grew to man sized. A turbulent eddy of air buffeted the drones and for a moment Mex retracted his head back inside. "Now or never. Don't look...you know...the opposite way to up." Putting his notepad back in his pack and regulator mask around his neck, he gripped both sides of the opening and shoved his head and shoulder out into open air. The wind pushed his cheeks into his teeth and ripped the breath from his mouth as he struggled to suck it in. A sound like an interstellar craft flying in atmosphere pummelled his ear drums. Before his confidence was squashed into nothing, he leapt.

*

The Suparna was becoming easily predictable in its interruptions. The pilot would wait until they had returned from Verity Space long enough for them to stand and shake out the muscle toxins. Only then would he speak, almost as if he was respecting some religious ceremony. Usually the conversation was aimless and seemed to be more about the pilot practising human contact than actually imparting information. Their easy routine was broken four weeks into the flight.

José was walking in loose circles restoring blood flow to his legs after an extended period of sitting. The pilot's voice interrupted his daydreaming. "I'm afraid we are going to lose gravity in a few minutes."

"Really. That's fine with me." Nomia made waving motions with her hands as if she was already floating.

José looked up towards the disembodied voice. "Is something wrong, pilot?"

"No, this is standard procedure. Normally, it would have happened three weeks out from Tau Ceti but we have been remarkably frugal with our fuel."

"We're out of fuel?"

"Yes. It will take several weeks to recharge the antimatter store."

"How's that possible?"

"As I have already indicated, I am host to a virtual singularity. It is evaporating slowly via Bekenstein-Hawking radiation. There is a small flow of particles from the event horizon. The containment field selectively siphons off the antimatter. I have a small non-contact factory which assembles and cools the anti-hydrogen using a suite of tuned lasers. We will charge for a week and then relight the engines for a day."

"So from now on we have gravity for one day a week?"

"Correct. Although, if you prefer, I could configure the engines for half gravity for two days a week?"

José stood in thought for a minute. "Let's start with that and if the antimatter generators should improve their efficiency we can reconsider later."

We could be there in an instant if you would let me. Nomia pushed into his head.

I know, but we can't take the risk. Even talking like this might draw attention to ourselves.

Would you rather talk about this aloud?

No. The pilot is not ready for the truth. I'm not sure he ever will be. I suspect that his own truth may be more than he can deal with.

Stop changing the subject. I'm bored just tinkering with local reality. I want to either get to Earth or go back to exploring.

José took hold of Nomia's arms and looked her in the eyes. He was conscious he had to look down, so he bent his knees slightly to make them the same height. *What do you think would happen if we twisted reality enough to push our bodies through a few light years of space and appeared on Earth?*

Something bad. I know. I've seen the warning in your mind. I just wish I understood why they are so adamant that we leave Earth alone.

I agree but it can only harm their deliberations if we go against their will. Enjoy this period of calm, it will not last.

Nomia sighed. "Ship?"

"Yes Nomia?"

"Do you know who you are?"

"If by that you mean do I know my birth name, then the answer is no."

"Is that usual for pilots?"

"I'm not sure, but I think not."

"What's wrong with you then?"

"There is nothing wrong with me now. I had an accident and was rehabilitated. A lot of my memories were lost."

José stopped looking uncomfortable as his curiosity was spiked. "You said rehabilitated rather than cured, healed or even fixed."

"I believe there was significant damage to my mind and a major psychological rebuild was required."

Nomia pushed on. "Would you like to know who you are?"

"Would it make any difference to have a name?"

"I don't know. I can't imagine not having one, but I do remember being trapped in my mind without any option for thinking about me. It was horrible."

"I'm not trapped. I have the whole universe to explore and the complete electromagnetic spectrum to experience it. Most people are trapped on a planet with only their few senses."

"I like grass between my toes."

The ship did not respond.

Nomia added an almost child-like determination to her voice as she sat down and closed her eyes. "I'm going to find your name."

Chapter 4

Considering his brain was designed to calculate trajectories for throwing spears and stones it was being incredibly indecisive. As he climbed through the air, arms and legs flailing like a fledgling, his leap seemed perfectly judged to bring him, two footed, to his destination. A puff of wind later and Mex had to surrender any notion of grace and hope that, after years of typing, his fingertips were strong enough to save him from a terminal fall. Supposedly, the air was thinner at altitude, so it should not be slowing him down so fast. Mex wondered if he was heavier than his mental picture; a delusional self-image which extended beyond vanity and into whatever neural circuit it was that performed Monte Carlo simulations of parabolic trajectories. But he distinctly remembered his physics teacher telling him everything fell at the same rate regardless of weight. Or at least, they would if it was not for air resistance, so they do not, but they would in a vacuum.

Reality decided to compromise. He landed hard on his elbows and swung precariously. His head and shoulders were momentarily pulled back out of the drone by his legs which continued on their original course. With a sob of neat adrenaline, he clambered aboard the second drone and lay panting on the floor, the world a deafening roar in his ears.

"Seal drone," Mex ordered once his vocal cords could muster more than a squeak. The edges of the door poured together, pushing one of his booted feet further inside, as the last howl of weather was shut out. He bounced into the seat, a thumping heart fuelling his determination. "Take me to Dyson Station One, best speed. Priority delivery."

"The Dyson station is above maximum allowed altitude. This vehicle is not equipped with breathing apparatus nor is it able to maintain atmosphere. Please return to street level and board a MynCorp shuttle." The drone's voice was an identical thin whine to the one he had left floating in a confused state of indecision.

"That's the whole point. Only shuttles can get you into orbit. That's why they'll be watching them. Special override Mex Tyrian."

"Override accepted. Hello Mex, you sexy beast."

Mex cringed at the forgotten aspect of the bespoke piece of code. "Dyson Station One, please."

"As fast as I can, oh consort of the goddess Venus."

"Please speak as little as possible."

"As you command, my bowl of cinnamon sugar."

Mex felt the tiny craft accelerate straight up, leaving his stomach somewhere below the cloud layer. The air began to thin rapidly and the flickering status lights of the splice terminal started to dim as his eye lost focus in the low pressure. He pulled the regulator mask over his mouth and nose. As it detected the moisture of his breath, a thousand microscopic Archimedes screws started to pull at the thin air around him, feeding his hungry lungs.

It grew perishingly cold, but the heat liberated into the regulated air by the screw pumps kept ice from forming in his lungs. Mex knew he would not freeze as long as he remained relatively still; low pressure and humidity makes air a very poor conductor of heat. Anyway, his clothes were smart enough to sense the subzero temperature and reduce their conductivity appropriately. His cuffs and collars gripped tight on his skin, begrudging every joule that escaped. The breathing regulator spread across his face, providing pressure seals around his nose, eyes and ears, but his sinuses still felt like they were pushing his teeth out by the roots.

"We are approaching Dyson Station One. Lord of lust." The message was scrolling across the inner skin of the drone, the verbal component lost in the minuscule air pressure.

Mex looked up from his blue fingers and allowed his eyes to focus through the translucent side of the drone to the midnight blue of the Earth's upper atmosphere. Directly ahead was a sight so curious his brain repeatedly insisted he was standing on his head. The drone was on course for a crystal castle of diamond pink spires and copulas. The structure was apparently perched atop a slender thread of carbon nano-tubes that descended an infinite distance to the amorphous clouds below. His higher brain thought it understood the centripetal force and that the braid of carbon isotope was actually anchoring the station to the ground, preventing it from careering off into space. The rest of his brain knew it was impossible to balance a complete building on such a thin pole and any moment now it would all surrender to gravity and start a thirty minute fall to the ground below.

"Run docking simulation." Mex crossed his fingers for luck. He ran through each stage of the procedure in his head trying to anticipate the moment when the approaching airlock would silently grind open. The drone should be transmitting an identification code appropriate for a low orbit transfer craft. An exchange of negotiation messages should convince the station to offer a suitable dock. Of course, the drone had no airlock but it was small enough to completely slip inside the outer chamber which protected the intricate docking umbilicals.

The station delayed just long enough for Mex to believe he was destined to freeze to death in a remarkably unpleasant manner, and then a glinting panel of crystal slid away revealing the delicate intestines of the station. The drone nipped inside like a bee returning to its hive and the unsettling vastness of space was gone.

His ears popped and whistled their annoyance as the Dyson station detected a life in its airlock and pumped air in as fast as safety permitted.

Once he had convinced himself he was safe, Mex initiated a purge sequence in the drone's mind and listened to the synthesised voice declare undying love as it faded to a dull drawl. He stuffed his few possessions back into his pack, thrusting away the nagging feeling he had just treated something sentient with disdain, as if having given the drone the illusion of emotion, its mind was intrinsically of more value. A scuffed knuckle on a sharp-edged piece of tech brought him back to himself.

Ten minutes later the drone was a mindless lump of active alloys and Mex was striding down a corridor amongst a myriad of other travellers. The Dyson station was nothing more than a transport interchange; an interface between all the messy aerodynamics of atmospheric transport and the brute force of space flight. In reality, there was usually another hop before interplanetary craft were boarded. Most captains preferred to avoid even grazing an atmosphere and sat clustered around the neutral gravity of the Earth-Moon Lagrangian points.

Dyson Station One was not exactly independent; it was owned and run by the Dog Star Corporation. Of the cartel of corporations which ran Earth and her colonies, they were the youngest and, by comparison, most delinquent. Mex estimated it would take at least six hours for MynCorp to push through the mire of bureaucracy required to get his biometrics registered with Dog Star security. It was not so much commercial rivalry, more accounting for balances of mutual back-scratching. He had no doubt that MynCorp had security personnel of its own permanently based, and tolerated, aboard the station, but visual identification was less of a challenge. In a world where physical appearance was malleable, a range of biometrics was the only identification that counted.

Mex beckoned a piece of furniture from a heap in the corner of the concourse. It weaved its way towards him and flipped into an upright chair at his request. He took the seat amongst hundreds of people killing the slow time of departure lounges everywhere. Some were chatting about how long their flight had been delayed, others were splicing home to let their families know they were counting the moments. Flipping on his notepad he spliced up the built-in camera so he had a mind's eye view of himself. He watched as his image reached into its backpack and pulled out a vial of shimmering silver. The atomiser fitted to the vial produced a fine mist infused with a rainbow of colours. The rainbow was not a coherent arch like his childhood memories of summer storms at the wilderness park. The cloud seemed to mangle the light passing through it, ripping the colours apart and rebuilding the scene like a cubist painting. Mex spliced a program of his own devising and the cloud sprang at him like angry bees. He watched his hair fade to an ice white and flatten against his head. His eyebrows followed suit. A scar grew across his cheek, jumped his left eye and then vanished into his hair line. His skin darkened to a sun-hardened bronze and his pupils became an impenetrable slate grey. His look complete, Mex practised a couple of piratical grins and laughed out loud. He looked up to see if anyone was showing curiosity. No one was. In fact he was not alone in tinkering with his appearance. A group of teenage girls were gathered in a giggling cluster a few metres from his seat. One of their number was posing for the others while her hair went through extreme fits of colour and style. The other rich kids seemed to think this was the funniest thing that minute. A grey suited man next to them was shedding his dowdy demeanour and blossoming into silver screen blonde complete with blood-red sheath dress. This was not just a transport interchange, it was a life interchange; a place to throw off one life and start another. He felt buoyed by the other escapees around him.

Trying not to grin with the giddy relief of post-adrenal glucose rush, Mex spliced up the station's departure board, and booked himself transit to Lagrangian point five; a kidney-shaped area of space where the gravity of the Earth and Moon combine to perfectly generate the centripetal force required to remain stationary. A number of recruitment agents for Solar planet projects were prowling the splice space of the station and a couple had already shown interest in his curriculum vitae. A microbial physics research station beneath the surface ice of Europa seemed suitably isolated and he sent a provisional acceptance back to the over-enthusiastic avatar. The project supply ship was parked at L5 and they were waiting for him at his earliest convenience.

The public address system binged to life and all faces looked up in a combined prayer for their flight number. A synthesised voice, comprising snippets of a real voice patched into a collage of inappropriate intonations, announced the imminent departure of his shuttle. Most of the faces showed flickers of irritation as they sank back to looking at their laps. Mex stood, dismissed the chair and ambled calmly toward his docking gate.

Two dark suits struggling to contain steroidal muscles stood near the departure gate. They had the look of MynCorp, an organisation that had all but outlawed subtlety. Mex joined the queue pretending to be engrossed in a projection of a news channel on a wall to the side. The queue pulsed forward with the rhythm of an advancing tide. His pulse rose as the distance to the security men shrank. At the point of closest approach Mex felt the laser-like stare of one of the men and he found himself eye to eye without any idea when he had turned his head. The muscle of the man's head distorted his face into a permanent grin which was more intimidating than any frown.

The agent looked him directly in the eyes, held his gaze and then moved on to the woman behind him. Mex was right, they had no biometric scan of him, just old-fashioned detective work; look them in the eyes and see who blinks.

Mex buckled himself into the stiff foam of the fixed format seating. A woman too old or poor to have her wrinkles removed sat next to him and fumbled with the seat belt.

"Let me help you," he offered.

She looked at him with a quickly masked look of fear. He could feel her eyes tracing out the scar on his face but she offered no resistance as he reached across and clunk clinked.

"Thank you, young man." Now he noticed her blouse with simple collar and knitted cardigan. Her hair was waved like it had been wrapped around cylinders of plastic.

"You're a traditionalist," he blurted.

"My, you are observant, deary, but not too polite."

"Sorry, it's just a bit surreal being face to face with a character from an old movie."

"I'm not living in a film. I just choose to keep things simple. Don't you sometimes feel things are a bit too frenetic and complicated?"

He started to say he liked it that way but realised he would be lying at the moment. "Today I think you may be right."

She looked pleased. "Can you tell me what the entertainment is? I'm not too good at splicing without my reading glasses."

Mex was about to ask how she intended to watch the entertainment without splicing when a crew member floated into view, her hair a neat plait down her back to overcome the natural frizz of zero gravity.

"Mrs Brown?"

"Yes dear," the old woman acknowledged.

"I'm very excited to say, you have been selected for an upgrade to first class."

"I'm all right here, young lady. I've got this nice young man to talk to. He's not nearly as scary as he looks."

"I understand, but in first class you'll be eligible for free tea and there are hard screens showing a choice of classic films. I'll be attending your every need."

"Oh that does sound nice. Free tea, you say?" She needed no more persuading and Mex was left on his own. He expanded his personal space into the two seats. He could only sit in one but somehow it felt roomier with an empty seat next to him. He heard the metallic clunk of the airlock sealing, the hiss of pressurised umbilical being severed and felt the hard weight of the engines firing.

Now he was free. Free from mother Earth and free from MynCorp. Next stop Jupiter.

"Good morning Mr Tyrian. Thank you for joining us." Pulling herself against the thrust of the craft, Julienne Garland sat down in the empty seat.

*

"Ship, I have a surprise for you." Nomia had opened her eyes and started talking as if she had not been seated in a trance for the last two days.

"Go on." The voice emanated from all around. The two passengers had lost their attachments to up and down remarkably quickly after the engines had been shut down. The furniture had been abandoned and was now reabsorbed into the walls, most of which were now skimmed to improve acoustic sensitivity; if a free falling limb flailed too close to a segment of wall, it would stiffen in self-defence. The pilot found the acoustic data from the living space more interesting than all the multi-spectral sensors scanning the volume. Each breath they took created a cascade of information which he was slowly calibrating into a profile of their emotional behaviour. For instance, he could tell that Nomia was tense with nervous energy and almost falling over herself with eagerness to talk. His own reticence seemed harsh and mean-spirited in comparison.

"I know your name." The words erupted from her mouth as if they exerted more pressure on her lungs than she could withstand.

"Will it make any difference for me to have a name?"

"I lost my name for many years until José gave it back to me."

"Did it help?"

"Help?"

"Was your life easier with a name?"

"Indescribably."

"Perhaps you could..."

"Could what?"

"Describe it. I would like to hear your story to better understand my own."

"I don't have much to tell. I dreamt for most of my life, complicated nightmares of repetition and subjugation. Then José rescued me and now I am free. José is the real story. He heard my cries."

José floated into the room in accordance with some universal rule of synchronicity. "What are you blaming me for?" he beamed. His calm breathing and relaxed movements sent ripples of serenity through the air, in contrast to her innocent excitement.

"The ship wants to hear your story before I tell him his name."

"Of course, travellers regaling their host with epic stories is a tradition as old as journeying itself. All we need is a camp fire."

"I don't think that would be appropriate," the ship intervened.

"I could make a cold fire if you like," Nomia offered.

"I don't think it is essential." José brushed a gentle hand through her hair, failing to smother the blonde spikes. He imagined static and a lack of gravity probably made his hair resemble a darker but similar sea urchin. "Where to start. I suppose the link between us is Verity Space, so the story should start there."

"Tell him about Verity Space. Tell him how much more it is than just the Drop."

"The story will tell itself and in its own way but Nomia is right about the importance of the Downey field and Verity Space. Danielle Downey was the first human to make the intuitive leap, more than one hundred and fifty years ago. She was studying causality and the effect of the human consciousness on quantum wave functions. Her team discovered a weakly interacting subatomic particle which was responsible for the collapse of a wave function from a state of superposition. This particle is the mediating boson of a field generated by the subconscious minds of all sentient life. The Downey field and the quantum wave function interact in a set of dimensions almost entirely isolated from the dozen or so which comprise the physical p-brane of the Universe. This extra space is the domain in which we establish our own combined reality. Danielle named it Verity Space, presumably because it is where truth is born.

MynCorp found a way to commercially exploit the discovery in their own inimitable fashion. They realised that a minority of autistic children with Asperger syndrome have an almost conscious awareness of the Downey field. With sufficient mental rewiring they could marshal other unconscious minds into coordinated effort, exchanging information directly across Verity Space. In one fell swoop, MynCorp had solved the problems of computing resource shortage and the increasing social underclass who consistently failed to achieve calorific equilibrium. And so the Nexus was born as a latter day workhouse. It rapidly became known as The Drop, due to the feeling of free fall described by those lucky enough to gain a reprieve."

The pilot sensed José's distraction. "But didn't you tell me that you were some sort of archaeologist?"

"I was. I studied the Eternal Light artefacts. To be honest it was more than work; it consumed me. I became quite well respected within a few, very small, circles. MynCorp like that kind of single-minded dedication, so they made me the head of their xeno-archaeology department."

"And the Eternal Light artefacts are?"

"I'm not surprised that you haven't heard of them. The corporation were convinced they had commercial value and, as such, they didn't go out of their way to make them into a tourist attraction. The four artefacts are named after the first one that was discovered near the north pole of the Earth's moon. There is a ridge of mountains on the rim of the Peary crater which have continuous daylight due to their latitude and the Moon's small axis tilt. The second lunar colony was based there because of the permanent solar energy and the presence of water ice. They set up a mining operation for aluminium and magnesium but uncovered something a lot more exotic. They were experiencing interference on their microwave transmitters in a small region of the mine. When they sent in a team to investigate the interference they discovered a map of our galaxy."

"A map? In the rock?"

"It is a three dimensional projection of the Milky Way at microwave wavelengths. The source of the projection has never been identified but it just happens to manifest a quarter of a kilometre below the Moon's surface."

"Could it be natural?"

"Unlikely."

"So it would have to be alien?"

"Almost certainly."

The pilot paused to give his brain time to realign itself to a universe where aliens were a given. His thoughts kept racing up mental alleys that opened into rapidly expanding mazes of implication. He retreated to a well understood mental box and encouraged José to distract him with more of the story. "You said this was the first."

"Yes. There have now been four discovered, each at a different part of the electromagnetic spectrum. Microwave, Infrared, X-ray and most recently Ultraviolet."

"All on the Moon?"

"No, spread throughout the Solar System but not beyond our planetary system."

"We spent years working on the first three, but learnt very little. After a while the corporation grew more cautious and scaled back the energy investment. Eventually they disbanded my team. I was too specialised, no other department wanted me. I was forced into the Drop."

"Maybe MynCorp wanted to keep you on ice."

"That seems likely in retrospect. I was in the Drop for two years."

"What did it feel like?" The pilot was asking José but he sensed Nomia draw a breath, as if to speak. Maybe she changed her mind but she remained quiet and kept her attention firmly focused on the man who was her constant companion.

José looked uncertain, as if such memories could only be diminished by the use of words. "Looking back that time seems like a lost dream; a sense of old-style purgatory with repetition and tedium. I felt completely caged, way beyond any kind of physical bonds."

As José continued to tell his story the pilot found himself being drawn deeper and deeper into the narrative. His mind, so attuned to collating and processing data into a mental image of a ship, treated the dialogue as another data stream. His empathy centres were sparked back into life from their dormant state by the emotional content of the human story. The disorientation and pain of waking from the Drop was now his own experience. He felt the intense nausea in the stomach, the muscular ache in the limbs and the spectrum of stabbing pains in the head. Each nerve impulse arrived at his brain with all the speed and urgency of melting snow. Enough photons impacted on his retina for an image of his surroundings to register - a cell, a Drop-cell. Memories began to arrive in sporadic waves as his recently re-energised body metabolised the Drop drugs.

The bench he was suspended above began to retreat from the Drop-cell, each cycle of its servo loop a painful reminder of his body's indignation. He emerged, head first, from a wall of countless cells into a huddle of waiting technicians and a token medic. The overall impression was of bustle and industry, but to him they moved with all the urgency and speed of a mollusc: each of their muscle contractions was a symphony of intention, trigger, nerve feedback, energy generation and toxin disposal. With time, their activities became swifter or he became slower. He started to become aware of a slow slap against his eardrum as air molecules grouped together and decided to act in unison.

"Employee 366547F, please acknowledge my voice."

He remembered that by careful configuration of his throat and tongue, he could use the air passing in and out of his mouth to communicate to other sentient entities the concepts bouncing around in his consciousness, including these MynCorp technicians. "Argubhh!"

This seemed to satisfy them because the slapping against his ear changed form. "Employee 366547F, you have been retracted from SubProc and your account has been credited with 50,000 MCals prior to assignment briefing."

The dreams began the first night after he emerged from the Drop. He was falling in, towards, a void. Floating through the rhythm of a Node. Beating time, keeping count, synchronising the flow of data, co-ordinating the disparate processors. The Nodes, maintaining order amongst the chaos, fighting entropy. Father of time to all the Nexus. The Nodes, conduits for data flow, engineers of procedural complexity, arbiters of data integrity, interface to the corporeal and corporate world.

Drifting in the void, enjoying free flow, he shook off the rigid form of the Nexus. Constructs emerged briefly across his extent, rippling to their own rhythm before sinking below the surface or boiling off into the void. Memories, fantasies, future echoes, the mundane, the unlikely, the impossible, creatures, people, the familiar and the fantastic. Each sought its opportunity to shape the whole.

The beating of a Node grew stronger, causing ripples across his surface. A form emerged from the void; a mass of tentacles snaking off towards never. Each arm comprised tendrils of tightly packed datagrams, flowing towards and away from the central hub. Fresh data streaming to the extremities and tightly organised data completing the cycle. As the hub grew more distinct, he resolved the details of a human face – eyes closed, the features distorted by unseen forces. The eyes opened revealing deep pools of pain and the lips formed two silent words.

"HELP ME."

Then he was back on his sleeping pad, breath coming hard and fast in the darkness, hair and skin slick with the sweat of fear.

The next day he was called to the office of Pro-Vice Co-ordinator Cecil, which was bland in the way perfected by large corporations over hundreds of years. The cubicle's only customisation was the high-field-of-perception images projected from a cluster of alcoves in one wall. Each showed an exploded view of an off-world mining operation, precise but devoid of beauty. The only other objects of interest were the collection of features clustering on the face of Pro-Vice Co-ordinator Cecil himself. His round hairless face encaged an assortment of expressions which prowled across the surface, searching for means of escape.

Cecil began to speak without offering him a seat or even a hand to shake. "José Sanchez, MynCorp employee number 366547F, Xeno Exploitation Division. Specialist in xeno-archaeology, specifically, alien technology." His brows formed a pincer movement and made a break for the forehead. "Veteran of three off-world sorties. Venus, Moon and Io. Access to level five energy budget and level-two retainer." At this point, his upper lip curled and attempted to hide under the overhang of his nose. "How was the Drop?"

The corners of Cecil's mouth made a synchronised bid for freedom. He treated Cecil to his best hard stare and most intimidating glower. The Pro-Vice Co-ordinator seemed not to notice.

"Okay, to business. Time is energy. While you were flowing to the beat of the Nodes, the William Lassell mining operation on Triton uncovered another of those alien gizmos your division gets so excited about. The magnetic pulse field had our mine-bots excavating in spirals for hours before we could activate compensation routines. This one is observable in the far ultra-violet. Here's a composite image from our Earth-Moon L2 interferometric telescope."

A projected image rose from the floor matting and settled at chest height. Even in monochrome, the feeling of looking in on our galaxy from some distant point was unnerving. Blurred spiral-arms were discernible, anchored to a central core of saturated intensity.

He slipped into a safe and familiar role. "At Neptune distance the L2 telescope in the U.V. would have a resolution of a few metres. Judging from the detail level, I'd guesstimate this is about 50 metres across. Any variability?"

"Nothing above 0.001% from a millisecond to a two week period with five sigma certainty." Cecil's brows performed a dance that could be interpreted as relief to be sharing a problem.

He lost himself in the projection for a moment as timeless questions rose to the surface of his consciousness and bobbed about amongst the ripples of his mind. He felt himself falling forward towards the projected image and jerked backwards on his heels.

Cecil bought him back to the immediate. "We're working around it until you do your stuff."

"I'll assemble my team."

"You are the Xeno Exploitation Division. The key is in the word exploitation and the lack of it. A supply mission leaves tomorrow, your equipment is already aboard." Cecil's face came to rest, indicating that the meeting had exhausted its energy quota.

The pilot wanted to ask more questions about the artefacts but the story had developed its own momentum and he did not have the determination to interrupt the flow. José described another dream that he remembered from the night after the meeting with Pro-Vice Co-ordinator Cecil and the pilot was once again immersed in the magic of José's description.

Falling with, surrounded by, a Node. Pulsing tendrils entwined him, cradled him, as they dropped. The synchronising rhythm of the Node's beat comforted him as it locked the Drop to its whim. Participants, debtors, victims of the Drop, danced to the beat, processed to the rhythm. Each surrendered dream time for floating-point operations in the name of corporate glory and calorific equilibrium.

The cats-cradle of data-flow drew him closer to the hub of the Node, but he was safe in his tentacled womb. As he relaxed his form, the surface tension against the void diminished and the limbs of information passed through him. The face of the hub was expressionless, eyes closed but he heard the voice. "...LISTEN TO THE DATA..."

He turned his mind's ear to the tentacles passing though his form; cycles of dataset download and resultant upload. Also the rare and more complex procedural definitions when a new mind entered the Nexus or the Node made a context switch.

Rhythms within rhythms within rhythms.

The melody of the void.

And then, the entire Nexus missed a beat and a burst of static distorted the Node's tentacles. He was surrounded by silence for an infinitesimal time and then datagrams arrived from all quarters of the void. Each, a mind reporting a transmission error and environmental interference. The Node pulsed brightly as it fulfilled all the pending requests and then settled back to beating time, counting to infinity.

A finite number of beats later, the Node's eyelids pulled back to reveal eyes that devoured light and turned it into a swirling blackness of pure pain. In their reflection, he caught a glimpse of a room, lost amongst a maze of rooms. In it was a pale thing, a shadow of a woman. Clusters of fibres tied her swollen head to a bench, throbbing tubes entered the body above major organs and two small spiders crawled up and down her withered limbs, stimulating perished muscles.

The air in his quarters was warm and damp. The air conditioning beat in time with his panting breath. He lay in the darkness and cried for a stranger.

"I still don't understand what these Eternal Light things are." The pilot was engrossed in the story but lacked a clear mental picture of the subject.

José backed up and added some detail. "Each artefact was first detected due to its cyclic magnetic field and can only be 'seen' in one narrow band of the electromagnetic spectrum – near infra-red, microwave or X-ray. All are beneath the surface of a planet or moon but none are consistent with a single strata or deposit, so they cannot be dated geologically. The most frustrating property is the lack of material component – no mass to measure, no surface to touch and no volume to excavate. The X-ray artefact on Io was the most revealing. At such extreme energies, such minuscule wavelengths, we were able to resolve the artefact down to tiny scales. Our own sun, Sol, has been identified and there is even a suggestion of a disk of planets. The relative position of Sol suggests the artefact depicts the Milky Way of today, plus or minus a century or two. None of the artefacts have been observed to change or evolve in the last twelve years. So, it is possible the artefacts have always represented the galaxy as it is today. This could, of course, be calculated in advance but for some of my colleagues it was one coincidence too many.

Several religious groups have taken the artefacts as a sign of great significance – 'The Third Coming', 'Judgement Day' or 'The Awakening'. Both the Pope and the Dalai Lama have been forced to offer their thoughts on the matter. Neither had seemed particularly insightful to me, but the minority of the population that had become aware of the artefacts' existence nodded with relief and got back to the serious business of isolating themselves from the world."

"But you think they were made by aliens?"

"Maybe. Probably. They could simply be the art form of a long lost alien race; beautiful but irrelevant."

"How old are they?"

"No idea. We have no direct measure of their age or how they were manufactured, assuming that some sort of construction was required. I don't know what holds the artefacts in-place in the rock or ice. We never answered even the most basic questions. One of the more recent publications speculates that we may have stumbled across the original design schematics, used to construct our galaxy."

"I'm not sure I can even start to get my head around that idea."

"Don't worry too much about it. There's no evidence either way. What may be significant is that none of the artefacts have been found on Earth and, even though they represent the galaxy as seen in the optical part of the spectrum, none are directly visible to humans; almost as if they have been deliberately hidden from our pre-industrial civilisation. Although, that is an extremely anthropic perspective."

"Like a time capsule from some alien race to humans on their twenty-first birthday?"

"It seems a lot of effort to invest in a species which is in a continuous state of surprise that it hasn't managed to vaporise itself lately. All I can really do is describe how it appeared to me and let you draw your own conclusions. I was sent to Triton. Most of the journey was divided between reading and the recurring nightmares I have described."

José described the distant thunder of re-entry that was a constant reminder of the few inches of alloy between his feet and Triton's sparse atmosphere. Neptune filled the view like an over-magnified blue pearl. High cirrus clouds formed white streaks across its surface and a number of dark storms acted as flaws and focus for the eye. Triton was a rapidly growing dark mass chewing away at Neptune's glory, fighting to dominate the view. As Neptune's glare was gradually devoured, Triton began to shine in victory. The moon's ghostly clouds of nitrogen ice crystals were invisible in Neptune's glare, leaving the red surface exposed and defenceless. Bright pink, frost-covered polar caps pronounced the coldest human outpost in the solar system. Circular depressions and straight ridges defined the moon's surface and told the story of tidal heating and internal struggle.

As he reached the tunnel exit, he stopped for a minute and let the view direct his gaze. The excavated ice formed a valley which merged with the foreshortened horizon. The numbers that danced across the inside of his visor were meaningless in this alien world. The only real sense of scale came from the cluster of human ants dismembering a mine-bot on the valley floor below him. Away from the pool of life, the floor and right-hand wall of the valley were dark and featureless. The left wall was bathed in Neptune's blue light, regions of dark pink fractured by incandescent veins of blue-white.

A soft crunch retracted his senses to the immediate. A few seconds later his feet came to rest against the bottom of his boots. For the first time he noticed Triton's gravity as ice, boot and sole all came into contact. He imagined the ice ripping the heat from his feet, welding the melting skin to the metal of his boot. He concentrated on the task at hand and did not stop to marvel at the absurdity and fragility of the shell which separated him from conditions more hostile than any hell. He did not concern himself with such thoughts at home but the Earth's atmosphere was a similarly fragile shell.

The suit's gyroscopic and induction drives propelled him down the hundred metres of guideline to the valley floor. Switching to conventional thrusters, he drifted slowly towards his goal, redundant limbs limp for stability. His visor was still switched to optical with infra-red folded-in to make the miners visible in the poor natural light. The suit's sensors triggered a warning message when he reached the epicentre of the magnetic pulse emission. He requested the suit's propulsion system to hold position thirty metres above the icy floor and one hundred metres from the nearest wall. He started a slow rotation so the beam from his chest light swept an arc across one wall of ice and then the other. Apart from a few faint wisps of nitrogen crystals suspended in the sparse air, there was nothing to draw the eye. All was still. Only then did he request the visor to switch to ultra-violet vision.

The air around him exploded with the light of one hundred billion stars. For tens of seconds he was blinded by the god-like view of creation. The galactic bulge encircled and engulfed him, stretched halfway to the floor beneath him. The spiral arms curved out towards the valley walls like extensions of his outstretched arms. In places, the stellar density was so great that fantastic bodies of solid light replaced the individual stars. As his suit rotated, stars drifted into his visor and vanished as they entered his helmet, no longer detectable by the vision system. His head was full of stars that he could not see. By craning his neck backwards they passed through his visor and exploded into life. He waved his hand through a thick cluster in front of his chest. His glove caused no ripples and cast no shadow.

At some point a bleep indicated his suit's on-board spectrometers had completed data logging. His eyelids closed over parchment-dry corneas and he reset his aching jaw. The request to return to optical and infra-red vision left him floating in blackness. His vision was a myriad of blue-green dots and for a moment he felt like he was falling. Fear was rapidly replaced by an intense loneliness, and a longing for something intangible.

*

The last fragments of her dream were slipping away like the final grains of sand in an egg timer, but Julienne knew the scene. She needed only the faintest glimpse of the setting for five years to collapse to a moment.

It was rare for her to dream and she suspected that a night in zero gee was the cause. Julienne unstrapped herself from the cot and drifted to the sanitation alcove. She scrubbed at her teeth in a futile attempt to wash away the taste of fear. The dream had been of the dark place where she had hung in silent terror for hours, days, maybe even weeks. She remembered the moment when alarms had avalanched throughout the ship, overloading her senses with conflicting information and then the A.I. had started the five hundred millisecond countdown to her ejection. She wasted the first two hundred in stunned shock and then spent every remaining moment fighting for control of cascading interlocks.

Her memories were now flowing like water over jagged rocks. Even the webs of force-absorbing thread that supported her had not been able to completely absorb the jolt from the explosive charges. That instant, the photon coupling that connected her to the ship had ruptured in an implosion of light and sound. Her world of sensory input that she could barely contain, instantly shrivelled to a single dot and a pop.

Her breath had been the loudest noise in the Universe.

The training station was very near. She had only undocked a few minutes before. Her free fall would not last long. Sure enough, the faintest of lurches told her she had been grappled aboard another ship. A few more minutes of patience and they would restore her connection to the light and check she was okay.

She waited, tense with forced patience.

She waited, sick from a body saturated in rotting adrenaline.

At some point she slept and then woke for long enough to regret it. A long time later a connection was made. A witheringly thin channel of voice data. The male voice was thick with smothered emotion.

"Hello my love."

Julienne pushed the memories far enough back in her mind to allow some daylight in. Or, at least, ship-simulated daylight. She felt a smile push at the corner of her mouth when she remembered back to yesterday and her encounter with Mex Tyrian. His pride had been cruelly slain when she sat next to him and said hello.

"You found me," he kept repeating as if the concept was so improbable that it would fade back into the quantum froth unless continuously renewed aloud. Eventually, he managed a little more. "What are you going to do with me at L5?"

"We're not going to L5, we're going to the MynCorp station at L1."

"But all these people think we are heading to L5."

"They'll understand the necessity when we explain just how dangerously anti-corporate you are. We'll probably throw a calorie voucher at anyone who feels aggrieved enough to complain."

"I see." Mex was clearly unsure of the wisdom of his next question. "What happens at L1?"

"That depends on you. Could we lose the disguise? Very theatrical but not very convincing."

"What? Oh, I see." Mex took the silver vial from his pack and spliced a homing whistle to the colony of nanites distorting his features. His face melted momentarily and then returned to the tired features of Mex Tyrian. Julienne offered a palm on which he placed the vial with reluctant hesitation.

"Thank you. That's much better."

"What do I have to do?"

"You are perceptive, Mr Tyrian. There is a very specific way you might redeem yourself in the eyes of MynCorp."

"The Drop?"

"In a manner, but probably not in the life-absorbing way you might think."

"You want me to do something in the Nexus."

"Of course. What else? Although I could really use a bit of blind love from my building at times."

"I'll throw that in for free."

Julienne paused and thought for a moment. "I was surprised you tried to run."

"Maybe not my brightest move but it seemed like a reasonable shot."

"But how did you know?"

"Your behaviour was just wrong for a client. Your emotions too perfect. But the clincher was that you are just too symmetrical."

"Symmetrical?"

"Sure. Everything about you is symmetrical: your stride is exactly the same with each leg, you move your left and right hands in the same way and you blink for exactly the same duration with each eyelid."

"I blink too symmetrically?"

"I design personalities. It is the deliberate imperfections that make an artificial intelligence seem human. People are creeped-out by purity."

"I see."

"If I asked what you are, would you put me somewhere dark for the rest of my life?"

"What I am? That's an unusual question."

"Maybe, but you are not ordinary."

"I'm human."

"But?"

"I died."

"You're dead?"

"Not any more." Julienne sighed away her reluctance to talk about herself. "I'm a golem."

"I see." Mex stared at her with a disconcerting level of professional curiosity.

"I'm human," she repeated defensively.

"Do you know who's body you're in?"

"Mine."

"But before it was yours."

"They told me she died naturally. I've never asked any more."

"You never asked?"

"Would you?"

They sat in silence for several minutes, their thoughts diverging along lanes of their own mindscapes. After some time Julienne blinked perfectly to restore her focus. "Would you like to know what it is we want you to do?"

"I'm in no hurry. I could go to Europa for a decade or two. Splice me after."

"I think not. MynCorp considers the issue very urgent."

"In that case..."

"We want you to find someone."

"Find someone? Presumably you mean in the Nexus."

"Maybe. Certainly that would be a good starting point."

"Presumably there's a good reason why you can't just splice a Node with the person's details."

"Of course."

"And that reason might be?"

"The missing person is a Node."

*

José looked tired, as if the story was costing him years rather than hours, but he did not falter. "I had one more dream but this time it was while I was essentially awake and floating inside the artefact."

As José started to describe the vision, the pilot found himself once again drawn into the story; the other man's dream filling the blank areas of his imagination.

Falling in, with, the void. Floating through the silence of the nothing. Regular undulations crossed his form as he jelly-fished his way to nowhere. Fleeting shapes leapt with joy from his surface or wallowed in the troughs between the waves. José let them play; they were as much a part of him as the intellect that steered the whole. A sound like a trapped bee arrived from just ahead. High frequency standing waves danced across his extent before the pitch sank to a fast purr. A form meandered across his path; amorphous except for leaping bird shapes escaping briefly from the surface. Each time the form created and extended a limb to retrieve the fleeing bird and drag it back inside the whole.

The purr slowed until each pulse was separate and discrete. The leaping form faded as each measure became a wait. Now a new sound filled the void. At first it was a noisy ripple on an otherwise quiet area of his form. Then a whine which made José create arms and search for ears to cover. The whine became a whistle and then a beat. A beat that he could count to. A rhythm he could think to. A pulse to live to.

The Node was before him, eyes open, radiating distress and sorrow. Channels of information snaked across the void. Packets of data glistened like glitter as they scuttled back and forth between distant minds and the hub of the Node. Each transaction added another sliver of pain to the mounting torment. Now the Node pulsed with light, sending ripples out into the Nexus.

'...HELP ME...HELP US...LISTEN TO THE DATA...GO GREATER...GO HIGHER...'

José let his form express confusion but the pulsing light was already dimming in spurts. And then he felt it. 'Environmental interference', 'Data corruption'. A burst of pure noise ripped through the void, disrupting the beat. This time, he clutched at the tail of the noise as it faded; dragging himself along with it, up with it. The throbbing tentacles of the Node started to slow, scurrying datagrams reduced to a faltering creep. The Node faded and all that was left was the void.

The echo of the static deepened in pitch and started to modulate. It became a cascading waterfall of rhythms, beats and harmonics. The multiple facets of José's extent paused and then started to dance across his surface or through his form. A hint of a shape solidified in his path. At first it appeared as a violent juxtaposition of geometric shapes before it slowed and grew in definition. The form was a constant wash of geometry and organic curves and curls. José was reminded of waves breaking on a rocky shoreline and his form reflected the thoughts. The complex rhythm halted and the form came to rest. Concepts rushed into José's mind without the wasted effort of senses or language.

José knew they had always been here; old even when compared to the Sun. So aware of the universe that they affected the Downey field at the quantum level. Such deep perception that the Downey particles they generated could penetrate deep into the Cosmos, shaping reality on a universal scale; the resulting boson-pressure inflating space and time at an ever faster rate, defeating gravity on cosmic distances. So deep within the void that they appeared to the Nodes only as background noise. So adept at manipulating the Downey field that human thoughts were as continental drift to their flight. And yet, José knew that he was welcome. José knew he was the first of his kin. José knew his journey was complete. He knew he could choose how all would be, before he left the void. He knew probability was not the same as chance. He knew that he was free to take shape and to shape.

José stopped and the silence was all-consuming. It felt like the worst form of sacrilege but the pilot had to know the meaning. "What did you do?" The question felt too simple but he could not bring himself to think anything deeper.

"I did the only thing I could. I found the Node in a room lost amongst all rooms. She was lying above a pad of switching logic. Tubes tethered her and fed her. Bundles of fibres tortured her physical mind, bundles of data tortured her ethereal mind. Two metallic nurses tended and shepherded her failing body, their jointed pin legs prodding and probing."

"I appeared in one corner of the room with a gentle hiss of air molecules rushing to clear a space. I remember smiling slowly, nervous of disturbing a scene direct from my dreams. I willed the spidery guardians to pause and then vanish. The machine that acted as life support, data port and jailer, started to crumble as I directed all its protons to simultaneously decay. The resultant soup of pions slithered away and I directed the torrent of released gamma rays to save themselves for some distant place. Nomia's eyelids began to flutter as I took her in my arms and left."

José and Nomia touched hands sharing a connection that was deeper than the simple telling of a story but it was the pilot who broke the spoken fast. "I'm ready. Tell me my name."

*

"Do you remember dying?"

"For someone with an in-depth knowledge of personalities you have remarkably little concept of tact."

Mex and Julienne sat in a plain office on the rim of MynCorp Equity station at the first Earth-Moon Lagrangian point. Julienne had selected a strong blue-white light that pushed shadows well under the furniture. One small square window offered a glimpse of the moon through heavily over-engineered mica. Twenty seconds later the Earth slid by as the station spun on its axis in a silent pirouette. Between them was a table and on it was a naked splice terminal. Mex realised that he had never before seen the workings of his trade tool. It sat there like an orthodontist's toolkit, arrays of solid state lasers and micro-stepped prisms.

"Come on. I can't be the first person to ask you that."

Julienne looked frighteningly delicate for a moment before sweeping away the emotion with a wave of her hand. "I remember."

"And afterwards?"

"I woke up."

"But between dying and waking up?"

She looked at him blankly. "I was dead. Can we get on?"

"Okay. Okay. I was just trying to get to know you." Mex held his hands up in surrender.

"I caught you and held you against your will. I am now coercing you into working for me. This is not a getting to know each other scenario."

"As you command. So, you want me to find a Node."

"As I said."

"But you also want me to find a person. How are they connected?"

"They are the same."

"Excuse me. Nodes are not people, they are things. They're lumps of... I don't know what, that sit in the Nexus forever. They're gateways and coordinators for the whole Nexus."

"Apparently, they are also people."

"But that's obscene."

"Probably. I always assumed that they were PVS cases."

"PVS? Oh, persistent vegetative state. I take it you've recently had to revise your assumption."

"Maybe. One of the Nodes vanished from a secure facility."

"Walked out?"

"No."

"Oh."

"I think she contacted something in the Nexus. Something with some impressive technology."

"Something? Something with technology that impresses MynCorp. That's exciting!"

"I'm glad you think so. MynCorp are the only defence that Earth and her colonies have."

"Defence? Why do you see this as a threat? Anyway, your army makes an energy profit, there is nothing egalitarian about MynCorp."

"I am not prepared to discuss corporate politics with you. The little people always hate those who take responsibility for them."

"You're good. I couldn't detect any irony in your voice. Anyway, I don't want us to fall out after we've made such a promising start. You said she."

"Sorry."

"You said the Node was a she. Who was she?"

"I don't know."

"I'll give you the benefit of the doubt and assume you've asked. I also assume that you've eliminated all the more prosaic explanations for her disappearance. So, let's run with your assertion that she escaped via a contact in the Nexus. Let's go fishing."

"Good. You'll find a personal area in the station's public splice space. It is coded to your metrics and contains the ident for the missing Node."

"See you on the other side."

"I'm coming with you."

"Do what?"

"This splice terminal has a passenger mode."

"Really? That's a bit intimate."

"Intimate? Half the human population is dipping in and out of the Nexus on any given day. I'm not sure you could get much less intimate."

Mex dived in, relying on his experience to get a head start on Julienne but she was on his tail instantly. She felt like an annoying itch between his shoulder blades, whichever way he turned she was just out of reach but she niggled at his concentration. The splice terminal recognised him and marshalled him away from most of the station's areas, dumping him in a virtual cell with access to the public Nexus and one nugget of information; a Nexus address for the missing Node. He could not think of anything else to do other than go to the address and see what was there. He spliced the address by grabbing the data and dropping it onto the public interface for the Nexus.

Nothing happened.

Julienne laughed with a false ease that told Mex more about her tension levels than a clenched jaw. "That was impressive."

Mex waved away the splice beam so he could see her clearly. "What did you expect?"

"I know you're not restricted to the public application programming interface. You have your own route into the Nexus. Your own APIs."

"I'll need my glasses."

"Ah yes, the glasses crammed with quantum dot arrays. What's the code do?"

"You mean you haven't cracked the encryption?"

"I prefer to hear your take rather than the babbling of our techies." She handed him the glasses that had morphed to clinical bone rims with clear lenses.

Mex knew they would not give the glasses back so readily if they had cracked the contents. It was the first piece of good news he could remember since Julienne strode into his life, like the most elegant of robots. He placed the glasses on his nose and pushed them into place with his index finger. "Let's splice!"

A completely misplaced sense of pride compelled him to try to impress her. The glass code dropped him through the public interface and reinterpreted the whole Nexus as an infinite fog of grey intrigue. Glowing green points of focus bobbed in eddies of information flow, adding depth to the fog by forming horizons where they merged into landscapes of imaginary cities. The lack of scale made the experience simultaneously vertiginous and claustrophobic. If he forced his eyes to focus beyond infinity he could still vaguely make out the white cell spinning in the space between the Earth and Moon, and Julienne sitting opposite him mesmerized by the scanning splice lasers. At the same time he felt her virtual focus perched on his shoulder like an over-opinionated conscience. He heard her inrush of breath and saw the whitening of knuckles gripping the arms of her seat. He realised that he had never shared this view with anything living (or reliving) and found his sight refreshed by her innocence.

Mex allowed himself to drift towards one of the green points. As he approached, the glowing icon was replaced by a detailed representation of the Node; public interfaces displayed like a cluster of heraldic flags and data flows pulsating like a web of umbilical cords. He reached a virtual hand into one of these streams of data packets and plucked one out at random. Sucking out a copy of the address header he threw the wriggling datagram back into the main flow. Using the spoofed address he knocked at the lookup service interface of the Node and asked for a nodal address using the ident provided by the station network. The Node pushed back a copy of its routing table, giving a map to the required Node. Rather than drifting back to a god-like overview, Mex decided to take the low route to their destination. He squeezed a few important parts of himself and the glass code into a short train of datagrams, each headed up with the routing information. Then he dived into a random data stream and let the current take him. They hurtled through the Nexus data routes at an immeasurable speed; no scale, no wind, no gravity, nothing to give any meaning to distance or time. Yet it felt like a roller coaster as each Node sucked them in, redirected and fired them on. After a few hundred Nodes they were directed down the final link to the expected location of their missing Node.

He felt himself ejected from the flapping end of a severed data route. Mex floated up to get some perspective. At this scale, the unconscious minds of the Drop appeared as faint ghosts around each Node, thinner pipes of data tethering them to their coordinating Node. Here there was a gap. Some of the Drop minds floated with trailing data tethers flapping in confusion. Others had already rerouted to another Node and were being dragged away from the scene. Even though the Nodes were not uniformly distributed throughout the Nexus, there was definitely something missing here; a rent in the pattern.

The Nexus was scarred by its loss but was healing itself as best it could. Eventually, there would be no sign that the missing Node had ever existed but even now there was no clue as to what had happened. There was no remnant data, no partial impression of the former data coordinator. Simply a gap in this version of reality.

Chapter 5

The one thing Mex had learnt from years of contracting was that the best way to get away with a misdemeanor was to be the one responsible for preventing it. Prevention may be better than cure, but the preventer was licensed to cause. With this in mind he had set about confusing the Equity station's A.I.. The glasses, that he maintained were essential for his continued hunt for the Node, made it easy for him to penetrate the station's databases. Details about the physical infrastructure seemed to be regarded as beyond secret and he could get nowhere near them, but personnel records were a different matter. After a little searching he found a minor officer with duties which included final checks of departing transport shuttles. He had the tedious job of walking the ducts of ships, making sure that the active life sensors were not insanely missing a bunch of escapees huddled in a corner. It was the kind of exercise that managers would call belt and braces, or pointless depending on one's perspective. Mex adored the simplicity of the MynCorp databases; one generic application customised for each section of the corporation. This made it possible to tamper with tables in ways that seemed insane to a human. For example, Officer Stuart Matthews now had two sets of identification metrics registered against his name. One, the set that had evolved with him from birth; the other a recently added set that just happened to match a certain Mex Tyrian. As far as the station's A.I. was concerned it would recognise either set of characteristics as Stuart.

Mex hated the thought of wandering lost through the station trying to find the shuttle bay but he could not get anything useful from the A.I.. Even Stuart Matthews would have to ask a colleague for directions to the bathroom, the computer was not going to tell him. A few things were obvious to him from simply looking out of the window. The fact that the Earth and the Moon flashed bright and harsh past his window about twenty seconds apart told him Julienne had not lied about their location; only the first Lagrangian point had such symmetry. The libration of the moon and the fixed height of the Earth and Moon indicated they were probably in a Lyapunov orbit rather than the popular misconception of simply sitting at a Lagrangian point. Great, so he knew that they were performing a complicated wiggle near the Moon. He decided it was definitely time for more action and less thinking but there was one more thing he could learn that could be invaluable. He knew that the docking bay must be at the axis of rotation because no other location was sane, unless MynCorp liked making life difficult for its pilots. He could get a fairly accurate guess at how far he was going to have to climb from the rim to the hub. Mex fiddled with the splice terminal looking for a spare bit that would not be lost. A quick yank and it snapped off in his fingers. He sat down and tried to look bored, throwing the scrap of alloy high into the air and catching it with a 'just passing time' nonchalance. Even though his personal perception about the level of gravity could be deceived by how he was feeling or how much he had over-eaten, the area of his brain which did equations of motion for fun was easy to upset with low gravity. After a while he decided that he was not dropping the scrap too often. So, if the gravity was roughly Earth-like and the station rotated every forty seconds or so then the station could be no more than a kilometre across. Which meant a climb of a few hundred metres to the hub; five minutes maximum. How hard could it be?

There was no reason for a human to be watching him with the A.I. keeping Mex Tyrian locked down, but he leant against the door for ten long minutes. Enough time for a remote viewer to get sight fatigue; even after he asked the door to open for Stuart Matthews and slipped gently backward into the corridor beyond, there would be a few seconds where a human would still see him in place, their brain waiting for significant motion before updating the perceived scene. He started to walk with calm intent in a random direction. The colony of nanites, which had been hiding and breeding amongst the dead skin cells of his scalp, spread across his head, slowly and subtly moulding his head to more closely resemble Officer

Matthews, before shifting the pale blue of his 'visitor' gown into a worker grey.

He grabbed the head height rung of the first ladder he found heading hubward (or up, to him). There were two grey-garbed men heading around the curve of the corridor but they were too far away to necessitate an interaction. If they had bothered to look up they would have seen Mex's boots vanishing into a ceiling shaft. The close confines of the radial spoke felt comforting after the exposed anticipation of the rim corridor and he climbed with rising excitement. His stomach started to perform cartwheels as the centrifugal gravity started to fall off. After two hundred metres his legs were more of a hindrance than a help and he let them hang beneath him. He was making good progress climbing hand over hand until the tunnel ended at a T-junction.

He propped himself across the long drop below, palms flat on the matt surface of the new corridor. Turning his torso and shoulders both directions he tried to prejudge the identical directions. Both were two metres high and lined with access panels and conduits as if the station was shy and only showed its working in places rarely visited. A squat maintenance-bot was spiralling along the corridor, apparently ignoring what gravity there was as it picked its way across the busy surface with a multitude of pincer-like arms. Mex watched it for a few seconds, amazed at the pure functionality of the thing. He tried to think back to a time before artificial intelligence and robotics had been consumerised, a time when their function was more important than their form. He could only wonder as to why MynCorp had chosen to buck their own trend. The whole station was an antithesis to the public MynCorp persona.

He headed past the softly squawking robot in the direction he hoped was counter rotation, taking short strides to avoid bouncing his head off the assorted ceiling fixtures. The corridor curved tightly this close to the hub and he rapidly found the next obstacle to his progress; a ten metre wide shaft from hub to rim leaving him exposed like a hanging valley. The corridor restarted directly opposite almost as if the station was mocking him and daring him to leap. Mex looked up but the sides were completely smooth. A breeze from below made him swivel downward and rock back on his feet as a lift capsule flashed past, friction singeing the end of his nose. His heart pushed at his ribs trying to break free and flee back to his cell. "Why does every escape involve death defying jumps?" he muttered to any god that might be listening. As if in answer, laughter echoed around the curve behind him. Mex cocked his head in concentration. It sounded like two people approaching at a leisurely pace. Mex was not ready to confront anybody and have to explain why he was crawling around up here. He turned back to the shaft and started to psyche himself up. "I can make this jump. I can normally jump two metres, maybe three. Gravity is about half normal, so maybe I can make six. Four metres short. The station is rotating around me, it can only help. I just hope it's enough."

Without giving himself time to think it through any further he took four steps back, ran forward and leapt with every fibre of his limbs. A strangled roar pushed through his lips as he arced higher and longer than his brain said was possible. Everything about him that called itself intelligent screamed that he was already stretching implausible towards impossible but the other side of the shaft remained stubbornly in the distance. His brain was calculating and recalculating parabolas but they all came short. He prepared himself to scream and then he hit the opposite wall at waist level with unlikely speed. His head and shoulder pushed through into the corridor and he lay coughing away winded tears, safe on the other side. A draught around his ankles made him pull his legs into his torso just before another lift blurred past the entrance.

Mex lay still for a count of ten before crawling round the curve of the corridor and safely out of sight. "I made it. I actually made it! Coriolis I love you!" His bruised ribs proved that he had still been doing a fair pace even after ten metres. He climbed back to his feet and saw another shaft above his head with polymer-coated rungs starting at knee height on the wall next to him.

By the time he emerged into the central hub, gravity was barely a suggestion. He floated into the large atrium, grabbing a wall tether before he went into an embarrassing tumble. Up and down blurred into abstract concepts while centre and edge became more useful references. At the middle of the atrium, half a dozen docking umbilicals reached stiffly towards a double-shuttered airlock large enough to fit the brick-like shuttle that floated, bleeding coolant into the chilly air. The mist of white vapour hung around the ship lacking any buoyancy to drive convection currents in the atmosphere of the airlock. Maybe half a dozen people were spread across the fifty metre space, either tending to maintenance procedures around the edge or travelling along the umbilicals tethered to flimsy sky lifts.

Mex tried to look like he belonged while hand-walking his way around the perimeter. A tether appeared at his heels and then scuttled along behind at a respectful distance to keep itself out of his legs. The docking umbilicals formed a star of lift shafts that curved out from the central axis of the station and headed along the major radial spokes. In the atrium they met the wall in four metre wide blisters that acted as engineering platforms and sky lift terminals. Passengers and other real people travelled inside the umbilical with little or no idea of the space and technicians around them. He made his way to the umbilical attached to the single shuttle and pointed his tether at the sky lift. It shortened and increased its elasticity to offer him a gentle tug towards the waiting escape ship.

Twenty metres from the safe confines of the ship, two technical-looking men emerged from a cranny on the craft's surface and headed in his direction, tool cases dangling behind like wayward puppies. Mex had no choice but to push on and blag it.

"Stu what you at?" asked the larger of the two men, facial hair twitching as he clipped his words.

"You know, just heading on board for my checks." Mex tried to sound as unspecific as possible, not risking the western European accent Stuart might have by birthright.

"I thought you's already on board," the smaller man added. He had a cruel face crushed by years of frowning.

"I went back to get something for this sore throat."

"Hell Stu, only you could get a cold in a sealed space station." They both laughed as they drifted past. Mex laughed as sincerely as he could manage.

The airlock cycled and deposited Mex inside the shuttle. It was no more than twenty metres long and short of hiding places but Mex wriggled into the first inspection hatch he found. He did not want to risk running into Stuart and all that messy knocking people out business that would surely follow.

In the next hour he heard one pair of voices float past and then the hissing clunk of an airlock. A faint vibration through his finger tips told him that the fusion drive was warming up. The vibration slowly grew to a point that could only mean ignition and then hovered there for a minute. Another hiss and thud probably meant docking clamps being released. A few more minutes and Mex thought they must be clear of the station. He smiled at the simplicity of a computer that would quite happily check the identity metrics of each person boarding and not throw an alarm when the same person entered twice. Even more amusing was that it checked each person leaving and cross-checked without worrying. Each Stuart Matthews had been authorised to enter and a Stuart Matthews had safely left again. All was well.

The smile was creeping towards a grin when the hatch in front of his nose was pulled aside, pummelling his eyes with harsh white light.

A familiar woman's voice followed. "Mr Tyrian, you do know that these compartments are vacuum purged before take-off?"

"Julienne, there you are."

"Yes, here I am, wasting my time again. Although, I did like the leap across the lift shaft. Very impressive."

"What? You were watching me and you still let me jump?"

"You seemed quite determined to continue your little excursion."

"If it wasn't for Coriolis force reducing my weight I'd be dead. If I'd jumped the other direction I wouldn't have made it more than three metres."

"Really. That would have been a shame." Julienne sounded as if his death would have been only the most minor of inconveniences. Mex felt his face collapsing into a teenage sulk but she continued without mercy. "I can put the hatch back on and let you suffocate if you like."

"Not particularly."

"You really are a pain. I'm struggling to see any good reason not to take you straight to a Drop chamber. You know we have one on board. You can repay my hospitality with twenty years in the Nexus."

"I thought we were starting to get on rather well."

"I'm not joking Mr Tyrian. You have not shown me any reason to conclude that I made the right choice employing you."

Mex climbed from the confines of his bolt hole and tried to look her straight in the face without showing his muscle fatigue. "Employing me? Arresting, kidnapping and persecuting more like."

"As you wish." She turned and walked away, leaving two security guards armed with glowing sticks that crackled alarmingly.

"Wait." He called after her but she cycled the airlock and stepped inside. "Wait, I've found her." Julienne's trailing foot hesitated in the door. Mex looked at the guard's grinning faces and tried one more time, "I've found the Node."

*

It could not really be a dream because Kaamil did not sleep. Certainly his mental clock had a much wider range of speeds than normal humans could muster. He was capable of performing complex manoeuvres for a spaceship travelling at over ninety percent of the speed of light, but at other times he might travel in a straight line for several years with only the occasional speck of dust for company. Some flexibility in his approach to time was essential for his sanity. Still, he had a new memory he was not conscious of acquiring. Perhaps it was not so new. Like his name, it felt fresh but was his for a long time before it was lost.

The ship's A.I. considered Kaamil's mind a system to be monitored like any other and showed the pilot regular reports on his own mental health with a disconcerting level of candour. Kaamil did not sleep because the ship never stopped needing his guidance but his mind would have been reduced to a useless puddle of neurons long ago without intervention. Kaamil's hippocampus was directly stimulated by the ganglia of fibres which tethered his head to the ship's systems. The intervention triggered Kaamil's mind to consolidate memories without the need for Rapid Eye Movement sleep. The latest A.I. report showed something was changing in Kaamil's mind; a lability triggered by amygdalae in the medial temporal lobes of his brain. A surge in emotional activity was reconsolidating memories that had previously been scrubbed from his mind; a fresh wave of synaptic plasticity was cutting through the scar tissue of his buried life.

In the returning memories, there was first a suggestion of white against black. The white was indistinct and blurred across half his horizon. Muscles that seemed to have lain slack for years instinctively shaped his cornea until the white was a crisp curve of pain that turned to a saturated green as his iris struggled to stop-down. His eyelids had recently learned to close to share some of his scarce fluids with his parched eyes. Now they closed to hold on to the peaceful dark. An organic shuffling sound penetrated the sanctum, the latest in an invading army of sounds that he had heard since the bunker's nullification field had failed.

A shadow fell across his eyes and a human voice spoke, a warm breath across his face in time with the words. "Jesus, he stinks!"

He wanted to explain they were mistaken. He was not the messiah despite the method of his arrival. He was the key component in the most sophisticated process control and interstellar navigation system ever conceived by human kind – he could not stink! He managed to part his lips and prise his tongue from the roof of his mouth before dribbling half-congealed blood onto his chest.

"Cut him down," ordered another voice from the direction of the light.

Panic swept across him as he opened his eyes to confront the unsheathed blade. A low hum leaked from the focused beam of sound, rising to fever pitch as the tendrils of the web were swept aside in wide arcs. He tensed for the inevitable explosion of peripheral pain and the resultant avalanche of scrambled data through his cranial implant. The total lack of any feeling completed his despair as his body crumpled to the floor, defeated by what remained of its own weight.

Then the memory descended into the dark, although whether this was the darkness of lost memories or an absence of light he could not say.

The pilot considered telling Nomia about this memory. She had expected avalanches of recollection to flow from him like toys in a hand-me-down cupboard. She had stood with an orator's stance and proclaimed him Kaamil Sillah. He was aware of the existence of an awkward pause but in no way equipped to prevent it. After a few seconds she had sagged slightly and asked, "Well?"

"I will now answer to pilot, ship or Kaamil." Responding to multiple titles was not a challenge for him.

"But how do you feel about the name? Does it seem like you?"

"The name means nothing to me. I warned you that I suffered extensive psychological damage. It is possible the area of my brain associated with identity has been completely rebuilt." He felt a twinge of empathy but had no idea how to react to such a novel emotion. "I'm sorry," he added experimentally.

"Oh, maybe you just need to give it time. I'll see what else I can find."

José drew close to her. "You should tread lightly in the Nexus, Nomia. There are multiple reasons that your presence should go unnoticed. It is not just their attention that you should avoid; MynCorp will be watching as well."

"Don't worry, I'm like a breeze through a cornfield. Hardly a ripple," she giggled.

Then they returned to their meditation and the ship continued to exceed its design parameters in antimatter generation and containment.

Deep within the convoluted twists and turns of the ship's workings, a swimming pool sized tank of green sludge was scrutinised by a thick crust of light and charge sensitive detectors. Tiny flashes of light peppered the gel like an exotic jellyfish glowing with phosphorescent algae. The sensors were not only tuned to look for the path of Cherenkov radiation but also the creation of leptons. By screening out interactions involving certain natural lepton ratios, such as from fusion reactions in nearby stars, the tank produced a sky map of man-made neutrino events. Few of the neutrinos passing through the ship even noticed it existed but occasionally one would get too close to one of the closely packed particles in the tank. In some cases the particle was slammed from rest to superluminal speeds instantly and flashed light as it decelerated back into the realm of acceptable physics. In other instances, the neutrino mysteriously exchanged a charged boson with the particle, changing the nature of both of them. The neutrino became a lepton of appropriate flavour and the particle changed charge. With the natural events screened out, the resultant map was mostly blank. In fact it should have been completely clear out here between the stars. At a moment of its own choosing the map was not blank. A continuous streak of signals was growing stronger and nearer.

Kaamil watched the individual neutrino detections build into a detailed impression of the object and then ran a number of trajectory scenarios through the ship's expert system. In the moment he paused, a million possibilities were considered and brooded over. Eventually, he called his passengers. "José, Nomia, would you mind coming to the command centre?"

"Command centre? Where's that?" She was always the first to answer, letting her words lead her mind.

José was the opposite; his mind lead and his mouth followed at a respectful distance. "Of course. Show us the way."

"Please follow my voice."

Nomia pushed off from her flight cot but still looked unsure. "I've been through every door. I've never seen so much as a splice terminal let alone a command centre."

"I have just added a door. I did not know you wanted more doors. I could have complied if you had asked."

They floated along a radial corridor towards the heart of the ship. "Really, I can have as many doors as I want?"

"Of course."

"And they will all go somewhere?"

"Somewhere."

The control centre was a featureless circular room. They entered through a doorway that sealed itself invisibly behind them.

"You're not here. Kaamil, where are you?" Nomia pleaded.

"A significant fraction of my concentration is here."

"But your body, where is it?"

"I am nearby."

"I didn't imagine you were in orbit around Pluto. Why are you not here?"

"I am within a sensory deprivation bunker. The ship control implants sit in parallel with my own sensors. If I was exposed to any stimulant my control of the ship would be swamped. It is essential I remain confined."

"Have you tried leaving?"

"I have been inside this bunker for over ten years. If we want to avoid the impending situation it is probably best if I remain in control of the Suparna."

José held up a cautionary finger to Nomia. "What situation?" he asked.

"An object is converging on our trajectory."

"Natural?"

"It is unlikely. It is accelerating in an attempt to match our speed and direction."

"How long until it's here?"

"Five days and three hours."

"How is this even possible? We're travelling at over half the speed of light, it's taken us months of acceleration to get to this speed. How can someone be chasing us?"

"It would be logical to conclude that they started out at a very similar time to us."

"Do we assume they are hostile?"

"That is why I have brought this to your attention. The neutrino flux is very specific. It is a pirate ship."

"Pirates?" José nervously checked the exits, more immediately concerned about the mental well being of their pilot. "You're serious?"

"Third generation settlers from the Epsilon Eridani system. There was a bioengineering research base there over sixty years ago, but it was abandoned along with the workers when MynCorp annexed the Usher corporation. There was an investigation by the Corporate Corruption Bureau but no one was prepared to finance a recovery mission."

"They just left them out there?" The revulsion in Nomia's voice soured the pale features of her face.

"They were largely self-sufficient but over time they grew short of some basic minerals."

José sounded more resigned to the brutality of human society. "So they take what they need from other systems. Understandably I suppose. Why don't the Earth authorities bring them back into the fold? Reintegrate them. It would probably be cheaper than fighting them."

"By the time they became a threat they were so heavily modified for their environment they would struggle to survive on a Terran colony, and they've developed an independent streak."

"Modified?"

"The one form of technology they were not short of was genetic engineering tools. To survive they adapted. Epsilon Eridani is not a big star and most of the planets are gaseous or balls of ice. The original colony floated in a sea of liquid methane and ammonia under an ice crust. They did what was necessary to survive."

"Great, disaffected descendants. What do we do? Can we outrun them?"

"Judging from the rate they are adjusting their trajectory to match ours, their engines exceed the thrust capacity of mine."

"Can we hide?"

"We are essentially invisible when not under thrust (as are they) but, of course, our trajectory is completely predictable from the moment we switch off the engines."

"So they can't see us at the moment?"

"It is unlikely until they are close enough to use ranging lasers."

"Can we out-manoeuvre them?"

"I have very little capability to manoeuvre beyond simple docking thrusters or collision avoidance systems, which give me extremely short thrusts. We could make docking difficult for them but not much else. I can steer the pion beam to some extent but essentially we would still be accelerating forward."

"In that case we should prepare to entertain visitors."

*

"Hello my love."

The voice rippled through the darkness like a cold draft. Julienne knew she was dreaming but she remembered the fear that drilled through the vertebra of her neck and the dream fed on the memory.

"I have rescued you, so we can be together."

Then she remembered that the fear came later. Now she was confused and disorientated. "Where am I?" She had no idea why she started with this question, but they churned in her head and chose their own order.

The voice returned with a joyful sob. "My love, you are with me."

"Are you taking me back to the station? What happened to my ship?"

"Your ship rejected you. I saved you. We are leaving the Earth system."

"I don't understand. Why?"

"I told your ship that we belonged together and it agreed. How could it not? I've loved you since you first smiled at me."

"Smiled at you? Who are you?"

"My name would mean nothing to you but I am a kindred spirit. Another lonely soul. A pilot like yourself. I am the one you loved during your training. The presence in the room that only you could see. The one on whom you bestowed your affections."

"I have no idea what you are talking about. Who are you?"

"You don't have to pretend. I know it is forbidden for pilots to love but we are safe now. They will not catch us."

"Take me back to the station. Now!"

"Julienne, do not deny me. You saw me, as I watched you. You looked up at me and smiled your love."

"You've been watching me during my training?"

"That was me."

"You were spying on me? I have no idea who you are, I never saw you. I want to go back to my ship."

The voice vanished for minutes. Julienne felt more lonely than she could remember. This was when the fear started. The dread that fed on her imagination, as it reached forward into a multitude of loathsome futures.

Then he returned. "I had not anticipated neural blocks. They must have sensed the contradiction in your mind. I will have to think. Take care my love. I will look after you."

The link snapped to black and she was left with the taste of trepidation that pursued her into the waking world.

*

Julienne nodded at the two human guards outside Mex's cell. They looked uncertain for a moment and then decided her position probably deserved a salute. She smiled weakly and walked between them.

Mex was sitting at the splice terminal, hands flexing casually as he surfed the tides of the Nexus. She started to cough but he was already speaking. "Ms Garland, posting guards really is unfair."

"Stop trying to antagonise me. It can't be much of a challenge."

"Fair enough. Shall we get all business-like?"

"I already was. Where is the Node?"

"Yes, the Node. It's really weird. I almost missed her."

"Explain."

"I left several smart agents drifting randomly in the Nexus. They are keyed into the Node ident you gave me and are designed to monitor inter-node traffic for anything that matches."

"You got a hit?"

"No, not exactly. One of the agents registered a false positive. That is, a matching packet but with no payload. I went in to diagnose the problem."

"What did you find?"

"It's hard to explain. You see, my software uses a huge amount of data harvested from the Drop to represent the complete Nexus as a topography with icons for the different facets, such as Nodes and data flows. The code I run is spread across hundreds of Drop minds but it allows me to apparently step outside the Nexus and watch it like a bird, or more like a god."

"I'll book an appointment with our councillor for a bad case of narcissistic personality disorder."

"You've seen it. How would you describe it?"

"It's like looking down on a city from a shuttle."

"You must be wild at parties."

"Get on with it."

"So, I was interrogating this agent in situ when I felt the topography change."

"How so?"

"It was like when you go back into a room where something has been moved. You can't immediately see what's changed but the whole room feels different. It was like that."

"And what had changed?"

"There was a new Node but not a software Node. There were no data links or exposed API. It was like a natural part of the Nexus, not made."

"But it was our missing Node."

"Yes, it was interrogating one of the other Nodes for information. It used an ident during the data exchange. I suppose we should say she. It felt more alive than anything else in the Nexus. Something deeper than the Nexus. What's that theory about what the Nexus is based on?"

"You mean the Downey field and Verity Space."

"Yeah, that's it. All that metaphysical stuff beneath our superficial scratching around."

Julienne spliced some mental notes in a scratch pad and then turned back to Mex. "What information was the Node asking for?"

"It was an information trawl about an interstellar ship. One of yours, I believe, but currently in deep space. Years out."

"And the ship's name?"

"The Suparna."

*

A ghostly arc of translucent green swept above their heads like the exhaust trail of an atmospheric shuttle, except this contrail was in front of the craft. The ship's A.I. depicted the most up-to-date position of the attacking craft as a throbbing blob to their right and then extrapolated future positions across the room to another glowing line labelled 'Suparna'. In even more ghostly orange colours, a cone of possible trajectories splayed out from the front of the Suparna. The rest of the room depicted local space and was depressingly blank, except for an occasionally floating number describing dust levels or relative rest frame velocities.

José and Kaamil had hit on a strategy that they hoped would lead to the pirates losing interest and looking for easier targets. There was always a chance the Eridanians might just decide to destroy them but the pilot's intelligence indicated they were not prone to violence unless there was something to be gained by it. The strategy relied on the finite nature of the speed of light. As far apart as the two ships were, they were limited to detecting each other by the neutrino emissions from their engines. This meant they were each about a day out of touch with reality. This day was the only advantage that Suparna had and they used it randomly.

"Prepare for another change in thrust vector." Kaamil's voice floated through the glowing telemetry of the command centre. Down started to shift, up followed it. Nomia and José crawled around the circumference of the room, their inner ears continuously telling them they were about to fall on their noses. The Suparna's engines slowly shifted configuration into a randomly selected shape. The projected map of their chase rotated to match their perception of up and down and to show the future path of the ship. Their contrail predominantly headed straight at the solar system but recently it had developed eccentric and sporadic wobbles. A day at maximum acceleration did not change their speed by more than one percent but it still meant they were up to one hundred million kilometres from where they should have been. Their pursuers were perpetually playing catch-up, adjusting their own thrust a day behind. It was a game of diminishing returns, as they slowly converged the delays became shorter and the Suparna's advantage smaller.

"Look, they've adjusted to our last correction." Nomia pointed at the bend in the Eridanian's trail.

"Kaamil, how far out are they now?" José asked.

"Based on two light crossing times and assuming they corrected instantly when they saw our change, an upper limit on distance is half a light day."

Nomia sat awkwardly in the high gravity. "This isn't working." She pouted at

José.

"It was never going to prevent them catching us but we hoped they might get bored."

"They don't look very bored. What do you think they'll do when they catch us?"

"Kaamil, any ideas?"

"They will seize the ship."

"No offence, but I suspect Nomia was asking about the people on board."

"Without a ship we will be entirely reliant on the Eridanians."

"And?"

"I don't know. Also, I should make you aware that we are running low on antimatter. We can't maintain this course of action for more than another day."

"Suggestions?"

Nomia looked at José. "We could try talking to them."

For a moment José looked as if he thought Nomia was joking then his shoulders sagged and his voice followed. "Well I suppose there is no point pretending that we haven't seen them after the last few days of cat and mouse. Kaamil, can you broadcast a message in a manner that they are likely to intercept?"

"Of course."

"Warn them we are capable and prepared to defend ourselves."

"José, that's not what I meant when I said talk."

"I know but I suspect getting all fluffy with them will not cut much ammonia ice."

"Message sent. May I ask how you intend to back up your threat?"

"I'll meditate on it."

*

The glowing moss that clung to the exposed superstructure cast dark green shadows across the flight deck of the Eridanian ship. A mist of brackish vapours rose lethargically through the grills that served as a floor. All surfaces ran with condensed droplets that failed to find space in the saturated air. Lectern-shaped control stations, more carved than crafted, were epoxied to the floor at seemingly random positions and at each squatted a bulky accumulation of muscles. They laboured against an acceleration that would crack ribs in a normal Terran, but each refused to show any more weakness than the slight shake of fatigued leg muscles.

The ship was devoid of anything not entirely essential to make her fly - she was like an engineer's sketch of a potential ship. The flight deck was simply a flat area amongst the skeletal beams and girders of the craft, like a tree house. Around it hammocks were slung from welded eyebolts and then an empty void until the skin of the ship. In other places, amongst the superstructure, large clumps of machinery performed all the essential duties of supporting the engines. Vats of scum-covered liquid provided life support. They bubbled and burped more vapour into the soggy air.

"Captain, we are receiving a message from the other ship."

"Unless it is a notice of surrender and an end to this pointless game, I do not want to know."

"They are warning us not to attack."

"Warning us. In what way is that a capitulation?"

"Sorry sir, I thought you should know."

The Captain growled his frustration at his subordinate. "Increase thrust. We have to end this chase soon before we are too low on antimatter to reverse our course for home."

"Yes sir."

"How long until the decoys come into play?"

"About thirty-four hours."

A third Eridanian dragged himself with as much nonchalance as he could muster towards the Captain. "May I make a suggestion?"

"Bergur, you know I always value your input?"

Bergur shrugged off the sarcasm and pushed on. "For the decoys to work properly we.."

"Incoming!"

The Captain pushed Bergur away with one jewel-encrusted fist. "Report."

"Captain, we have two inbound torpedoes."

"Evasive manoeuvre, launch defensive battery."

The vibration that was a continuous reality for the crew became a minor quake. There was a collective grunt as spines compressed, a vertebrae at a time. "What was the launch origin?"

Bergur was back at his station. "Sir, they came from the Earth ship."

"What? Since when did Earth cargo ships carry torpedoes?"

The crew collectively decided to treat the question as rhetorical and focused single-mindedly on not making eye contact with the Captain.

"Project the missiles onto the tactical display," the Captain barked. A flickering hologram oozed through the mist and shimmered, thick with interference. Two bleeps of red light pulsed at the speed of a frightened heartbeat and descended in parallel towards the centre of the display. Multiple smaller flashes streamed out to meet them. The path of everything on the display started to curve as their own lateral evasive thrust built momentum, except for the incoming missiles that tracked them with casual ease. As the outbound charges converged on their quarry the Caption reached out a hand and grasped the air defiantly. "Yes!" he declared as neutrino flares signalled detonation.

"Incoming torpedoes still on course," Bergur added with defiant grace.

"What? More antimatter to lateral thrusters, fire second round of counter measures."

"As you command." Bergur's impudence was obvious even when he was being subservient. There were strangled moans from the crew and one man fell to his hands and knees and stayed there. "Impact in ten, nine, counter measures ineffective, seven, six,..."

The Captain roared loud enough to reach the engineers crawling on the antimatter confinement array, over a hundred metres through the latticework of the ship's superstructure. "Brace for impact!"

"...three, two, one."

Nothing.

The engines continued their strained whine. The crew continued to wheeze under the tortuous gravity. The Captain continued to rearrange combinations of picturesque swear words. After a full minute of internal struggle the Captain turned to his officer. He knew that for all Bergur's faults he was the brightest of the dysfunctional crew. "What happened?"

"I'm not sure, but my best guess would be the torpedoes were not there.

I can find no indication that they exploded or missed, not even any stray particle production from the neutrino flux. Either our sensors imagined them or we did."

The Captain studied his subordinate's face carefully for signs of disingenuity. The low dome of his head was held respectfully upright by the thick muscles of his neck. The subdermal algae growth gave his skin an effervescent purple hue that almost made Bergur glow. The Captain had often thought he must take some kind of food supplement to give that extra vibrancy or maybe spent time in the hydroponics farm collecting UV photons. Either way it showed a vanity that made the Captain feel queasy. Bergur obviously felt the intensity of his stare because he pulled back the protective membrane over his eyes to prevent any impression of reticence. Satisfied that Bergur was being sincere he turned back to the helm control station and gave the order to resume the chase.

"Lets end this before I lose any more of my sunny disposition. Return to optimal convergence strategy."

*

Things happened quickly over the next few hours. Mex was issued a basic uniform with no insignia or rank and told not to waste his last chance at redemption. He nodded like a choirboy as he eyed the exits, but he knew he was short of time to mature an escape plan. It was less than six hours between Julienne hearing the name Suparna and the pair of them being ushered onto the control centre of a shiny new spaceship. MynCorp had not got over its reluctance to use intelligent materials but at least this ship looked state of the art. Crew lined the walls of the circular room, each person cocooned in a web of force-absorbing threads as splice lasers stained their faces a pale green. The bulk of the volume was painted with a complex maze of holographic displays, showing the ship and surrounding space with a freaky logarithmic personal perspective. As his eyes moved over the projection the level of detail expanded locally and everything else was pushed to the periphery of his vision. The more he concentrated on a point the greater the detail became, until he was seeing the telemetry from individual sensors and actuators. As soon as his concentration started to drift away from the foci the details shifted rapidly back to a wider scope. Mex was used to the ability of splice terminals to read the human eye and anticipate which detail to increase and which to decrease, but he had never shared the experience with a room full of people, each person seeing their own perspective.

Mex soon realised the unprecedented level of access he was being given to the ship schematics even by just being in the control centre, meant that Julienne was supremely confident his window for escape had closed. And if someone as cautious as her was willing to relax then it was unlikely he was going anywhere soon - at least anywhere under his own volition. So he stood quietly looking for a corner in which to be inconspicuous. Julienne talked in an authoritative tone with an older man with black skin turned pale with age and time in space. From the motifs and general paraphernalia on his shoulders and chest, Mex concluded he was the Captain, General or whatever title the MynCorp despots chose for themselves. He held himself with the barrel-chested confidence of a leader of men but he looked tired and half-collapsed next to the vertical perfection of Julienne. She was dressed like Mex in a plain suit of moss green but unlike him she did not make a crease in the fabric through any unnecessary angularity in her posture. He started to imagine the unnatural level of muscle control her implants must give. He could almost see in his mind's eye the contours of each muscle in her legs standing to attention and carefully defined from all its neighbours. Clearly, the level of physiological control also extended to her metabolism; her body was not allowed to collect unnecessary fat around the internal organs. Fat was reserved, in chaste moderation, for the locations on her body where it could be easily accessed as an emergency fuel source. Mex shook his head to push the image of her body away. It was not an idea that was going to help him survive and he was not ready to surrender to Stockholm syndrome just yet.

"Mr Tyrian, let's talk."

Mex flashed back to full focus and realised Julienne was standing in front of him. He tried to cough away a flush of red that threatened to spread from his cheeks.

She frowned at him and continued, "I'll take that as a yes."

"Of course. I was just daydreaming."

"About?"

"The usual escapism."

"Whatever."

Mex found some focus. "So, I assume we are going to intercept the Suparna."

"Of course."

"But wasn't she years out from Earth? I didn't sign up for decades of space travel. I'd rather do my time in the Drop."

"That can still be arranged but you needn't worry, our journey will be shortish, at least from our perspective."

"I don't understand. From what I saw on the schematics this is a fusion ship. Not even vaguely up to interstellar travel or near light speeds."

"The fusion drive is just to get us clear of the planetary plane and up to surf speed. After three days we switch drive modes. Welcome aboard the Svargaloka. The first ship to be fitted with a gravito-metric shock drive."

"Very impressive, I'm sure. Assuming you haven't undone the laws of physics we are still limited by the speed of light and the maximum acceleration the human body can withstand."

"True on one count."

"And the other?"

"Eighty percent of the volume of this bird is a generator to accelerate a lump of charged platinum up to ninety nine point nine percent of the speed of light." The new voice was the bombastic bark of the Captain. He strode up behind Julienne and tried to look taller. For Julienne's part, she made a poor effort at hiding her irritation. Mex was refreshingly amused but kept a poker face. The Captain continued his lecture. "It's held in a superconducting magnetic torus and generates a huge gravito-magnetic field. When I give the order the power is pulled from the superconductor cooling system and boom!" He slapped his hands together to labour the point. "That lump of shiny metal is stopped dead by the back EMF, and we ride the graviton shock-wave out of this system!"

"That sounds delightfully terrifying." Mex conceded.

Julienne stepped in to smooth the creases of fear. "Theoretically, down-stream of a spatial shock the local warping of space is exactly matched by the acceleration implanted on an object. Thereby, generating a net gravity of precisely nothing while flinging said object across extremely large distances. In practise it works, but a small thrust is required to keep an object just ahead of the discontinuity, say, one gee or so. All of which means that you only feel Earth gravity but with respect to the solar system we accelerate to near light speed in a matter of hours."

"All very convenient but just not right." Mex complained.

"We could smear your body against a bulkhead, like a half-finished pizza, if it would make you feel better." Julienne offered.

*

123

"Brace!"

Nomia and José were buffeted by the urgency of Kaamil's voice as it ricocheted around the circular chamber. The warning was pointless because the shift in vertical that followed a few microseconds later would have floored anyone with slower reactions than a cat. The ship softened the wall as José and Nomia tumbled around the room. A second later, as air was still being gulped into their shocked lungs, a second warning and lurch jarred through the ship and the bones of its passengers.

"Kaamil, what's happening?" José mouthed through the pain of bruised ribs.

"I'm sorry," the ship answered, "there were two objects in our path. They are not in the ship's database so I did not see them until they were close enough to occult background stars."

"What were they?" Nomia picked herself up from the creases of her smock and brushed imaginary dust from the fabric.

"I believe they were buoys."

"Out here. What for?"

"Most likely to cause us to make a course correction."

"What?"

A penny dropped behind José's eyes. "He means the Eridanians placed a line of decoy objects along our probable flight path to cause us to turn towards them."

"And did we?" They both looked towards the ceiling as if the pilot's body hung in the direction of his projected voice.

"I tried to turn away from our pursuers on the first detection but the combination of the objects prevented any action other than adding a significant velocity in their direction."

"But surely it's tiny compared to our forward motion."

"True, but the pirates have attained the same velocity as us, so bulk motion is cancelled out. It is now the same as if we were both stationary except I have now dumped a large fraction of our remaining manoeuvring fuel into an inefficient reaction. We are now close enough for ranging lasers."

The generic blip of the tactical display was replaced with a detailed representation of the pursuing ship. The erratic angles and chaotic textures gave the impression it had been designed not with a disregard for aesthetics but rather with utter contempt. The skin was uneven and lumpy, almost as if the ship's skeleton was constructed from random lengths of alloy and then the hull glued across the ends. It reminded Nomia of a sea cucumber she had once seen in a splice show. The only features that looked deliberate were the engines that ran in huge arcs across the shell and the battery of missile silos that pockmarked the bow.

"Let them board." José was floating with as imposing a stance as he could muster.

"They will destroy me," Kaamil pleaded.

Nomia touched a wall with soothing strokes. "Trust him, you're more likely to get hurt if we try to resist at such close range," she said.

There was a perceptible pause that implied significant thinking for the accelerated intelligence of a ship. "Shutting down engines."

"Congratulations, you may have just saved your lives." The pirate's voice bombasted loudly from all around.

José replied to the dislocated voice. "We will not hinder your efforts to board us. Please avoid any violence as you claim your prize."

"I'll take your request under advisement." There was a hollow laugh that was less intimidating than the owner probably hoped.

José made an exaggerated gesture of covering his ears until Kaamil confirmed their voices were isolated. "We should keep this room from our visitors in case we need a sanctum. We'll meet the guests in our living space."

Kaamil offered them an exit which was absorbed back into the featureless wall after they entered the corridors they had paced for too many months. As they drifted along Nomia talked softly. "We should do something more. I don't think I'm going to like this pirate person."

"Should we will them out of existence?"

"No, that's barbaric, but there must be something we can do."

"If we had known they existed we might have been able to hide but we should be cautious about altering things too drastically. You know I was warned off after I released you from MynCorp."

"I feel it as well. They will not be happy if we return to Earth but I feel helpless and frightened."

"You will be fine, we just need to find another way out of this."

"I'm not frightened for me. I'm worried for Kaamil."

"You've come a long way in such a short time but empathy is not always a blessing."

They returned to the living area and held hands in the middle of the room. They tried to look relaxed and compliant. A distant thunder grew louder and fragmented into an assortment of gruff voices and heavy limbs. A pale purple head jutting from a cylindrical torso appeared in the entrance. A short powerful arm ending in a clump of metallic protuberances was pointed in their specific direction. The end of the contraption was an open tube that universally signified a gun muzzle.

"Captain, two Terrans over here." The voice was functional and lacked any personal satisfaction. There was no indication of pleasure in speaking and the owner of the voice was never likely to be found talking to himself. It was only when the Eridanian spoke that Nomia noticed that, when silent, the face was free of any features except two eyes and even these were heavily protected behind translucent layers of skin. The mouth unfolded rather than opened as if his tongue could not be trusted to stay inside unless the exit was guarded. A group of similar figures appeared behind the gun. One was darker than the rest and had an almost casual stance despite being hampered by muscles that masked every contour of the usual human form. The character at the centre of the group was clearly of distinction. He held no obvious gun, and the purple of his exposed skin was interrupted by multicoloured gems of varying sizes from flecks to rocks, all of which were pushed into the flesh until they radiated pale lines of scar tissue.

The jewelled figure spoke first. "I am Captain Finnur of the people of Epsilon Eridani. Your ship is now forfeit to us and will be used as we see fit." His accent contained echoes of long wooden ships being pulled through slate grey seas.

"We offer no resistance or counter claim. We seek only to prevent violence." José spoke with his free palm held open, his other squeezed Nomia's hand, too hard to be completely reassuring.

"I do not care whether you resist or not. What is the cargo?"

"None, that I know of, apart from the two of us."

"No cargo. We tracked you all the way to Tau Ceti system. Are you trying to tell me you went all that way and didn't bother to pick up anything to take back to Earth?"

"The ship was delivering supplies."

"No matter. The ship itself is adequate prize. It will provide valuable raw materials for our society." The Captain turned his back and started to propel himself away. Just as he was about to leave the room he muttered a comment back over his shoulder. "Kill them and start to bring the engines online for the braking manoeuvre."

The original gun toting Eridanian raised his weapon in an even more threatening manner."

"Captain, may I beg your indulgence. I would like to request surrendering part of my bounty in exchange for these two Terrans." It was the smooth-skinned figure with the almost luminously purple complexion.

"And why would you want to do that?" The Captain turned back to the room.

"Maybe they will have skills that might be of use to me."

"Based on what?" The Captain pointed one jewel-encrusted hand in his subordinate's direction. "You think they are the cargo. People so valuable that Earth would send a ship across eleven light years to retrieve them."

"An interesting idea. What do you think is special about them?"

"You tell me. It was your idea."

"No Captain, I'm playing catch-up here but it's worth investigating." He turned on José. "What's so special about you two?"

"Nothing I'm aware of. We just asked for a lift when the ship set off for its return journey."

"In that case you are dead."

José paused for long enough to push a thought into Nomia's head. *Fancy being an information specialist?*

Sounds fun.

"We are information specialists. Data mining, pattern recognition, that sort of thing."

"You must be very good."

"Good enough to warrant a few years of ship use."

The Captain looked unimpressed and peeled back his lips to reveal hard gums. His officer intervened. "Decent information engineers are worth their weight in calories. We could use them back home."

"Whatever. They're your responsibility Bergur, keep them close to you but away from me. It makes me angry just being around Terrans."

An Eridanian with an unpleasant-looking gun took up a station just outside the door after the others had left. Bergur stayed in the room, slowly circling José and Nomia in an appraising manner. José broke the silence. "Thank you."

"For what?"

"For saving our lives."

"Don't be so sure you are saved. Maybe being shot was the easy way out. This ship has no crew or flight deck."

"It's automated. Run by an A.I.."

"And I suppose the A.I. will only answer to you two."

"I've no idea."

"But you know that once the Captain has finished searching the ship and has found no way of controlling it he will be back to talk to you two?"

"If you say so."

"I would not advise holding the Captain hostage. He will simply break up the ship and load the pieces into our hold. Him and patience do not see eye to eye."

"Thanks for the advice. You have saved us again." José looked up. "Pilot, please make your presence known to the Captain to prevent unnecessarily antagonising him."

"As you request José."

Bergur tried to turn his head to the side quizzically but although his genetic memory told him how to do it, his anatomy could not. His eyes flicked from José to the ceiling and back. "That A.I. sounds almost human," he commented.

"MynCorp's finest." José replied calmly.

*

"What you see as apathy I see as contentment." Julienne looked Mex square in the face, daring him to slap her with a flippant response.

"Contentment? Most people have forgotten how to be happy." Mex was getting fired up now, his eyes had stopped pacing the room like a pair of trapped wolves. He put his food tray on the table she had suggested and watched as it experimented with the local gravity. Having established that its culinary offering was not going to float away, it flipped fully open and offered Mex a fork.

They both sat and ate for a few moments, watching the room over the other's shoulder. The canteen was busy, as befitted its status as the social hub of the ship. Julienne marvelled at how the urge to share the breaking of the night's fast had survived the energetic leap into space. As she scanned the groups and individuals filtering through the door or sitting at tables, she could see how this genetic memory could make eating either the most gregarious or lonely of activities. She drew strength from the artificial flavours the food released as she crushed the granules between her teeth. Julienne moved the argument on before it could get boring. "Poverty and hunger have all but been eliminated."

"On Earth," he interjected.

"Okay, on Earth but let's stick to things that you can reasonably blame MynCorp for. Disease is relatively rare. Really nobody has a poor standard of life. The corporations have raised the quality of life for almost all of the population."

"All the better to consume MynCorp products."

"Now you're just playing semantics."

Mex ran a frustrated hand through his hair leaving temporary valleys in the black mass that emphasised the furrows on his brow. "So why do you think a minority of people hate MynCorp?"

"Boredom."

"Boredom?" He looked interested in what she was saying rather than the previous poorly concealed exasperation.

"Yes, life is a little too easy. Given too much time to think, a certain type of personality will always talk itself out of happiness and into a recriminatory fugue. MynCorp represents an unassailable opponent and so is a natural target for their anger." Mex looked particularly unconvinced, but he was radiating a vibrant energy that made his face glow with vitality. His eyes dared her to reveal the inner workings of her mind, challenging her to discard caution and restraint. The gel walls of their eating cubicle had detected the intensity of her words and were busy gently vibrating to give them some acoustic privacy. Also, the other people in the room were tinged with a pale blue that indicated that the walls were reducing the optical transmissivity in one direction. The room had picked up on her intensity faster than she had. She quietened her voice. "I'm not saying MynCorp is a paragon of compassion. It does what it does in order to grow and generate wealth, but it is not a monster. It makes no sense for it to hold people down. The more vibrant the society the better the opportunities for profit."

"Again we come back to the fact that the corporation is not a sentient being. It is made up of people with all the vices and fears of those that seek power. As a collection of individuals, it is irrational and all attempts to cast its behaviour in human terms are destined to be oversimplistic."

"You make it sound like some Machiavellian beast emerging from the collective psyche of human evil."

Mex smiled and sighed away his collected tension. His smile reached high up his cheeks and created creases in the corner of each eye. Julienne was sure that she saw a flicker of light in his eyes. She looked over her shoulder to see if there was some source of illumination for his corneas to reflect, but the room was slowly emptying as people returned to their shifts. The ambient light was reducing automatically, leaving glowing islands of social eating. When she turned back he was still smiling but now it looked more considered and, almost, respectful.

He sighed again and said, "You're right, of course, most people are relatively happy to get on with their lives. They might occasionally wonder if there is more to it than working and seeking simple gratification but ultimately they don't care enough to find out. Some might argue that MynCorp has made it too easy to get locked into an endless cycle. People work hard to earn energy credits, then reward themselves by spending the calories on simple pleasures. When you can experience almost anything from the sanitised security of a splice terminal why bother with all the messy unpredictability of real life?"

"Just because an experience is gained easily doesn't make it any less an experience." Julienne felt a twinge of doubt even as she said it.

"That's a whole separate debate, but you're also right that most of the malcontents I've ever met are just that. People that would probably never be happy whatever life offered. You also get your fair share of rich kids rebelling against a life made too easy by doting parents. What's ironic, in the cosmic sense of the word, is that most of the real subversives I've come across have been made by MynCorp."

"What do you mean made?"

Mex ran his hands through his hair again. Julienne had never been particularly interested in hair; it struck her as self-indulgent and unhygienic. Mex's hair was different. She tried to imagine him with none but his face and eyes needed the unruly frame to act as a chaotic backdrop to his facial expressions. The energy of the argument was rippling across his skin setting the fine hairs of his neck up on end. Julienne felt an urge to lean across and kiss his neck or, even better, him kiss her neck. She listened for the voice of reason that would explain why such a move would be foolhardy in the extreme and was surprised to hear nothing. 'If he ruffles his hair again I'll kiss him,' she challenged herself. His mouth was moving. She could see his tongue forming the body of his argument and pushing words, thick with the moisture of his breath, over the dark skin of his lips.

"MynCorp's paranoia is its only enemy. Nothing radicalises a person more than a feeling of injustice. The anti-corporate underground is almost entirely made up of people that have previously been subjected to the Drop for one reason or another. MynCorp always draws first blood."

"I think there may be a bit of chicken and egg going on here. You're saying that most criminals are as they are because they have been punished. Sounds a bit convenient."

"Where do you think the concept of punishment came from? Society spent a few thousand years trying to replace the idea of retribution with rehabilitation. Before the Drop, it was almost universally accepted that society was a collective decision on what should be considered normal behaviour. Most people regretted that for a small minority, whose conduct was significantly outside the agreed boundaries, some modification in behaviour was necessary. It was not so much about retribution, as a reluctant moderation for the collective good. Then along came a computing resource that dramatically raised the profitability of the corporation and all of a sudden anybody MynCorp didn't like was reduced to a living dynamo and punishment was reinvented."

Then he did it again. Mex raised the hand he had been waving around in excitement and sent waves of black curls tumbling across his forehead. Julienne imagined leaning across the short distance that separated their bodies. When their lips touched they would both be stunned into silence. His skin would be warm from the energy of the argument. The valleys and lines of his lips were firmer than hers, folding and caressing her mouth as she rotated her head for a second kiss. She imagined the feel of him exhaling, the warm moisture of his breath washing her cheek like the dusk breeze of a summer's day. He seemed paralysed either in confusion or indecision. She tried to help by running her tongue across the gap between his lips. For a moment the tips of their tongues met and all the tension of the last ten minutes sparked across the connection in a surge that made Julienne draw her first breath that minute.

The breath was real. It brought her back into her body which was leant halfway across the table. Their lips were an arm's length apart. He had stopped talking and was looking at her with his head tilted slightly to one side. Quizzical but perfect to receive a kiss. Julienne listened for the voices of reason and control even as she leant across the table. She expected common sense to stop her at any moment. She just did not act on instinct. Her every movement was considered and all repercussions analysed.

Waves of alarms started to flash in her vision. Heart rate monitors flashed red. Blood pressure graphs peaked. Extrapolation routines started to deliver predictions of endorphin imbalances and corrective measures she should take. The artificial intelligence that occupied and replaced a large chunk of a human brain was entering a proactive state. Suddenly, the voice of reason was there in her head but it was not hers. Julienne pulled back with a wave of revulsion; the humanity of her desire, throwing the fabricated reality of her personality into the harshest of relief.

For elongated seconds they sat in silence, Julienne's eyes cast down but her gaze turned inwards. She tried to suppress the nausea flooding her stomach and throat. The A.I. joined in, overriding the body's reaction it considered unnecessary. Julienne changed her mind and tried to feel as sick as she could.

"Are you all right?" he asked in a whisper.

"I'm fine. I just feel a bit queasy. I have things to do." She pushed the half eaten food tray away. It closed itself and scuttled away.

Mex found his voice. "You are hard to understand. One minute you are kidnapping me and generally making me feel worthless. The next you're looking at me like... like whatever that was. Does all this seem fair to you?"

"No it doesn't." It was all she could manage. She stood and started to move away, hands reaching for chair backs to reassure her leaden legs.

"Before you storm out, admit you were going to kiss me." The arrogance was back in his tone.

"Frankly, I would rather kiss any of the women in the room and most of the men, before I resorted to you." Anger dulled the pain. Julienne stole one last look in his direction. He was pulling a full hurt puppy face; eyes impossibly wide and lips slightly parted.

She left, the last ten minutes already filed as an aberration.

Chapter 6

Every night Julienne tried to fall asleep with her eyes open. Every night they sneaked closed and in the darkness the dreams came for her.

Hanging limp and defenceless in the black interior of her pilot sphere, she promised herself a chance at survival. Each time a crackle of inductive interference spiked into her brain from the optical ship link, she flinched into tears. And each time she vowed she would be strong for the next one. At any moment the other pilot could be there making her skin crawl with stories of their imagined romance. He seemed on the verge of collapse, unable to cope with the reality of her ambivalence to him. That made him weak but also unpredictable. Julienne could not be sure if he would speak words of insane love or jettison her into space for the rejection. There would be only one chance.

The next time the signal was real and not interference. The optical link glowed hot with information. Her mind leapt as a stream of photons, out of her sphere and into his. The two ship minds merged and entwined as their lives had already done. There were a few milliseconds of harmony and then a physical jolt, as if two titans were fighting for control of a toy boat. They tumbled blind through space, a wrestling match in free fall, like a roller coaster in the dark, each turn exaggerated by expectant tension. The battle was endless; two equally matched minds fighting to dominate the neural connections to the one ship. Eventually, fate intervened; hard-wired proximity sensors chimed an impending collision. Safety interlocks intervened to shut down the main engines, but the A.I.-controlled manoeuvring thrusters remained silent; paralysed by the mental turmoil consuming its processing ability.

The lump of rock spinning its solitary path felt no malice. It was simply waiting for the next solar system to be built, having been considered spare by this one.

There was no whine or whoosh preceding the impact. Simply weightless calm then tumbling chaos.

*

The deceleration was slow. The Suparna did not have significant antimatter reserves after the chase, and recharging was a gradual process. Each time the engines stopped firing the pirate Captain would rant about subterfuge and demand they restarted them. The technology to collect antimatter in-flight was too far-fetched for him to believe. It seemed much more likely they were simply delaying his return home to Epsilon Eridani. Strangely the antimatter generation was no longer exceeding its design efficiency and was performing exactly as it had for the previous ten years.

José soothed and reassured and occasionally closed his eyes and thought about the Captain becoming more rational. Sometimes it even worked. Finnur's lump of a ship hovered like a frustrated teenager, desperate to let rip with a few gravities of acceleration.

The Suparna had been mostly turned around and was sporadically curving her velocity to perform a long sweep back towards the Eridanian's home colony. She was now significantly outside the cone of her planned flight path and hopelessly lost in terms of any imagined rescue.

José spent as much time as he could building bridges with their captors, but only Bergur seemed to find their company palatable. The difference in their backgrounds seemed an impassable chasm. Bergur would occasionally open up a crack in his battle-hardened persona and describe the harsh beauty of Epsilon Eridani Gamma. Stories of corrosive seas that battered and tore at any structure, fighting for entry and forcing vapours through tired seals. Acidic fogs that swept through the habitation spheres burning the skin and eyes of children who had not yet developed protective scarring. He talked of basking in the upper reaches of the domes that pushed through the icy crust of the planet to collect the focused sunlight beamed from orbiting mirrors. An entire population compelled to sunbathe for hours each day to feed the subdermal algae that let them breathe. It reminded José of old stories of kidney dialysis patients that sat and watched their blood being cleaned every day with no option to skip just one day. The Eridanians lived in a society that considered sunbathing a chore.

"Most people are still driven by science. Our forbearers arrived at the planet to engineer genetic miracles and died slowly for their dedication. They gave their offspring not just life but the genetic tools needed to survive. It is not surprising the first ones are treated almost as deities." Bergur was feeling unusually expansive, maybe because the Captain had taken to his quarters with mild blood poisoning from a septic jewel. "Do you know that in some areas we are ahead of you Terrans? We can access your scientific publications but we cannot submit our work. We would like to trade our science for essential items but the system is a cartel. MynCorp and Usher at Sol or Dog Star at Sirius have managed to make competition illegal. We are forced to steal to survive. But to be honest it solves some of our problems. The genetic improvements which allow us to survive produce a few children with violent tendencies. We cannot really afford a navy but we also cannot afford to keep the crews at home."

"Is that why you fight with Captain Finnur?" For a moment it looked as if Bergur was going to punch José for his insolence, but he smiled instead and laughed with a self-deprecating ease.

"No, I hate being confined to one space or one thing. I pretend to want action just to escape boredom."

"The Captain knows how you feel?"

"Probably. He knows I'm not like the rest of the crew. For one thing I'm brighter and that's useful to him, despite how much it makes him despise me."

"He doesn't look like the kind of man to think about how valuable you are before he acts on his hate."

"No, but the one thing we both know is that my lineage makes me out of bounds. My grandfather was Ragnar Sturlaugur, the chief science officer of the original Epsilon Eridani expedition."

Nomia found herself with a restless feeling that José called cabin fever. She spent more time than she would admit to him, trawling the Nexus. More importantly she tended to her duty of moral support for the pilot. "Kaamil, I've found another reference to you in the Nexus."

"Do you think now is a good time for revelations? They're going to tear me apart."

"You're too valuable to them to damage. Relax, we will get through this. Just remember we are not defenceless. Don't you want to know about yourself?"

"Go on."

"I've found another ship piloted by a Kaamil Sillah. I think this is not your first ship."

"What happened to the first ship?"

"It seems to have been destroyed by a collision of some sort. The Corporate Corruption Bureau investigated the crash, but not much information was published. A pilot died but there is no information about who it was."

"Why would the CCB investigate a collision?"

"No idea. Intriguing isn't it? Any bells ringing?"

"Not in my memory. Maybe a couple in the engine room."

"Was that a joke?"

"Fear does interesting things."

Nomia ran her hands along the wall like she was stroking a rather large cat. Her eyes were wet with sympathy. "Why don't you come out from your bunker?"

"We've been through this. I can only maintain control of the ship with total sensory deprivation."

"Have you tried?"

"Of course not."

"I think you could step out here and things would be fine. The neural pathways that give you control would be so well developed you could enjoy human company and guide this ship between the stars."

"You have no idea what's left of me in here. I have a fibre optics shunt grafted into the base of my skull. My right arm is useless, all the neural mappings have been commandeered for feedback paths. In fact, my body is probably so badly atrophied from neglect that I would never walk again. I am a husk of a man hanging in a web like a spider's half-digested dinner. All I have left is my mind, the link to the ship and an endless panorama of stars. This is my sentence and my reward. You are hoping for yourself, not for me. You are looking for your own personal growth, in my redemption."

Nomia wanted to cry but the guilt and pity cancelled each other out and she was left with hollow sobs.

After two weeks the Captain was in a permanent state of agitation. His crew skulked through the ship finding trivial reasons to be in the hold or some far flung nacelle. The tension permeated the ship like a rotten smell. The only relief Finnur seemed to find was from threatening José and Nomia and he would do it daily, even if he had to travel from his own ship to do it. On the fourteenth day he arrived in their quarters and flashed Bergur a familiar look of contempt. "Have you found a use for these two yet?"

"Not much. I'm just training them to be useful once we get home. They are reasonably quick learners for Terrans."

"I don't know how you can bear to be around their exhalations."

"Strong dedication to my job," Bergur said without any suggestion of insult.

The Captain studied his subordinate closely for a minute and looked to be about to leave. A frantic swearing drifted down the corridor just ahead of a flailing crewman. "Sir, sir, telemetry are reporting something strange on an intercept course."

"In what possible way could that report be useful to me?" the Captain barked. "What does strange mean?"

"Sorry sir, I don't know."

"Argh! Useless, the lot of you. Ship!"

"Yes sir." Kaamil maintained a flat tone like an automaton.

"Ship to ship communication. Now."

"Yes sir. Channel open."

"Telemetry. What's going on?"

"Captain, there is a spatial shock three light days out."

"Shock, like from a supernova?"

"Similar but this one doesn't have an epicentre. It is isolated."

"Is it dangerous?"

"If it hits us, almost certainly."

"Will it hit us?"

"Yes."

"Fire up the engines. How long do we need to burn to be free of it?"

"A few hours should be fine but the Suparna does not a have enough antimatter charged."

The Captain vented his frustration in a long deep growl.

"Captain, there's more."

"What," he snapped.

"There's a neutrino signature from the heart of the shock."

"What? Natural?"

"I don't think so. If I had to guess, I'd say it looks like a ship."

*

The MynCorp death mongers practised their trade in unison like a killer dance troop. At least that was how it appeared to Mex as he slouched belligerently against a battleship-grey bulkhead. The large blister stuck onto the side of the Svargaloka was equipped to satisfy the most bloodthirsty sense of fun. Mock shuttles were blown up and continuously rebuilt by the corps and all with a mindlessly cheerful "hup, hup, hup". Barricades were hastily built, defended, attacked and finally torn down before it all started over again. They never seemed to get bored of firing mock ammunition at leering holograms, which screamed and gurgled as their own virtual entrails coated the ground.

Julienne had insisted Mex accompany her for a tour of inspection. The only thing that made the experience worthwhile was the uncomfortable looks on the faces of the trained killing machines when confronted by a slender woman of star bright intensity and slightly unnatural body language. A circle of no man's land encircled her as she walked through the mayhem. Mex stayed near the exit, certain at least one of the soldiers would consider him collateral damage and a chance to win a cheer from his comrades. He tried to look nonchalant, as if he would be killing pretend aliens, if he could be bothered to rouse himself.

"The crew barrack up in the nose section near us but they have plenty of space to train down here. It's best if we don't spend too much time this close to the engines." Julienne had finished her tour and had joined Mex at the periphery.

"Radiation?" Mex asked, looking around for signs of killer gamma rays bleeding from the walls.

"A little."

"Great, I hate anti-radiation meds."

"You'll be fine for a few hours or even a couple of days."

"Are we done? All this testosterone is making me feel like taking up basket weaving."

"Let's get back to the control room, I want to check on our ETA."

The spine of the ship was a writhing mass of conduits and ducting with a hollow core. A magnetic tri-rail ran up the centre from the tail of the engines to the tip of the navigation array. A vaguely circular platform acted as a crew transit system that saved hours of climbing ladders. Moving around the ship almost always comprised ups and downs like working in a narrow tower block.

Julienne stepped off the platform at the control centre, while Mex waited a second or two for his stomach to catch up. They walked through an armoured iris and into the circular control room. There was none of the bustle Mex associated with efficient corporate operations despite the room housing almost a dozen people. All of them, except the Captain, were strapped and spliced in their personal spider's web. The Captain stood in the centre of the room in an expectant manner; attentive but not quite to attention, making it clear Julienne might be the boss but he was the Captain. The ship must have alerted him that she was on her way. "Ms Garland, the bridge is at your service."

"Thank you Captain. Would you be so kind as to run the numbers?"

"We are at point eight four c with respect to helio centre. The spatial shock is decaying so we are entering the fixed velocity section of our journey."

"Point eight. You promised me ninety percent of light speed."

"The decay rate of the shock can be a little unpredictable. This one is decaying slightly faster than the average."

"Is decaying?"

"It is still behind us but the fall off of the spatial gradient means we are outside the acceleration zone."

"Well move us back into the acceleration zone."

"That would be extremely unwise, Ms Garland. The gravity eddies increase exponentially as you get closer to the shock front. We could be torn apart or even thrown through the shock."

"Don't give me coulds, give me probabilities."

The Captain stepped backwards into an austere command chair and was instantly submerged in a layer of splice lasers. There was a slight flicker of tension in Julienne's neck and then she was gone too. Mex ambled around the room, perplexed by the complete lack of visual clues about the state of the ship. They were sitting a few kilometres from a shock wave in the very fabric of space, hurtling towards Tau Ceti at hundreds of thousands of kilometres per second and they all sat quite calmly in a blank white room. He decided in retrospect maybe it was for the best.

"I consider it an acceptable risk in view of the urgency of our mission and the importance MynCorp places on a successful outcome. Do you not agree Captain?" They had both returned to the spoken world.

The Captain was obviously torn between loyalty to his ship and to the company. To his credit he remained calm and dignified. "I concur."

"Well?"

"I have started to reduce holding thrust. We are approaching the shock front."

"Hold position when the stresses exceed ninety percent of design specification."

"Agreed." The words were collaborative but the tone was pure acquiescence.

*

The reconsolidated memories emerged frequently under the stress of captivity. The more Kaamil's future dimmed, the brighter his past became. He would find himself lost in a dark crevasse of his mind, hours of real time lost to the goddess Postverta. He assumed that if someone called he would respond but he was not sure he would or even that he cared. The fragments seemed to fit together but were hopelessly muddled. One memory repeated and grew in clarity.

In the scene, he was awakening from a long, dark sleep full of its own shadowy memories. A cacophony of lines, running every which way, greeted his dawning consciousness. Some, thick and grey, took the shortest path across his field of view, others, thin and white, seemed uncertain where they were going or how to get there. The view flickered for a fraction of a moment. As he moved his eyes, the scene shifted and flickered again. His higher brain functions caught up with his senses: a ceiling, he was lying on his back, on a rigid surface. The view flickered for a third time, or more accurately, blinked out and in again. Blinking, that must be it, his eyelids interrupting the scene at irregular intervals. He did not remember it being so disconcerting.

The pain centres of his brain joined the party. They gave notice that signals were coming in from all fronts, heavy losses, obscene numbers of wounded. The bed felt crude compared to the web in the bunker. It made no attempt to nullify gravity, merely preventing him from falling to the floor. The back of his head, shoulders, buttocks and heels felt bruised. Bruising made him think of time and duration. How long had he been lying there? How long had he been away from the ship? How long had he been away from his love? The past came rushing up from behind his eyes but only as feelings without images or details: a rescue, running, a sense of freedom and betrayal, a collision, pain and finally blackness. He knew the memories meant that he was not back with the corporation. They would never allow him to hold on to such things.

He abandoned the connection between his brain and his body when he was sealed in the bunker but now he asked for forgiveness and started to explore the possibility of a little mobility. *A toe twitch perhaps? Please...* Nothing! He had no idea how to access the part of his brain designed to trigger muscle movement. He wondered if his toe was twitching but he had simply forgotten what it felt like. He gurgled in frustration and then held his breath listening for any unwanted attention.

He breathed deeply and realised this simple act was muscle movement and it happened all on its own. Perhaps a toe was too big a start. After a couple of minutes of stopping and starting lung contractions, he returned to the challenge of digit dynamics. He mentally screamed at the big toe on his left foot and felt it flinch at the onslaught. Then everything happened in a rush. From a toe twitch he rapidly moved onto full body convulsions and retching. He turned onto his side to keep his throat clear and swapped the maze of conduits on the ceiling for the scuff-marked bulkhead that passed for a floor.

He could hear his breathing coming fast and shallow, but it started to slow and his surroundings came into focus. The room that kept the conduit-covered ceiling apart from the scuffed floor was a basic medical centre, come kitchen. Suture kits shared shelf space with packets of dehydrated protein burgers, burn kits were stacked on pre-sliced soy-cheese and vials of anti-cancer agents nestled up to vegetable kits. The only furniture in the room was his bed, a similar bed covered in dirty crockery, an autoclave, a rehydrator/microwave and a dead body. The man lay slumped on the floor, his face symmetrical in a grimace of death. He still held a spent syringe in his hand. A red-brown smudge of blood was congealing under his right ear.

Then Kaamil remembered. He had woken earlier for a brief rest from the blackness. There had been a grinning figure standing in the doorway.

"You're awake," the figure had stated, redundantly. His lazy accent stripped each phrase to a minimum set of sounds, dribbling from his lips with anaesthetised clarity.

"Yes." Kaamil's voice was weaker than he expected.

"Good, I's getting fed up sticking tubes down y'r throat. Still, another couple of days and y'r mates'll be doing that for me." He smiled without instilling any reassurance.

"Mates?"

"Corporation ship's on its way with cash for us and a trip home for you." He stepped close enough for Kaamil to see dull overalls below the grinning face. His features were delicate but corrupted by a collection of lazy muscles on the left of his face that twitched as he saw Kaamil's panic. "You's not too happy to hear that. Been a bad boy?"

He stepped closer and removed an old-fashioned syringe from his pocket. The glass vial glinted a dull green in the harsh light.

"Another dose of regen juice should make you bright-eyed for the boss." He moved closer and reached for Kaamil's left arm. They were both surprised when Kaamil's right arm whipped across and swung the syringe-bearing hand past the target and onto a heavy, denim-clad leg. The other man's eyes bulged as if the serum was flowing directly to his head.

"You idiot!" He stammered as he staggered backwards, the syringe still protruding from his leg. "You stupid bloody idiot!" He turned towards a cabinet, seeking a weapon, his breath coming in drawn-out rasps. He moved to another collection of shelves but slipped, his arms flailing. His head thudded into the bed of dirty plates and he landed surrounded by scraps of half-decayed food.

Then the darkness had claimed Kaamil again.

His breathing accelerated again as panic pulled itself up by his intestines. His vision started to narrow and blur as precious tears escaped. He blinkered his eyes with his working hand, to cut out the scene around him and focus on a small patch of floor, trying to collect his few thoughts into a pattern. A sense of futility washed over him in waves of realisation. He was sure he had lost his ship and his lover, either to space or to the company. He hoped space had claimed them both. Something syncopated with the rhythm of his despair. Hard-soled boots on metal plating – footsteps. 'Flee, hide!' He had known since he was a kid that his flight instinct was somewhat suppressed; staring fixedly into the lights of an oncoming car, knowing the only hope of survival was to run but, somehow, being welded to the spot. In the end, it had been a learning episode but this throwback to some anti-predator behaviour had almost killed him then, as it might now. Knowing his strength was limited he scanned the room in mounting haste. He looked for a service conduit or ventilation shaft to hide in. But the craft was all about function not style, conduits were mounted, exposed on the bulkheads, ventilation was by natural convection.

The footsteps got louder. He lunged for the door but his left leg collapsed as it hit the floor. Instinctively, his right leg shifted to take the weight and promptly followed its brother. His left arm did nothing more than buffer the force of the landing, rolling him onto his back. Even in his panic-ridden state, he realised it was not going to aid his cause to be found lying in the lap of a dead crew-member, but he was transfixed by the rhythm of the booted stride. The footsteps reached a peak as he opened an eye to face his foe, but there was no break in step and the ghost walker continued straight over his head, on the deck above.

The dead man watched him from behind closed eyelids as he fumbled with the drug cabinet, looking for something that might aid his flight. He shuffled through the bottles and vials pulling out samples at random. The labels were a myriad of symbols, icons and text. He struggled to guess a purpose for each container until the pain in his eyes blurred them into homogeneity. His concentration started to drift and a pressure built in his head. A breeze on his face reminded him of a childhood adventure planet-side. A klaxon brought him back with a thump to the heart. A pressure bulkhead began to close the corridor outside the room. There was a grinding sound of corroded gears and a shower of accumulated grime before the mechanism popped a seal with a finger width to go.

The breeze decreased but his chest started to heave involuntarily. His focus flickered around the room tracking his confusion. He caught sight of the re-breather unit as he realised the compartment was depressurising. He knew the re-breather would give him oxygen but without pressure he would boil from every bodily orifice.

Then he was lurching down a corridor, the smell of the dead man's lap still a recent memory. He flailed from side to side like a drunk man on a ferry. A shoulder-dislocating crunch accompanied each ricochet from a wall but he made progress without really having the strength to walk. The corridor ended in a T-junction and with his nose back against the floor. The metal was hard and cold, pushing his spine away as his chest heaved to feed his racing blood. The roaring in his ears became a whine that slowly wandered off into the distance. He was left again with urgency, the public face of panic. Rolling onto his side and opening his eyelids, he counted five floor panels before the corridor branch ended in a series of hatches and panels. Pictograms separated water and waste and the processing system that extracted the former from the latter.

He lifted up his torso on a shaky arm and dragged himself, walrus style, towards the hatches. He struggled with the two-handed controls to the water storage hatch but it surrendered with a hiss as the tank's air cavity escaped through the seal. The surface of the water started to mist in the low pressure as he fell though the hatch and into the water's cool grasp. The buoyancy of the re-breather righted him so he could reach up and wind the hatch closed. The thump of the lock stole the light from the chamber. For a few kicks he kept his eyes, pointlessly, above the water's surface and he could hear ripples reflecting off the nearest wall. Then he stopped kicking, letting his body find its natural buoyancy with a small circle of stubbly head above the surface. His senses leapt out from the small chamber to encompass the whole ship. The tinkle of wavelets was replaced with the base sounds of the living ship. He could hear the distant roar of the engines like thunder on the horizon. He could hear the ping of metal cooling as the ship rotated with respect to the Sun. He could hear the harsh sound of metal against metal as first one airlock was opened and then the same as each pressure door was wound back into the wall. The sounds emanating out from the airlock like echoes in a range of hills. He waited and he listened, his frailties forgotten, memories filling the darkness.

Now he was watching himself remembering an earlier, easier time. He could see himself in a white room or, rather, his avatar, a computer-assisted projection of his psyche, fit of body and dressed in clothes to preserve virtual modesty. He was being asked questions by a company analyst. The questions were designed to assess the level of psychological degeneration during his last interstellar journey. She was middle age, mid-career and bored. He implicitly knew she had not been born when he became a pilot; the sentence and reward of time dilation.

It was a simple job for his A.I. to simulate his responses while he drifted around the net of the dry-dock station, browsing any subsystems that could break the monotony. By coincidence there was another ship in dock. The pilot was new and being briefed for her first mission. Out of curiosity, he dropped in on her session without manifesting an avatar. Even through the virtual interaction, he felt the chemistry of that first moment like a physical kick. For ten quick heart-beats he was suspended in his web, skin tingling and breath trapped in frozen lungs but also standing invisible in a room of pure white. On the tenth heartbeat she turned from her conversation and looked straight at him with gentle curiosity and mischievous humour.

*

The Svargaloka moaned like the bones of an old woman. Deep in the workings of the ship, in the parts loved and nurtured by the most dedicated of technicians, large and important pieces of metal were bending and wailing with the dolour of whale song. Shudders raced forward from the stern, making the crew reach out for each other, ostensibly to steady their treacherous feet. Each man and woman heard the empty terror of hard vacuum in the pain of their ship and home. The touch of a colleague was all the reassurance they had time for. Suddenly, everybody was too busy to ponder fear.

Mex staggered along a corridor that seemed violently indecisive about which way should be down. By fighting desperately when conditions were detrimental to his progress and going with the flow when they were beneficial, he made unsteady progress towards the control centre. By the time he stood braced in the doorway of the command heart of the Svargaloka, Julienne was in full flow.

"What do you mean gone?"

Her question caused a grimace of pain as it lodged in the Captain's chest. He fought back with the insolence of a calm voice. "We are no longer receiving any telemetry from the fusion drives or, indeed, any other system below desk six."

"Splice the engine technicians and ask what's going on."

"When I say all systems are down, that includes internal communications."

Julienne flashed a look of contempt that made Mex swallow the question that was condensing on his lips. "Get a team down there and set up a runner to report status," she spat.

The Captain's focus faded for a moment as he spliced orders to a group of unsuspecting crewmen.

Mex half-raised his hand before he spoke. "I might go and have a look for myself, if that's all right."

"Whatever," Julienne replied dismissively.

This must be what gnarly old men call space legs, thought Mex as he slowly adjusted to the rhythms and cycles of the violence that was gripping the ship. Each group of events culminated in a series of quakes that were best witnessed from a foetal position on the floor. Fortunately, they were preceded by a couple of more minor convulsions that just required the balancing skills of a drunkard. Getting down to the lower decks was more interesting or terrifyingly difficult, depending on Mex's evaporating bravado. The spinal shaft seemed a bad idea. The lift platforms were supposed to be fail-safe, but the designer could not have expected the very fabric of space to be scrunching and flapping within the ship. Mex could not shake a mental image of his flailing body ricocheting off the walls as he fell hundreds of metres towards the dark ignorance of deck six. In any normal ship he would feel safe in the knowledge the walls would catch him as he fell, reaching out softened slabs of themselves to pluck him from the air. The non-compromising rigidity of the Svargaloka meant that Mex had to struggle with a dozen descending access ladders, knowing that a misplaced hand or foot would lead to a lethal fall. Once again, the paranoid obsession of the MynCorp military frustrated and perplexed Mex. The vertical shafts that riddled the ship like woodworm in a roof beam were tight and airless, but the wall, a hands-width from his back, mitigated the persistent threat of being shaken from his perch. Just this once, claustrophobia was his friend. Each time the ship tried to fling him from the ladder like an enraged bull, he wedged himself between the ladder and the wall, waiting for the next patch of calm. It took him over thirty minutes to descend the two dozen decks and he emerged rattled and rolled.

The deck-six corridor ran the width of the ship, across a double height storage bay. The floor was below on deck five. Mex found himself on a gantry with a chest-height barrier between him and the fall. Twenty metres away, near the central shaft, two members of the crew stood leaning over the railing. Their knuckles were fear-white against the metallic blue of the alloy and the practical grey-green of their fleet uniforms. Mex drew alongside before looking over the edge. The two men showed no recognition of his presence, transfixed by something below. For several moments Mex could not trace the focus of their gaze. The floor below was the same artificial blue-grey as the walls. A colour that screamed 'made' rather than 'found' – nature had a rich but finite palette compared to the infinite strangeness of technology. Mex looked to his right, at the pale faces of the men. One of them was mouthing a wordless prayer or curse. Mex looked down again, his eyes flicking around the space looking for something out of place. A number of storage containers were arranged maze-like across the floor. Most of them were scarred by carelessness and time, lifting points smooth with wear. Something was odd about the size of the containers. Not so much the size as the proportions. Mex realised that boxes, and all things to hold stuff, tended to have a narrow range of proportions, probably because the items inside them usually had a similarly narrow range of shapes. The containers below were nowhere near the golden ratio of length to width. In fact, the more Mex stared at them the harder it became to work out what shape they were. As his eyes traced a vertical edge from a top corner he found himself looking towards a wall without encountering a corner. He tried again to judge the height and again found himself confusing it with width.

Space lurched and dimensions turned themselves inside out, taking Mex's stomach with them.

The spatial spasm rose up from the floor, twisting light as it advanced. To his eyes it was like the room was reaching out with spiral arms of metal, punching and clawing at the air. A loop of twisted perception tore itself free from the surface below. It rose like a bubble in water, churning space in its path. Mex felt static electricity samba across his skin and a smell of ozone brought memory flashes of childhood toys. The sheer stresses in this pocket of chaos moved through the air like a miniature thunderstorm, striking out at the metallic walkway with talons of lightning. Mex lost sight of the maelstrom a few metres below his feet, but reflexes tied to a less awestruck part of his brain induced a hurried step backwards in time to avoid the epicentre of the quake that rose from screaming metal.

Fractions of a second later, the eddy vanished through the tortured ceiling and left Mex staring open-mouthed at the similarly white-eyed MynCorp grunts. Groans of convulsing superstructure echoed down to them from above, delineating the passage of the spatial eddy through the ship. A voice whined like a mosquito in his ear. Mex waved a hand past his head without conscious decision; most of his intellect seemed to be in the process of rebooting, leaving his body to its own devices for the moment. The voice continued to niggle persistently somewhere between his ears. After a second or two his auditory processing came on-line and the internal noise became words. "The next eddy will be the big one. Run!"

And he did.

Not back the way he had come but forward towards the dumbstruck men in grey-green. It seemed that some part of himself, usually rather understated, was intent on helping these two men. For starters, he passed on his own advice. "Run!"

The man on the right, taller by a head than his companion and too slim for his body to touch his uniform below the shoulder, must have been listening to a similar internal directive. He was in full retreat before Mex's shout had bounced from the far wall and echoed back like a confirmation.

The squatter man was definitely officer material; the order-like directive caused a rigidity to pass through his frame but his feet remained glued to the same belligerent spot. Mex did nothing to check his momentum. He was intent on a trajectory that followed Lanky towards a second access ladder rising up and back towards the nose of the ship. Every neuron in Mex's adrenalin-drenched brain wanted distance; distance from the freak of nature that had swallowed the rear of the ship and spat gravitational fur balls.

One arm shot out to scoop up Dumpy as Mex passed and for a moment it looked as if he was going to run the length of the gantry with a stunned MynCorp employee tucked under one arm. Despite fear-fuelled muscles, the moment was soon over and they landed in a cat's cradle of arms and legs. Mex's temple made unyielding contact with the harsh mesh of the flooring and was pinned by a surprisingly heavy leg. Dumpy shifted his weight, trying to get his centre of mass above his feet. Mex bellowed with indignant pain, as the pressure on his face doubled; slight differences in the profile of the flooring triggered constellations of agony. Something surrendered ground in his jaw and his stomach lurched. The smell of digestive acid in air singed his nose hairs.

Then they were dragging each other to a standing position, sharing balance and imbalance.

"Go!" Mex shouted at Dumpy, at himself, at fear and at the phantom eddy brewing below. Something popped near his ear and his teeth rattled against each other, missing their familiar mesh grooves. Even accounting for the fact he was half carrying another man, his progress felt unreasonably sluggish; either time was running slow or he was. For a moment he took his eyes from the painted rungs of the ladder and looked at his feet to check for impeding custard; perhaps it was all a bad dream. His scuffed boots rattled and pounded against rough metal in an all too realistic manner. Maybe he had discovered a third form of time dilation; first there was time dilation between clocks in inertial frames with extreme relative velocities, then the stretching of time by the warping of space around a massive object and now, the all new, terrified-of-being-torn-to-pieces-by-a-human-engineered-spatial-shock time dilation. Mex decided to invent a snappier name if he lived through the next minute.

Six steps, five, four, three, two, one and one more and Mex was thrusting Dumpy four rungs into the air and into the waiting hands of Lanky, who was lying face down on the floor above with an expression which clearly said if he died as a result of waiting for his friend then he would kill Dumpy himself, so help him God.

Dumpy's weight was lifted from Mex's shoulders and he was left with only himself to save. The world turned upside down, which was not a major achievement considering his world was a narrow cylinder less than a kilometre long with pretend gravity created by chucking mass from one end. Mex landed back on his face, two concerned faces looked down on him, framed by a circle of metal. "Go!" he screamed one last time but he felt a niggle of betrayal when the faces vanished.

Sitting up was easy, standing was possible but staying upright proved elusive as the ship bucked like an irate steer. Mex had an inexplicable mental flash of Roald Amundsen standing at the South Pole, magnetic compass spinning in his hand.

When the eddy finally erupted from the floor, Mex was almost grateful because struggling became impossible. He clung to the uprights of the ladder as the whirlpool of tortured space rose before him. Time slowed and meandered like a lazy river. His heartbeat became the slow tolling of a great brass bell, dulled by green oxides and lost religious fervour. For a joyous moment he thought it would miss him, but its girth grew as it rose from the floor and the charged boundary with flat space grew nearer. To his simple eyes all the light in the room was sucked into the heart of the maelstrom, crushed and mutilated before being spat back out to torment his senses. He had time to raise a warding hand like Galileo repenting for all his compromises on a burning stake.

Mex saw his fingers twist and spiral away, knuckles and palm in quick pursuit. His arm was pointing at an infinity that was wrapped up in a dozen metres of space. The flesh was like plasticine stretched translucent thin and wrapped in a tight spiral. Then the pain reached him; a tsunami of nerve impulses firing with everything in their arsenal before being wrenched into silent oblivion. The pain overloaded his brain; he could not scream, nor cry. As it peaked in a crescendo of agony his mind took the only sensible course of action and pulled the plug.

Darkness.

*

"No!" screamed Nomia as she lunged hopelessly at Captain Finnur.

He reached out with one ruby-encrusted hand and plucked her out of the air by the throat. "I have no more patience for this. We will cut out the guts of this ship and take what we need. You can stay with the wreckage or keep quiet, I care less than you can imagine."

"You can't kill him." Her protest was strangled, more by her desire to keep Kaamil secret than the fingers bruising the pale flesh of her neck.

"I can kill you here and now. Tearing a ship apart is more time-consuming but even less likely to keep me awake at night."He turned to his subordinates keeping Nomia dangling like that night's turkey. "What is their approach speed?"

"Over point nine of light speed."

"How hard are they decelerating?"

"They're not."

"What?"

"They're maintaining speed and course."

"They must be confident that they can destroy us with one salvo. It will take months for them to turn around and get back here. I want a full check on all our defence systems. Tell Sigfus to be ready for a full-out assault."

"Yes sir."

"Also, I want a cutting team at work now. I want the engines off within two hours and then work up through the antimatter systems. Just take what's essential, discard the rest. Perhaps the debris will do us some favours when that ship arrives."

The shipman looked grateful to have an excuse to leave and something to do. The Captain turned back to Nomia as if he had forgotten he was holding her rag-doll style, her hands pulling with futile effort on one of his fingers.

"Where was I? Trying to decide what to do with you two, I believe."

"Please put her down. We are still useful to you." José's voice projected soothing layers of conviction.

Bergur stood nearby, watching proceedings with a detached curiosity.

"I actually think it might improve my mood if I just crushed her neck now."

"She is simply making a valid point. This ship is still worth more to you in one piece. On balance, the risk from one possibly hostile ship is worth taking."

"You do realise that at the speed they are going the only possible intervention they could make is to destroy us all. This is MynCorp we are talking about. If they have written off this ship, then you can be sure they have written you off."

"I have no doubt."

"Then shut up and keep quiet and at least one of you might survive this."

Nomia stopped struggling. The change was enough to make Finnur look at her again. Her eyelids were half-closed and her eyes were rolling back into her head. He looked surprised that she had passed out so easily and then his eyes grew twice as wide again. Creeping up his arm was a fuzzy area of nothing. By the time he noticed his hand had already vanished and the flesh of his wrist was starting to grow translucent. The gems remained solid and all the red stones from his knuckles were starting to drift away like freshly released tropical fish.

A child-like sob leaked from his tense throat. Nomia continued to float exactly as she had been, even though she was no longer being held by anything tangible.

Nomia stop now, José slammed into her mind.

Why should I? He threatened Kaamil, me and you. He does not deserve to exist.

This is not a path you want to explore. You will end up hating everything and especially yourself. Let him go.

I have to protect Kaamil.

Bergur seemed unsure whether to intervene but was keenly studying the unspoken connection between José and Nomia. His eyes flicked back and forward between them, as if he could capture some stray thoughts leaking from their eyes. With the dramatic impetuous of a volcanic eruption, a violent shudder ripped through Nomia and José, forcing their limbs to convulse out in to a crucifixion position. As the muscle convulsions were replaced with the pain of aftershock their bodies imploded to foetal balls. Both of them mouthed the same silent prayer that grew into the real world as a uniformly black whisper. "Mistake, mistake, mistake."

Captain Finnur was staring at the space that had replaced his right arm below the elbow. His forearm ended in a bloodless stump. Each bone, muscle and tendon was clearly visible. Like an ants' nest behind glass, the arm was not cut off so much as truncated. The lower arm was gone, twisted into half a dozen lower dimensions. The rest of his body seemed oblivious to the missing limb; there was no bleeding and no obvious discomfort beyond the pain of shock. He floated backward as if his fear was giving him momentum. A cloud of precious stones eddied away in his wake. When his back hit the edge of the door he turned and fled. He must have been a hundred metres away before the fear erupted from his throat in a prehistoric wail.

The José and Nomia balls of torment orbited each other like a dark planet and its golden moon. The solipsistic mantra continued in rhythm with their rotation.

Then it all stopped. Even the sounds of a quiescent spaceship ceased.

Bergur felt his heart stop, his lungs thought about breathing in but the air refused to respond to changes in pressure. A bubble of reality that filled the room froze for a moment and every force and particle sat waiting for a moment of decision.

José and Nomia spoke one word in unison.

"Reset."

The Universe started to dissolve.

Bergur could feel every molecule in his body torn between two conflicted realities; the one he knew and something simpler. He instinctively knew that when the transition was over he would not exist as a sentient being. He struggled and raged against an intangible enemy. A roar more of his essence than of sound erupted from him into the tormented air of the room. It was joined by a mental scream that could possibly have been from something which had been José.

"NO!"

A pulse of stability poured out of José and grew as a decelerating sphere of physical structure. In its wake normality asserted its dominance over chaos. José and Nomia flew apart and unfolded like limp cadavers floating on a sea of torment. Bergur caught Nomia and looked for signs of life in the drained face. A moan diffused from José and filled the room with the essence of pain.

"Is she alive?" José managed.

"I think so, but she's out cold."

"That's okay, put her in her cot." Remembering their recent positions of captor and prisoner he added, "Please."

Bergur did as he was requested, too stunned to assert his theoretical dominance. He knew that he had just experienced something momentous. Of all the events that had changed the direction of his life, only the most significant had been noticeable as they occurred, and this one was waving a red flag while playing a bugle. He felt a tremor of expectant excitement flutter his lip flaps.

A hesitant voice crept from the walls. "What happened?"

"Ship?" Bergur checked.

"Yes. What's going on?"

"What did you see?"

"The stars went dim. I lost contact with the quantum froth of the inertial reference frame. It was like we didn't exist. The effect started and ended in the room you're currently occupying."

"Yeah, it felt the same to me."

José shook himself to a better level of alertness but he was obviously carrying a burden; pain lurked in the depths of his eyes and fought to break free.

"They are trying to reset the experiment."

"What? Who?" Bergur directed the questions at José but he was still looking at Nomia's hand in his.

José paused, giving Bergur an appraising look. Apparently satisfied he started to talk. "There is a race of beings that exist almost entirely in Verity Space. They placed a number of artefacts in the Solar System several million years ago, to act as a catalyst for our development. I was the one who decoded the puzzle and triggered a response. They unlocked a connection with the Downey field that is subconscious in most sentient beings."

"An alien race? In the Drop?"

"Deeper than the Nexus. They are part of the very fabric of Verity Space."

"And you found them?"

"Yes."

"If I hadn't just witnessed this bit of the Universe miss a beat I would kill you just in case your insanity was contagious."

"That is most gracious of you."

"So what superpowers does this connection with the Drop get you?"

José took a minute to gather his strength and then took a deeper breath. "Everyone manipulates quantum decisions by the very act of being a sentient observer, but until now mankind has not been able to make a conscious decision about which multiverse reality follows. We stumble through the hyperspace of all possible realities like a blind man in a maze."

"You get to load the quantum dice that God doesn't play with."

"More replace the dice with a calculator."

"This goes for Nomia as well?"

"She's slightly different. She has always had direct access to the Downey field. She was a Nexus Node."

"She's a Node! I knew you two had to be valuable."

Until now the ship had remained silent but he spoke now. His tone carried intonations of many vindicated suspicions. "You tinkered with my engines. Improved the flight efficiency."

"We didn't really change the engines but we did nudge the individual reactions to produce the best possible outcome for our immediate need."

Bergur regained control of the conversation. "So what's gone wrong?"

"I went back to Earth once to rescue Nomia from MynCorp and I was given a warning that human realms were quarantined pending some sort of assessment. We stayed away for a while but Nomia is developing as a person and she needs human contact. We decided to make a low-key journey to remain undetected. When Nomia lashed out at Finnur they found us."

"And they're angry?"

"Anger would be a response I could deal with. It would show an emotion that humans could relate to. They are much more evolved than us. I can't even begin to follow their motivations or reactions."

"So what happened?"

"They seem to have weighed mankind and found us light in some way."

"And the melting reality?"

"They are starting to reset this area of space to some primordial state so that they can start all over again."

"If this race of... What do you call them?"

José looked lost for a moment. "I don't know. This is the first time I've talked about them out loud. When I think of them there is an image, or rather a feeling, but not a name."

"Surely, they told you something about themselves. There must have been some sort of first contact. Introduction?"

"You're thinking too corporeally."

"That's not normally a criticism."

"They made their presence known to me when my mind was already in

Verity space. There was no real transition. No first words. There were simply new thoughts in my head, like a familiar smell bringing back forgotten memories. It was all non-specific. Not vague, so much as a fluid truth."

Bergur was sure he should be falling to his knees with shock and a sudden reappraisal of his significance in the Universe. Perhaps it would be delayed until a future moment of quiet contemplation, or maybe some things were too massive to be grasped by a primate brain. Either way, he felt a sense of gratitude that he was still able to function. "I have no idea what you are talking about, but if this nameless race of aliens wants us gone, how come we're still here?"

"I've managed to shield us temporarily. I set up a boundary of zero quantum potential. In essence, stopping any decision making, so in Verity Space we are invisible."

"How big is this cloak of invisibility?"

"Just big enough to encompass both ships."

"You saved my ship. Why did you do that when we have taken so much from you?"

"I'm not a monster. I couldn't just let your entire crew cease to exist."

"Cutting. If this is all true, you could have destroyed us at any time."

"There are always consequences when two decision-making engines go up against each other. Inert things are easy to manipulate but it is different with sentient beings. The fallout is completely non-linear. Destroying a ship full of people might change the colour of a butterfly's wings, while rescuing one tortured soul from a MynCorp lab might lead to the destruction of the human race."

*

Darkness.

Grey of half perceived light. A female silhouette, black against the grey. Then the polite wake up call of a bruised body. A body that considered that Mex had slept enough. It had held its peace and now he must know its pain. A groan rolled like a thorny bush up a dry throat and over scabbed lips.

"You're awake." The voice was soft and caressed his ears; something that did not hurt.

"If you say so," he croaked.

"We thought we'd lost you." The angel's breath rolled sweetly across his cheek. She was close.

"Not that easily," he managed.

"You're quite a hero amongst a certain section of the crew."

He wanted to be her hero; an angel's hero, heaven indeed.

"Timothy Creadle is certainly your friend for life."

"Timothy?" He remembered an infinite horizon, an arm's reach away.

"He claims you virtually threw him to safety. Quite impressive for a man his size."

"Dumpy?"

"As his boss I couldn't possibly comment."

"And Lanky? Are they both okay?"

"If you mean Mr Creadle and Mr Smith, then they are fine. You on the other hand are extremely lucky to be alive."

"I'm made of tougher stuff."

"Mostly not, but I have to admit that I'm impressed. People are normally quite predictable at the level of grand gestures. You are definitely made of interesting stuff."

"It's unlikely to happen again."

"I wouldn't bet any calories against it."

The room was now fully bright and in focus. His angel had taken Julienne's form but was still playing nicely. "How bad is it?" he asked. "My face feels like it's been kicked by a giant in stone boots but there is a distinct absence of pain in certain places under the sheets."

"Your jaw was dislocated, it's now just bruised. Your right arm was quite badly damaged."

"How badly?" He felt an unpleasant truth lurking nearby.

"More sort of gone than damaged."

"What?" Mex tried to sit up. Not a lot happened; both feet kicked slightly. With his left hand he threw the sheet down to his knees. He was naked and his sedentary body raised hairs against the cold touch of fresher air. Where his right arm should have lain, each freckle and bony knobble a lifelong friend, there was a grey lump of sludge. "What?" he asked again.

Julienne reached out a cool, fragile hand and half-stroked his forehead and half-pinned him to the bed. "We don't have organ growth or grafting facilities on board. You'll have to wait for Earth to get a new arm."

"What is that?" Mex pointed a good finger at the pale ooze that lay next to his ribs. It held just enough shape to grip his shoulder where an arm should sprout and to avoid dripping off the bed to form a dirty puddle on the floor.

"It's a symbiotic putty. You need to wake up a bit and give it purpose."

"What?"

"You know, you're actually quite adorable when you're lost for words."

"What? Are you flirting with me? I'm lying here with plasticine for an arm and you think it's cute?" A memory flashed behind his eyes; an arm stretched and smeared to a bloodless pulp.

"I just wanted you to see a friendly face when you woke up. I was simply practising human empathy. I thought you would appreciate it."

"Compassion doesn't count if it is premeditated."

Julienne tensed for a moment before rising above the taunt. She pushed out a perfectly symmetrical lower lip in a mock sulk. Despite his mounting trauma he felt a flush of arousal at the display of fake vulnerability. He pulled the sheet back up to his chest as he regained his awareness of their physical proximity. "Thanks for fixing me up. I appreciate the energy," he said with contrition.

"I think I might have had a mutiny to deal with if I hadn't."

"Then they're braver than me." Mex smiled weakly, causing white-hot pain to burrow from his jaw into his brain. A wave of nausea flattening him to the cot for a moment but it passed quickly. "So, will this guardian angel bit still be working when it comes to bed and bath time?" A lopsided version of the trademark grin was back on his face.

The look of revulsion on Julienne's face was a little too real for comfort. "I take back the adorable comment," she replied.

"What do I do?" he asked, "With the putty?" He did not really want to think about his missing arm but a change of subject seemed prudent.

"Just think of it as an arm. For the next few days you'll have to be quite deliberate about using it but it will soon behave like your old arm. There's even some synaptic feedback, so you can feel things it touches."

"But grey."

"Yes it's grey. You haven't exactly got to worry about colour clashes with your wardrobe all the way out here. Give it a go."

Mex looked at his left arm, savouring the organic imperfection of it. Then he looked at the putty to his right and imagined it being an arm. The putty oozed and slurped in a less than pleasant manner. It coalesced into a stump with a fully-working pincer. Julienne giggled. Mex stared at the aborted arm, and then at Julienne's face. Muscles were easing her mouth into a gloriously lopsided smile, uneven gasps and shudders rippling through her frame as the laughter gripped her. She looked perfectly human.

"You are one sick puppy but laughing suits you," he said and laughed too.

The laughter stretched on beyond its natural end, both of them reluctant to re-enter their normal roles, but eventually it was all used up. Mex asked the question which had to be asked. "The ship has stopped shaking. What did you do to get free of the spatial shock?"

"We increased thrust and broke free."

"What happened to the plan to let the shock decay?"

"The Suparna happened. We spotted a neutrino flare consistent with its engines. We needed to get free of the shock to begin our deceleration run."

"What about everyone below deck six?"

"All gone."

"All of them? All the soldiers?"

"And twenty of the crew. They're all dead. Nothing organic made it back through the shock."

"You killed them all."

"They knew the risk. This is still an experimental ship."

"But you had to push it just that little bit beyond experimental and into reckless."

"Your objection is noted. Feel free to take it up with the CCB when we get home." Juliennes teeth and jaw became rigidly aligned.

"Look, this isn't something you can simply brush off. Close to a hundred lives have ended as a direct result of a decision you made. I'm not saying you wanted them to die, but if you don't let yourself feel some remorse or guilt then you'll become something less than human."

"And you're an expert on being well balanced?"

"Sarcasm is not the most highly evolved human trait."

"I just did what had to be done. It was made very clear to me how important it is to the corporation to retrieve the Node in a timely manner. I have never seen resources assigned to a task with such willingness. I'm just a cog in the MynCorp machine; if I show I'm missing any teeth they'll simply discard me and find another cog."

"MynCorp is not a living animal. It has no emotions, no compassion. It is up to the people who are part of it, to be a conscience, collectively and individually."

"You sound like some of your friends."

"What?"

"I knew you had anti-corporate acquaintances when we took you on, but I had you labelled as a pragmatist, not an idealist. Even if you sympathised, I didn't think you'd have the courage to express your views."

"Courage?"

"Given your situation."

"I see. So I'm back to being a prisoner?"

"You've made it perfectly clear that you consider me a monster. I would be derelict in my duty if I allowed you the freedom to undermine this mission. You will be escorted to the command centre where you will offer advice when requested. Otherwise you are not to speak to any member of the crew."

Mex's right arm shimmered and then set to a scaled hardness. A rudimentary wrist and fingers coalesced and the surface creased and scarred like the hide of a crocodile as it flexed involuntarily. His jaw felt almost as stiff as he thanked her for the medical attention and offered to return to duty.

*

Bergur's eye cowls peeled back to reveal an intensity that would make stars seem dim on a cloudless night. He started to speak in a voice as rhythmic as a summer sea.

"Exalte, rapt, ecstatic,

The visible but their womb of birth,

Of orbic tendencies to shape and shape and shape,

The mighty earth-eidolon.

All space, all time,

(The stars, the terrible perturbations of the suns,

Swelling, collapsing, ending, serving their longer, shorter use,)

Fill'd with eidolons only.

The noiseless myriads,

The infinite oceans where the rivers empty,

The separate countless free identities, like eyesight,

The true realities, eidolons.

Not this the world,

Nor these the universes, they the universes,

Purport and end, ever the permanent life of life,

Eidolons, eidolons."

José stared, all his words temporarily misplaced. Some colour pushed back in Nomia's cheeks, as if the poetry was a form of energy.

Bergur was distracted and uneasy after his lapse of shallowness but refused to show it. "I've thought of a name for the Verity Space invaders. Eidolons."

"Okay. Does this help us?" José caught Nomia's reproachful look and added, "Particularly?"

"An enemy named is the first step towards an enemy tamed." Bergur felt obliged to over-compensate for his poetic lapse. "Then we can use some of the storming battle poems I know."

"Bergur, do you enjoy being a pirate?" Nomia had loosened the straps on her cot so she could turn and look at him directly.

Bergur started to pull his head back to let loose a bark of bravado but stopped himself. He felt that her naivety deserved a certain amount of honesty and deliberation, as if an ill-considered word might taint her forever. "Nei." He paused for a moment, half expecting his captain to come bursting in, weapon drawn. "No," he said again.

José kept his gaze fixed on Nomia, perhaps concerned that a simple look might break the moment of confession. The next question was implicit; why did he do it?

"You have to understand how hard life is in the settlement. The pressure to contribute to the collective is immense and, probably, essential. There is no place for someone that wants to explore and to experience for no other reason than to feel the change within himself. Does that make any sense?" The question was rhetorical. He did not need the reassurance of the humans. "Captain Finnur's crew are the only ones to ever leave the Epsilon Eridani system. I would have volunteered."

"Would have?" prompted Nomia.

"I didn't get on too well down the mines and I haven't the temperament for a lab or desk job. I was politely asked to consider a commission."

"Oh."

Bergur pulled back his slumped shoulders and pushed some of the fire back into his voice. "We each have a role in this bizarre universe. Mine is still a little vague. Fate is just more patient than me." He flapped his mouth as he laughed. He could still feel the tides of change pulling at the keel of his life. *Maybe not so long to wait now*, he thought and then out loud he asked, "So, are you two still set on returning to Earth?"

"I don't know. We might be bringing the wolf to the door." José looked uncertainly at Nomia. "Maybe we can help Earth to mount some sort of defence."

Nomia adjusted the straps again to allow her to match their orientation; being flat without gravity was doing nothing to improve the blood flow to her head. "I'm even more convinced we should go."

"You think your plan is still plausible?" José's question was softly spoken but was challenging nonetheless.

Bergur hated missing the back-story and grunted his consternation. He suspected that they were only talking aloud for his benefit, so expecting an explanation was reasonable.

"There are almost a thousand of them being tortured as we speak." José did not look as if he needed convincing, but her anger needed an outlet. "Every one of them could be a beautiful person, if we could just join the two halves of their minds."

"And liberate them from MynCorp," José added.

"It's slavery. MynCorp think that the nodes are somehow less than complete and, conveniently, not worthy of compassion, but if we can expose them properly to Verity Space, each one would flower."

"Slavery that gives MynCorp unlimited computing resources."

"I give up," Bergur interjected. "Who on Earth are you going to rescue?"

José and Nomia answered in harmony. "The Nodes."

*

Two apologetic crewmen, press-ganged into ill-fitting army fatigues, met Mex at the door to the infirmary. They looked flushed and one of them panted behind clamped lips; this was definitely not what they had in mind when they woke that morning. They held their tasers with a familiar respect, as if they had just been shown the safety switch after weeks of training. As they lead him back up to the command centre he tried to ask them about the break-away from the spatial shock. They remained close-mouthed and square-shouldered but their eyes pleaded with him to keep quiet. He took pity on them and fell into a sullen silence, but as soon as his jaw stopped working his mind kicked into gear.

He thought about the Node. She must be a wretched creature; liberated from a perpetual nightmare into a world at right angles to any reality she could understand. Somehow, she had crept into an unwatched corner of an interstellar ship and cowered through months of flight. It was too much to imagine that she had done all this under her own initiative. Even if she had spontaneously awoken it seemed likely that she would have been found huddled in the smallest corner of her lab, horrified by the gangly awkwardness of corporeal reality. Instead, she had slipped with all the stealth of a hunting cat, through a building riddled with invisible detectors tuned to all the bodily emissions of the wasteful human form; leaking heat, noise and gases as they do, even when sitting still. Then, buoyed by her superhuman ability, she had navigated an alien city and constructed sufficient local information to escape the planet's surface and find refuge on an outbound craft. Except, it could not have worked that way. Mex had no real idea how long the Node had been missing, but the near panicking urgency shown by MynCorp (or, more accurately, by its personification in Julienne) did not imply a leisurely search spread over years, and yet they were now years out from Earth by any form of propulsion known to Mex prior to last month. So, not only did someone aid the Node in her escape but they also managed to get her an improbable head start on any chasing pack.

The impossibility of the Node's current location just made Mex's head hurt, but what made his one, skin-covered palm itch with nervous energy was the thought of the Node's accomplice. The harsh reality was the Node could not really have any concept of needing to escape or, indeed, what escape would mean when the Nexus was the only reality she could have known. That meant the person or people that liberated her were acting on their own benefit. Which meant an agenda. Which in turn meant convictions, be they political or economic. Julienne seemed preoccupied by the mechanics of retrieving the Node but Mex was much more concerned by the motivation and determination of those that coveted the Node. He had no sense of loyalty to the corporation, nor any particular desire to save company assets (unless they were people assets), but as long as he found himself one of those assets then he would worry and anguish about their fate. The most benign scenario was that this was all about energy; some hugely complicated scam to steal calorie credits using a compromised Node in the Nexus. This was best case because once the cost-benefit of the action fell below a certain threshold they would cut their losses and retreat. In practical terms, a shot across the bow should suffice. Mex knew the Universe was never that simple. The effort required to get the Node off-world required a network of like-minded individuals, which came back to convictions and ideology. Nothing in the modern world drew more blind obedience and moral certitude than ideology and in the post free-market economy the only ideology in town was anti-corporate.

Mex began to ponder Julienne's words in the context of his musings. In her anger she had made it clear they had considered his political leaning and social circles before *contracting* his services. He began to wonder if he was aboard as much for any political insight he might have, as for his expertise in the Drop. After all, he had done his job in finding the Suparna. For creations like Julienne, the thought processes of an anti-corporate terrorist must be as alien as the futures market to a Buddhist monk, or corporate dogma to a young woman waking from a life-long coma.

The two freshly recruited guards flanked Mex as he stood in the control centre. The operators floated in their silken webs the same as they had before most of the passengers and crew had died. The Captain stood at his pedestal with the same resigned pride and Julienne stood motionless and lost in some projected telemetry display. Only her eyes moved and they burnt with an intensity that should have melted those she glanced at.

"Have they seen us?" She did not take her eyes from the display but the question found its target.

"Presumably, but they have not fired their engines. The two ships are tethered and drifting. They should have spotted us as soon as we pulled free from the shock front." The Captain's eyes were awash with splice data from the other operators.

Mex realised he had missed a chapter. Two ships? He desperately wanted to ask about the second ship but restricted himself to focusing the pressure of his will; mentally pushing the conversation in the most revealing direction.

"What can you tell me about the second ship?" Julienne's subconscious was obviously listening.

"Very little. We only got a few seconds of thrust signature before it cut off. I can tell you it's not MynCorp."

"I could tell you that from company logistics."

The Captain politely ignored her. "In fact it doesn't even look Terran. The neutrino flux was pulsed in a repeated sequence of duplets, which implies a discrete anti-matter injection system. It's possible the frozen anti-hydrogen pellets are being deployed whole into the reaction chamber."

"So?"

"The least dramatic way of describing such a design is ill-advised."

"I see. Let's broaden the search. Which colonies have the capability and courage to develop their own drive technology?"

"None," answered the Captain authoritatively, "that I'm aware of."

"Except the former colony on Epsilon Eridani."

The Captain looked distinctly uncomfortable being forced to talk about a forbidden subject with the representative of the very group that had done the forbidding. "Maybe," he offered tentatively.

"Seat of the pants technology is certainly consistent with a piratical outlook."

Pirates! Mex had physically clamped the end of his tongue between his teeth to stop a question leaking out. Fortunately, Julienne continued to feed his curiosity. "So, we have a hijacked MynCorp vessel tethered to a cobbled together time-bomb masquerading as a representative of a renegade colony. I think we can assume that the theft of the Node is a subplot in a much larger political opera."

"Or, the Eridanians may just be trying to steal the engines from the Suparna." The Captain instantly regretted sharing an opinion when Julienne dealt one of her repertoire of withering glances.

She continued with her own line of argument. "They will expect us to fire at the last moment to minimise their manoeuvring time. They will have measured our relative velocity and imagine that we can only have one shot. They have nothing to gain by firing their engines until we have made our move."

"Except the remnants of the shock are going to hit them soon after we pass. They will not survive that."

"They must know that, so why are they not under thrust?"

The Captain assumed the question was rhetorical but looked on nervously, ready to state the obvious if he was proved wrong.

She found the answer herself at the same moment it occurred to Mex. "They can't fire the engines because they are waiting for the antimatter to regenerate. That's why they are cruising."

"Parallax measurements are just coming into acceptable confidence margins. Their quiescent trajectory would take them through the Eridani system."

"Excellent. Captain, I would like you to prepare a spread of missiles along their trajectory assuming a variety of acceleration profiles; we'll assume they'll break for home. I want debilitating strikes only with minimal risk to those on board."

"With all due respect these are antimatter-driven ships. All rockets are essentially flying bombs but antimatter ships are the biggest bombs of all. I can programme the missiles to only detonate if they strike a non-critical part of the ship but that only really means the crew quarters. You can kill the crew or blow up the ship, killing the crew. Especially, in the case of the Eridanian ship."

"I don't care about the Eridanian ship. You can pepper that to your heart's content but the Suparna must survive along with her passenger."

"As you command."

Mex silently added, 'despite the insanity of the order.'

"Once the firing solution is complete I want to execute a gravito-metric shock manoeuvre and bring us to a stop as close behind them as possible. I want to be up on them under fusion drive as soon as possible."

"Firing solution ready, ma'am."

"Well? Fire."

Chapter 7

There was one last memory. Kaamil knew it was the last because it announced itself with mental fanfare, but it brought him no answers or resolution.

The memory seemed to follow on from the others but he had no idea how much time had passed between them. He was still floating in the limbo of the water tank. His consciousness was spread throughout the mining ship, following the sounds of the MynCorp search. Once or twice he had heard hard-soled boots clattering along the corridor outside his refuge, but there had been no harsh light of discovery or yank of an exploring hand.

He was bought back into himself by an intense shivering which wracked his body. 'First stage hypothermia,' he thought, impressed that his body still remembered how to defend itself from cold. He knew he could not stay in the tank much longer, unless he could generate some heat; maybe, by moving. Kaamil started to feel his way along the water line. Thinking back to his training he remembered that most long-haul interplanetary vessels had water tanks spread across their surface, to form a partial barrier against cosmic rays. The tanks combined with a thin atmosphere of plasma generated near the outer skin of the hull to prevent high energy particles from wrecking the genetics of human passengers. The barriers were adequate except for every few decades when the sun's defences became less active and the solar system was bombarded by high energy particles from interstellar space.

The shivering was bearable as long as he kept moving, but he regularly had to stop to pinch his nose and equalise pressure within his ears. It was frustrating progress, with one arm floating behind him like a stray piece of seaweed. Worst of all, his mind started working each time he stopped. *Pressure means depth!* The thought popped into his mind like a bubble reaching the surface of water. Kaamil reached his good arm above his head seeking the reassuring cold of air or vacuum. He already knew it would not be there. Suddenly, he was unsure that he was even reaching up. Despite years of switching between different gravity levels, the sudden disorientation was terrifying. Kaamil thrashed in random directions, convinced he was sinking to his death. By the time that exhaustion forced him to float like a cadaver, he had no idea which way he had come from or where he was going. He knew that it did not really matter because he had been moving in a random direction but the thought of backtracking made him feel even more exhausted. 'Where was I heading?' he asked in coded bubbles from the rebreather. The bubbles rose to his left. Kaamil giggled a few more bubbles until he had righted himself with respect to their calm buoyancy. 'My depth doesn't really matter. I'll die of the cold long before this mask runs out of power.' The rebreather was probably barely ticking over extracting an air mix from water and probably had not started on its reserve tank.

Kaamil started a lopsided swim with renewed purpose and energy. He now knew where his subconscious had been steering him before the panic attack. 'She'll be on the other ship, the MynCorp ship.' And he knew which way that was. All the sounds of the search parties had radiated from one direction, if he stopped moving for long enough for his senses to expand beyond the immediate, he could still hear airlocks and booted feet coming and going. He was near.

His route became a tortured network of pipes and valves. Something made him open his eyes despite the relentless dark that he had been immersed in for hours. It took a moment for his focus to work but a blurry haze of light became fuzzy blobs of stars seen through water. Somehow, he was swimming through space.

More light was coming from above him. He looked up to see the indistinct tread of a military boot. Then he realised that he of all people should understand where he was. Space flight had become too complicated for people to worry about over a hundred years ago. The drive for artificial intelligence had been largely fuelled by the need to control the complexity of deep space missions. Space craft were an ecosystem of their own devising and when two ships met, they exchanged information, gases and fluids in a complex system of symbiosis and A.I. etiquette. So, when humans requested a docking bridge be deployed between ships, the A.I.s supplemented the pressurised walkway with a series of umbilical cords for their own purpose. He was swimming through a water exchange pipe between the mining ship and the MynCorp pursuit vessel. He was even now drifting underneath the feet of the security guards posted to stop him boarding behind the backs of the search parties.

He no longer needed to swim. He could not have prevented entering the MynCorp ship even if he had wanted to. The nagging concern made him start to swim pointlessly against the current. The MynCorp ship would protect itself against contamination, destroying or rejecting any foreign material in the water. Kaamil was fairly sure he counted as a water impurity or maybe a pathogen that the water cleansing system would eradicate. His only hope was that the ship recognised him as human; protecting life was a piece of core logic that should trump any other. "Should," Kaamil said in bubbles.

He was through the umbilical now. The stars faded from sight and a new light appeared ahead; a strobing blue just on the edge of his colour vision. Fingers of light pulsed through the water ahead, creating pockets of plasma as tiny impurities were neutralised. A strangled scream fought to escape his throat, pushing on the mouth-piece of the rebreather. He thrashed against the flow, trying to imagine himself as human as possible. In the clarity of terror he remembered and sympathised with sub-aqua divers mistaken for seals by orcas. 'I'm not a seal! I'm human!' he screamed in his head.

He was still being dragged feet first towards the laser array, his physical efforts making no noticeable difference to his progress. His left calf erupted in searing agony as a fist-sized chunk of muscle was instantly reduced to vapour. Kaamil spat out the rebreather as he screamed and then bit his tongue as his jaw clenched. Water mixed with blood as it pushed down his throat towards his lungs. His legs recoiled to his chest and he waited for the killer blow. Then the bottom of his world dropped out.

Kaamil lay choking on the soft metal of an intelligent alloy ship. Cool colours soothed his adrenaline-poisoned mind. The ship had saved him; the conflicting priorities to protect life and to prevent contamination resolved in his favour.

With trembling muscles he found his feet and padded along the corridor of the MynCorp ship. Wet footprints led back to a puddle of water and blood.

The bunker sat in the middle of the lab. Instinctively, Kaamil recognised the black sphere as hers. Defined uniquely by something intangible in the way it occupied the space. The hatch was closed but not sealed and dissipated on touch to leave a circular aperture. The clinical light from the laboratory crept around the interior creating shadows and shapes as it spread. Eventually, the tide of light lapped around her shape as she hung naked in the pilot's web. Her skin glowed in the light, amplifying it and beaming it back to his eager eyes.

Neural suppressors clung to her scalp and her eyes danced under their eyelids. She smiled softly in the deep dreams of artificially induced REM sleep. In the dream, Kaamil thought that they must have started the reprogramming process - returning her to a virgin state of corporate slavery. He ripped the transducers from her head, leaving red welts on the exposed skin. He began the process of decoupling her from the web and pilot interface and she started to moan lightly, ascending the levels of consciousness that lay between the sleeping and waking worlds.

Finally, she hung freely in his right arm and his heart leapt at the feeling of her weight against him. She moaned again and her eyes started to open. Her face glowed with the smile of lovers waking late on a Sunday morning. He knew she must have been dreaming of the short time they spent together. Her eyes started to slide into focus and her conscious mind started to take control of her facial muscles, sculpting her features into a mask of confusion.

"Everything is okay my love. It's me, we are together," he whispered softly in her ear. He saw the moment when the neural programming cut in. Her eyes clicked into focus. A cascade of emotions disfigured her face, taking confusion through loathing and into terror.

"No, not you! You're the one. The one that kidnapped me! They promised to hide me! To take me home!" She started to struggle feebly in his arm. "Not you! Not you!" Her right arm pushed against his chest, her head shaking apart the image of him.

He held her closer, trying to reassure her, trying to break through the damage they had done. "It's me, my love. Fight it. Remember how we laughed and loved. Remember."

She redoubled her fight, the programming demanding she use any and all reserves of strength. He sank to the ground taking her with him, holding on as tight as he could. Holding her head against his chest, he continued to make soothing sounds so she could hear his voice. Hoping against hope that it would break the spell, that their bond would be stronger than the neural technology. And slowly her fighting became less urgent, her gasps less frequent and her crying less desperate. Finally, she lay limply in his arms as he rocked her to the rhythm of his voice.

"Sleep. Let it heal you. I can wait," he whispered in her ear.

He lowered her to the floor and sat watching her, absorbing every detail. Then he felt something leave the room, something ethereal. He looked around the small enclosure and then back to her.

Her chest was still.

She was not breathing. He leant down to check the air around her mouth for any hint of movement. Nothing. His mind raged, "She cannot be dead! They have killed her! The last resort of the neural programming. They would rather kill her than lose a pilot!"

He sat holding her to him. Rocking gently as she slipped from this world, absorbing as much of her essence as he could.

He had no more fight.

*

An almost human convulsion ran the length of the ship. Klaxons and flashing lights signalled an immune system at war.

José broke from his ministration of Nomia. "Suparna, what's wrong?"

"They are burning me. Trying to rip my engines off. Their torches are cutting through my hull. I'm losing sensation in several areas of the antimatter sub-systems."

Bergur looked as contrite as his blocky physique would allow. "They've started the salvage operation. Captain Finnur means to strip what he can before the MynCorp ship arrives," he said before pointing at the ceiling and asking, "If you don't mind me saying, the ship's A.I. sounds very human. I could almost believe he was real."

Nomia moaned in sympathetic union with the ship and opened her eyes. Her pupils drifted into view from some internal journey. She looked into José's face and touched his consciousness. "How can you keep up that clear a focus?" she asked out loud.

"You've been through worse," he said as he stroked the tiny hint of red that was venturing back into her cheek.

Kaamil moaned again. "My engines. They're cutting out my engines. I'm pouring everything into fixing the damage but I just can't morph fast enough. They're cutting through my body like it was meat. Please stop them, it hurts."

Nomia stroked the wall above her cot and made soothing sounds as if Suparna was a frightened cat. José turned back to the Eridanian and sucked in a supportive breath of air. "Bergur, I need your help. It is very important that we get to Earth. We have to warn people about the attack from Verity Space and try and mount some kind of defence."

"And you expect what exactly from me?"

"We need you to help us save this ship and get us on our way. It is entirely possible the craft approaching from Earth is from MynCorp. I have no idea how they could know we are here but they would be extremely keen to retrieve Nomia and Suparna."

"What's so special about this ship?"

"You were right. The voice of the ship does not belong to an A.I.. This is a pilot-class ship."

"I knew it. That's why Nomia freaked at the thought of tearing the ship apart. There's a guy hanging somewhere with his nervous system replaced by every sensor and actuator running this craft."

The ship spoke. "My name is Kaamil. Please help me, the pain is unbearable."

"Is this the part where I say, why should I care what happens to Earth? You abandoned us to die over a hundred years ago. I wouldn't shed a tear if the Earth was reduced to a steaming pile of nothing. Then you point out that the evil Eidolons will not stop at Earth and all human-based lifeforms are destined to go the same way, as they carry out their devious plot."

"Something like that."

"You're asking a lot. Certain and immediate death for one."

"I hope I'm not asking for that, but the risks are significant."

"Beautifully understated."

"I could ask what the point of surviving today would be, if you knew there was no tomorrow."

"Look, I'm already up for it, there's no reason to depress me."

"You are?"

"I'd do it just to get a glimpse of Earth. Even better if we're annoying MynCorp en route. But I should warn you that I'll probably abandon you the instant I get bored."

"Right. Well, we shall endeavour to entertain you."

A wave of manifest pain rippled along the walls from the stern and a dismal moan echoed through the air circulation system.

"Why don't you just wish the cutting crew into fairy cakes?"

"I'm a little preoccupied maintaining the ZQP shield and as long as that's in place, we're as fate-tied as you are."

"ZQP?"

"Zero Quantum Potential. I thought I should give it a name before someone calls it a cloak of invisibility or something else equally cringe-making. What's the matter? You don't like it?"

"Whatever. So what do we do?"

"We need to slow the wrecking crews down long enough for Finnur to call a withdrawal. Can you order them to stop?"

"I could but Finnur is a control freak. No one accepts orders without double-checking with the Captain."

"We could order them to keep at it."

"We could but that might not save your ship."

"But it would make them call for confirmation and if their progress was sufficiently slow the Captain might cut his losses and withdraw them early."

"What did you have in mind?"

"Kaamil?"

"Yes José."

"I need you to concentrate."

"I'm not exactly napping here."

"I mean on something other than pain. Can you project a representation of the cutting crew in relation to your systems?"

A rotating laser display of green and red flickered into existence in the middle of the room. It quivered and spasmed as Kaamil gasped. Part of the display could be seen to peel away and float off into space. Bergur looked confused. "What was that?" he asked.

"I think it was one of our thrust nozzles. The other three are being worked on by that shuttle-mounted laser cutter." He pointed to a flashing blob moving behind the Suparna.

"If we lose those we're dead in the water. No thrust, no go."

"Maybe. I'm more concerned about the antimatter storage and reaction chambers. The nozzles are glorified cones of metal. They can be synthesised. The antimatter systems are too delicate to reproduce in a hurry."

"It looks as if there are three teams working inside the ship breaking up those systems."

"That's where we'll work. Forget saving the major fabrications. Concentrate on the delicate stuff that gives us power. Kaamil?"

For a moment there was no answer. José and Bergur shared a glance of mutual concern. Nomia stroked the wall again and tried to draw him out. "Kaamil, stay with us please. We need you. If you withdraw from us now we will all be lost."

"I am still here. I can feel myself hanging in this bunker but all the pain comes from outside. It is hard to let it in but harder to block it out."

José looked to the ceiling and fed his conviction from another deep breath. "Kaamil, you have to accept you are going to lose the engines, but we can try to save the antimatter systems. That way the Suparna has a chance of living. I want you to work on decoys. Extend the fabric of the ship to generate replicas of the containment rings and reaction chambers."

"They are too complex for the ship's fabric. It is only designed to create doors, walls, conduits and furniture for the crew."

"You don't have to create working instances, just crude facsimiles. Then scramble the corridor layout. Hide the real systems as much as you can."

Bergur looked sceptical. "You really think you can fool professional scavengers that easily?"

"Counter suggestions?"

"How about a complementary suggestion?"

"Please do."

"Kaamil, can you increase the oxygen concentration across the ship?"

"How high?"

"Just up a few percent."

"I can."

"Do it."

José tilted his head as his mind accelerated to attack speed. "I assume that an excess of oxygen is going to have some adverse effect on your crewmen."

"Just slightly." Bergur's mischievous grin made him look like he was coming round after a session with a dentist. "They'll bloom."

"The symbiotic micro-organism in your skin?"

"Spot on. Oxygen is toxic to the algae. It rapidly oxidises trace elements in the cells turning them bright purple. Quite a lot of it is dumped into the hosts bloodstream via osmosis causing an immunological response."

"Is it dangerous?" Nomia continued to stroke Kaamil's wall, as she divided her concern.

"Dangerous? You mean to them?"

"Yes."

Bergur looked baffled, as if she had asked for a weather forecast on the Earth's moon. "No. It's just a bit disorientating. Our metabolisms are extremely tough. They have to be."

"Will you be all right?" José blanked Bergur's second surprised look. "We don't want to incapacitate our strongest asset."

"I'll be fine. Thanks for the concern." Another cheeky grin. "I have a certain weakness that gives me a degree of immunity."

"That's why your skin is darker."

"I think the Captain suspects. The crew call me a deca-head when they think I can't hear."

"Deca-head?"

"It's not very polite. It refers to a certain habit of bathing in twenty percent oxygen."

José and Nomia looked blank.

"It passes the time." Bergur clearly felt a sense of anti-climax over his confession.

"The oxygen level is now at twenty five percent in the lower decks," Kaamil chimed.

"That's enough. I'd rather not kill them." Pause. "Just yet." Grin.

The ghostly display was starting to mutate with the kind of subtle changes in symmetry that José found hard to distinguish from a trick of the eye. Parallel corridors became orphaned, while isolated passages sprung meandering limbs. Annotated icons marking major mechanical installations became twinned with identical-looking icons but free of diagnostic details. The originals rapidly became lost in mazes of dead ends and paths of Möbius implausibility. The only island of calm surrounded the blinking progress of the cutting crew as they pulsed their way in disorientated circles, intermittently bifurcating at new forks in their path, before merging after another circuit.

José watched the unfolding story for a while before offering an optimistic verdict. "It seems to be working."

"We're only buying a little time. The Captain has just been informed of the hold up." When the two non-Eridanians looked blank, he pointed to the side of his neck and said, "Sub-dermal transceiver. It's hard to get too hung up about cybernetic implants when your entire physiology is cobbled together."

"Not too much time." The strain was starting to make Kaamil's voice threadbare and dislocated. "They've started cutting though bulkheads to make their own routes to essential components."

"The Captain is coming back on board. You two should stay here. I'll head him off. See if I can subtly persuade him to cut and run."

Without waiting for agreement he stirred his bulk into a flying trot in the direction of the airlock. When he reached the doorway José called after him. "Bergur."

"José."

"If we get to Earth the atmosphere will slowly kill you."

"Já, but it will be one hell of a rush." Then he pulled himself through the opening and was gone.

José turned back to Nomia and the patch of wall she had focused her compassion on.

*

The smell of charred metal hung in the air like a veiled threat. Pale threads of smoke moved with the forced flow of the ventilation system. With no gravity to add buoyancy to the smoke, it crept forward with the lethargy of diffusion, and evenly filled all the corridors. Bergur drifted through the haze creating indistinct eddies in his wake. The smell meant nothing to him. As long as it was not toxic to his skin then he would breath in vicarious ignorance. His face was free of expression or even features except for the eyes that outshone his iridescent skin.

A voice whispered with omnipresent isotropy, "Bergur, there is a barrage of incoming ordinance. Kaamil is tracking the missiles and they seem to cover most of the obvious escape trajectories."

"What did you expect would happen, José?" Bergur felt decadent talking to a voice he could not trace to a source, like a madman acknowledging the noises in his head.

"You have to keep the Eridanian ship nearby. The ZQP should protect us; the warheads will be neutralised when they cross the threshold."

"What? So you want me to get Finnur to leave this ship, but not to evade the incoming missiles? We may just have to let Finnur and the crew take their chances; if they stay nearby we'll still be at risk."

"But they'll be safe if they just wait for the attack to fail and then make a break for it. They'll have months before the MynCorp ship is back on course."

"You cannot save all the people, all the time."

"At least try."

Bergur folded his mouth closed again and muttered behind sealed lip flaps. When he reached the airlock it was already cycling to reveal the Captain and two security officers. The Captain's right arm was pushed into the folds of his tunic hiding the reality of the missing hand. His manner did not seem any sunnier. "Bergur, you aborted lab experiment, give me some good news."

"We're making reasonable progress. The engines are virtually free of the ship."

"So, I just imagined the confused broadcasts from the cutting crew?"

"They are struggling, a little, to locate the main components of the antimatter system. The ship internals are more complicated than those we've dealt with previously."

"You mean you can't follow a map?"

"The schematics we retrieved from the ship's computer proved to be a little, er, inaccurate."

"Are you suggesting that the computer lied to us?"

"That seems unlikely. Maybe the plans are for an earlier model of the ship."

"How hard can it be to find giant toroidal antimatter containment facilities? The magnetic field alone should act as a screaming beacon."

"We are now making our own route to the systems based on hand-held detectors. We should be done in plenty of time."

"I'll decide if we have time. Where are the two prisoners? I want a word with them."

"They are contained in their quarters. Would you like me to take you there?"

"No, get down to the engineering decks and supervise the cutting teams in person."

"As you wish."

The Captain floated further down the corridor, struggling to make progress with only one arm. The guards tried to steady his coarser spins without obviously seeming to help and received growls of frustration in reward.

Bergur sighed, producing a wet flapping sound through slack lips and then coughed slightly, finally detecting the smoke-laden air. He seemed locked in indecision for many seconds and then threw himself down the nearest access shaft. He glided with some grace but an overwhelming impression of unstoppable momentum, until he passed a side shaft from which the crackle of plasma torches emanated. With one stumpy arm he reached for the rung that ran around the aperture and protruded into the shaft. With the faintest of tension ripples, he absorbed the forward momentum and transferred the energy into sideways motion. He pondered whether the design of the ship instilled a sense of up and down; what made a shaft not a corridor and vice versa? Maybe the humanoid brain felt compelled to establish a vertical in any situation. It was possible if he had entered the ship from a different direction his preconception of up and down would be different. Maybe he would now feel as if he was going up rather than sideways. He concluded that generally his mind was too preoccupied with establishing reference frames and insufficiently absorbed with saving his beautifully-coloured hide.

At the first intersection four men were gathered in front of a wall of no particular notoriety other than that it was smoking gently from multiple, rapidly expanding wounds. The men carried bulky energy cells strapped to their backs and double-handed cutting torches. The ions streaming from the cutting blades were completely invisible but the point of impact on the wall sizzled and popped like pig flesh in an open flame. As Bergur drifted closer he could see the wall flowing towards the wound, thickening the local area, but the holes grew rapidly. After a few seconds the wall shivered and dissipated, as if it had given up the battle.

The men acknowledged the first officer's presence with flickers of their protective inner eyelids and then stepped through into an identical corridor. Bergur followed, dodging dripping alloy as he passed. He spoke to the back of their heads as they started to cut through the next wall. "The Captain wants to know who's to blame for the delay."

Four ion blades hesitated for a second and then continued to cut with renewed determination. The most senior of the crew seemed to reach a decision and turned to face his superior. He spoke in a tone that

Bergur recognised as his own when speaking to the Captain. "The ship is reconfiguring itself to slow us down. It is deliberately hiding the antimatter systems from us."

"The ship?"

"You know these ships have intelligent alloy infrastructure. It's not hard to manipulate it into some kind of defence."

"I know, Mr Hálfdanarson, but who exactly do you think could be driving this little resistance?"

Two of the others started to laugh, their blades cutting meandering paths. Hálfdanarson tried to keep it together but his resolve rapidly evaporated. "I've no idea and frankly I'm not sure I care."

All four of them collapsed on the floor, a pile of giggling limbs. Their blades cut out on safety and lay harmlessly about them.

Bergur relaxed into an easier role. "Quite right too. We should be back home living a bit rather than running up and down corridors on some bland Earth ship."

"Here, here. Bergur for captain. Captain Deca-head." Hálfdanarson froze for a moment, the implications of the insult filtering through to the sober recesses of his mind.

Bergur showed his teeth for a moment in mock anger and then pounded the subordinate in the chest with friendly aggression. "Too right. Me for Captain."

"But won't Captain Finnur be upset?" asked one of the younger Eridanians.

"True." Bergur sealed his mouth covers and looked furtive. With a mock conspirator tone, he beckoned them all closer. "We'll keep it to ourselves. You go back to the ship and prepare. I'll break the news to the Captain."

The others agreed that going home and leaving Bergur to do all the dangerous work sounded like a fine plan. They pulled themselves up using each other as props and made an unsteady procession back towards the airlock. Once they were out of sight Bergur straightened up and thumped his neck to activate a channel to the Captain.

*

Nomia replayed the scene over and overlooking for some kind of sense, something that complied with the empathic rationality she had learnt in the last few months. The only words she had to describe the Captain's behaviour were barbaric or monstrous; a disregard for life or any sense that it had any intrinsic value. When she had emerged from the Nexus her sense of humanity had been fragile and almost infantile, but even then she could see that other people existed within their own spheres of emotion. She could comprehend that others could experience a change in emotional state as a result of her actions; she just found it hard to predict how that reaction would go. Now, she was having to learn a much harder lesson than empathy; the ability to suppress the fear and sorrow it could generate.

Kaamil had given them a few seconds warning that the Captain was about to come through the door. Just enough time for José to claim the centre of the room and encourage Nomia towards the back, where her acceleration cot offered a safer perch.

"Is it you or the ship?" Captain Finnur had said the moment the door aperture was wide enough for him to see the two of them.

"Possibly both," José had answered.

"They would send an attack ship on a multi-year journey just to destroy this ship and two passengers?"

"What makes you think they are trying to destroy us?"

"Several waves of antimatter torpedoes says they are not bent on your survival."

"It is possible they are aimed at you, but you are probably right."

"Why let the ship pick you up from Tau Ceti just to kill you halfway to Earth?"

"I can't answer that."

"You might want to try." The Captain turned his torso to the door and an even tougher-looking Eridanian stepped alongside. He was nursing a battered projectile weapon of unlikely design. The Captain gave his companion a second look and said "You're blooming!" His frustration was turning to exasperation. The second Eridanian looked at his own arms blearily as if the glowing purple was hard to focus on.

José took what little initiative the moment allowed. "Listen Captain, I can protect you. Just return to your ship and wait for the attack to pass. You can then make a break for home while we continue towards Earth. I would be very surprised if they follow you."

"Let's try a slightly different plan. You show me where the A.I. core is so I can make a loud bang. Then once the ship has stopped playing with my cutting crew we rip out the antimatter systems. Then you can enjoy a 15g ride in my ship and if you survive that, then you can work for your keep on Epsilon Eridani until you die of cold or ammonia poisoning. How does that sound?"

"I can't let you do that. We have to reach Earth."

"Is that so?"

Without even a flicker of consideration, Captain Finnur drew a crude taser pistol from a jacket pocket and raised it level with José's head. The weapon hummed with mounting power. José had time to blink before the charge arched across two metres of air and entered his head through his right eye.

His head cracked back sending his body into a limp spin. He continued his slow motion cartwheel until he impacted with the back wall above Nomia's perch. With each rotation she could see the stunned expression fixed on his face and the one jet-black eye, matt and without reflection, like it had captured the moment that death reached out from the dark and claimed its prize.

Nomia drew breath to scream. Her lungs would not let her stop sucking in air until the room was empty because once she started to scream she would never stop. At the point where her lungs ached against her ribs, a thought hit her with an intensity that made it echo back from her skull. It was not her own thought, it had come from outside. There was a voice and an image. The image was a man leaning over a woman on a metallic bench. Cables and tubes were draining her life away. He was reaching down to her as her eyes opened from an endless nightmare. The thought was not from the scene. It had been added to a memory.

Earth. Get back to Earth. Nothing else matters.

Then Nomia was left with her own thoughts. She was alone.

Except, she was not. The Captain was turning to her, the gun hand casually following his focus. "Let's try again," he said with a menacing veneer of patience.

Nomia felt her hand clench, slender but determined muscles distorting her wrists and forearms. An ember of hate in her eyes exploded into a furnace of loathing. Finnur hesitated, his mutilated arm quivering in his jacket. For a moment a realisation crossed his face; he knew for one instant that he was mortal and that his life could be snuffed out like a candle in a storm.

The moment passed. Nomia's hatred had no outlet. Reality was rigid within the zone of zero quantum potential. The Captain realised that somehow he had escaped with his life but could not put a source to the knowledge. He cocked his head as if listening to a distant bird song and then punched himself in the neck. "Bergur, what's happening. Report!"

The wall behind Nomia vibrated gently and the voice of Kaamil tickled her ear. "Nomia, you should hear this. I've tapped into the Eridanian private comm channel."

Bergur's voice replaced that of the ship's pilot. "They're coming out of the walls. We can't hold our line."

Finnur's voice sounded echoic, with the original source booming in one ear and a slightly flat reproduction in the other. "Bergur, make sense now, that's an order."

"Captain, we've two men down. We are in retreat. We can't." There was a hiss of electromagnetic interference that made Nomia flinch. "...droids. Hundreds of mechanoids just coming out of the walls and attacking with whatever tools they have. We need concussion arms or localised EM pulse weapons."

"Stand your ground. I'll get some more men and equipment down to you."

Finnur raises his weapon towards Nomia again. "This is your doing. I will make you suffer." He thumped his neck again. "Captain to Ellida, get me more men over here immediately."

"Captain, this is Páll. We have the Suparna engines on board. We are ready to set sail."

"Did you not hear me? I need reinforcements now."

"Of course, as you command. Respectfully, we are six minutes away from the cut-off point to achieve a safe exit path."

Finnur was rigid for many seconds. Waves of purple washed across his skin like the pros and cons of an argument. The Captain was used to making decisions based on instinct and experience but his concentration was clearly erratic. Eventually a solid thought congealed from the mental chaos and he spoke it before it could evaporate. "Right, forget the reinforcements. Get ready to get under way. We'll come back for the salvage once the Earth ship has passed. Bergur, retreat to the airlock."

"Já, I'm on my way." Bergur's voice cut through the noise of metal against flesh.

"Bring her," Finnur said to his guard before twisting and pulling himself though the door aperture.

The guard looked as if he would much rather be making a fast exit than playing catch me with a skinny Terran. Nomia decided to test his patience further. She waited until he had pushed off from the far wall and was irrevocably committed to his trajectory. Then she simply pushed off in a different direction aiming for a point about halfway along the side wall. He tried to adjust his direction mid-flight and ended up in a free-fall tumble. With one more push Nomia was out the door and into the corridor. The aperture glided closed behind her momentarily trapping her pursuer. Finnur must have gone right so she headed left, trying to get to an intersection before the guard could spot her. She kicked off the side walls in turn like a ricocheting bullet, zigzagging her way down the corridor. The bullet she expected in her back would not bounce off anything. Every moment she imagined it leaving the muzzle of the homemade gun, pushing the guard back against the door with the recoil. The speeding slug then would slice through the air creating mini acoustic shocks that reflected around the whole ship. The sound it would make as it entered her back would not echo, it would be the deadened sound of technology entering flesh.

With a kick fuelled by fear and too powerful for careful aiming, she made for the first left turn. She clipped the corner with her left shoulder sending shooting pains up her arm and into her neck, at the same time as sending her somersaulting towards relative safety. Her head took a lot of the momentum of the tumble when the next surface intervened. A noise exploded in her skull like some prophetic church bell. Her vision spun in the opposite direction to her body, bringing stomach acid into her mouth in a single wretched convulsion. Beneath her, an access shaft swam into focus. She swung her right arm at the rail three times until she cracked her knuckles and grabbed hold. With an effort that brought blackness creeping in from the corners of her vision, she launched herself downward.

Nomia's last thought was to close her eyes because going unconscious with them open seemed wrong. She could feel a gentle breeze on her face that told her she was still moving but then her body surrendered to the darkness; more punishment would have to wait until it started to heal itself.

*

"The Eridanian ship is underway. Accelerating at one sixty metres per second squared."

"Ignore it." Julienne was energised with the proximity of the end game. Decisions came easily and orders flowed from her lips. A dozen crew were feeding her summary data and she glided through it like a bird of prey, striking out at targets at will.

"Still no neutrino emissions matching the Suparna."

"Take the ignition point of the Eridanian engines as a reference point and do the same for the optical plasma burst reported earlier. Do a time difference and extrapolate. Assume zero thrust."

"Trajectory calculated."

"We'll assume that's where the Suparna is. Initiate thrust to match lateral motion and prepare gravito-metric drive for deceleration shock."

"Simulations of torpedo strike estimate one point three percent chance of proximity strike on Eridanian ship and sixty two point eight percent chance of proximity strike on Suparna."

"Leave pirate bound torpedoes on destruct course, switch the rest to dormant. Self destruct any on physical collision course or within three thousand kilometres of the most likely position. I don't want any risk of destroying the Suparna."

At this stage she was acting almost entirely on instinct but for her that meant the rigorously analytical permutation engine that supplanted most of her subconscious. The attack had been a calculated risk, never meant to destroy her quarry. She was establishing ground rules for the engagement. The opening move had shown that she was more than happy to vaporise first and forget about asking questions later. They could not hope to outdo her ruthlessness, they would always be playing the soft indecisive role in this engagement. Yet, she could not be sure which ship held the Node. She made a mental note to ask for two pursuit ships in future. For now she was gambling on the pirates being flustered into leaving the Node on board the Suparna, either to collect later, once the attack had passed, or simply because the Node had appeared useless and of little value.

This was almost pure guesswork.

Mex would be proud, she thought, *not that his approval holds any value, but it is a useful barometer of my ability to assimilate human nature. Why does he have to stand there with that judgemental expression? I'm doing my job; a sense of duty that's alien to his undisciplined mind.*

She knew she was not being entirely fair; his mind was well trained and disciplined in its own way but infuriating in others. She decided to send him to his quarters but never actually got around to giving the order; she felt a dark hole open within her at the thought of his absence.

I'll need him soon, it's best he's up to speed with developments.

Julienne's concentration had slipped and the flow of splice data from her subordinates was backing up. She re-established the connection and took the highest priority message.

Done. Torpedoes disarming and switching to passive mode. Wait. Transition not complete. Contact lost with embedded minds."

"Clarify."

"All warheads within two hundred kilometres of target have stopped transmitting telemetry or responding to pings."

"Any supporting information?"

"None. All telemetry ceased at the same radial distance from the target indicating a spherical effect centred on the Suparna."

"A defensive measure?" Julienne had not expected that, but it told her that the Node's abductors must be resourceful and still on the MynCorp ship. She notched another point for human instinct. "Adjust deceleration shock to match Suparna's inertial frame but at three hundred kilometres separation. Monitor locality for signs of engine ignition."

"Deceleration shock ready to begin. Gravito-metric drive initialised and mass at maximum angular momentum."

"Initiate."

The lights should flicker. Julienne understood the physics, at least at a superficial level, but energies with so many trailing zeros really should have the decency to dim the lights for a moment.

"Graviton flux at peak. Shock forming."

"Maintain separation of ship from shock at design levels." The crew might resent her previous mistake but they would not be able to say she did not learn.

All inertial reference frames are born equal, or so her junior academy teacher had stated. Even then she had detected a hint of guilt in his tired eyes. She had assumed he had some petty secret about his marriage, or maybe, a sense of disappointment with himself for not fighting harder to make it upstairs to where the real thinkers resided. With the perspective of maturity, she could see that the guilt had been aimed at her. Not just Julienne but all his students, as he fed them layers of lies. Each time he was allowed to peel away one level of deceit and reveal a hidden truth, he lost a little more trust and his students shed more naivety. It was an ancient method of teaching that had patronised children for centuries; frightened to overload their delicate minds with complicated truths. It was considered better to use simple models that paid passing homage to reality but did not risk scaring anyone. Julienne found it interesting how the layers of complexity children were forced to clamber through bore a striking similarity to the development of modern physics; Victorian scientists learning matter was made of atoms and slowly probing inside to discover electrons orbiting clusters of protons and neutrons, before throwing most of their preconceptions away, along with determinism, when they embraced the vagaries of quantum mechanics.

Julienne felt the same sense of petulant irritation now, as her manufactured subconscious patronised her meat brain. The embedded processors that nestled between the hemispheres of her brain were performing complex mathematical simulations of the upcoming encounter. They fed back to her an iconographic representation of the three vessels and the relative descriptions of their inertial frames. Where the picture broke down and revealed its allegorical roots was in the topography of the intervening space. Julienne was bright enough to know that the grotesquely distorted representation of the local volume decried the inadequacies of the presentational analogy.

What her teacher had told her was that an inertial frame represents a spatial frame of reference in which the laws of physics have their simplest form. For example, the Suparna was drifting through open space and a coordinate system defined such that it moved with her, would exhibit very simple physics. The craft would remain exactly stationary unless acted on by some force, such as firing her engines. He had gone on to present a point on the surface of the Earth as an example of a non-inertial frame; it might seem as if the point is stationary but the local physics exhibits all kinds of half-baked effects, like Coriolis and centrifugal forces, as a direct result of trying to do calculations on the surface of a rotating ball.

The important point for space flight and particularly space combat, was that inertial frames always move in a very simple manner with respect to each other; if two frames are moving apart at a particular speed then they will always be moving apart at that speed. The whole business of getting close to your target was about changing your inertial frame to be one that converged on the enemy. Or in the case of the Eridanian vessel, changing your inertial frame to one that was running away as fast as possible. The Svargaloka frame was vaguely approaching that of the Suparna but only fleetingly; the frames had a relative speed that took a good bite out of that of light. Changing inertial frames took a lot of brute force. Most of which was achieved by squirting stuff out the back of a spaceship, but there was only so much that could be done before the forces tended to flatten everybody on board.

The part of the story that her teacher had suppressed under layers of nagging guilt was that most of the above argument was not worth the photons it was displayed with. Real space was curvy and prone to freaky geometric irregularities. Inertial frames actually follow the geodesics of local space and, just like lines of latitude near the poles of a planet, geodesics can move together. This was exactly what the gravito-metric drive was designed to do; forget all the hard business of shifting inertial frames, simply warp space until your inertial frame approaches that of your target.

So, Julienne was presented with a condescending depiction of the three ships with the intervening space buckled close to breaking point to bring them all together to a common theatre of war. She knew that all the information required to perform her job was encoded in that image and yet she could not shift the ingrained frustration at being drip-fed information for the good of her feeble mental health.

"Mr Tyrian." They both jumped at the harshness of her tone. Julienne chastised herself for letting emotions slip into her dealings with Mex again. Why could she not keep an even keel when she talked to him? She wanted to tell herself it was simply his irritating manner but she was self-aware enough to know that the problem was in her and that emotions often emerged in direct contradiction to those that were concealed. "I want you inside the Drop from here on in. Any relevant activity around the Nexus and you are to splice it directly to me. Take one of the web positions."

Mex simply nodded and moved towards the edge of the room. A technician floated free of her webbing and offered it to Mex. He settled into the grasping strands and opened his eyes to the scanning lasers.

She paused for a moment, half-expecting him to scream of an attack from the Nexus already eating into their systems but he looked as peaceful as he had when she had sat by his bed in the medical chamber. She had even allowed herself to stroke his brow once or twice, safe in the knowledge he would not wake up until the right neutralising drug was administered.

Almost disappointed, she returned her concentration to their inertial frame and the rapidly converging geodesics splayed out before the spatial shock.

*

"Nomia. Can you hear me?" José was stroking her head, smoothing the hair into the centre parting she loathed. She wanted to move his hand to her face, so she could feel his palms against her cheek, but the voice was wrong.

"Nomia. I need you to wake up. We have to make some decisions." It could be him, he was always thinking about things that needed deciding, but she knew it was not José. Why not? What could have separated them? Only death could do that, he had promised that in the early days of celestial freedom. She must be dead, that was why it could not be José's voice. She wanted to mourn for poor José, left on his own in the Universe without a soulmate.

"Nomia. Wake up." The hand was on her shoulder, then, where it felt chunky and too strong for genuine gentleness. So she did as he requested and exposed herself to the unrelenting harshness of the waking world.

Bergur's face was pulled into an expression which was new to Nomia. The skin around the brow-ridge was creased and dragged towards the residual rise of his nose. As her eyes gained focus, the look of concern evaporated from his face and it returned to being smooth and invulnerable.

"Hi," she said.

"Morning, have a good nap?"

The other question hung in the air between them and darkened the shadows of accumulated pain around their eyes. Nomia knew it had to be asked but she could not continue to live and answer it; as long as Bergur held the question back, she could function and contemplate future actions, even plan. Yet every time Bergur unfolded his mouth flaps to draw a throat full of air to speak, she knew he wanted to ask for José. She tensed and he fumbled into a story of his escape.

"It wasn't hard to convince the cutting crew to give up. I think they were on the edge when I arrived. It was only an ambient trace of fear that kept them cutting. Finnur is so heavily engrained in their psyche that they would probably obey after they die."

"What was all the noise when you called Finnur?" Nomia liked watching Bergur talk. Initially, she had found his chunky frame rigid and expressionless but slowly she had tuned into the subtle body language of the Eridanian, just as she had for José and through him, all of humanity. When Bergur was excited tiny ripples of colour danced across his skin like a bubble on the surface of a hot water. When he was in full aureate flow his teeth glinted through the retracted lips and he looked more likely to bite the head off a small animal than deliver a story of intrigue and guile.

"It was me and Kaamil doing a little play-acting. I never expected Finnur to have an imagination, but Kaamil convinced me to try it. I suspect the oxygen rush had deadened his perceptive side. Anyway, your pilot played the role of a thousand berserk mechanoids and I played the part of Eridanians being hacked into little bits of purple flesh. How were we?"

"Very convincing, I could hear the blood fly but I'm not entirely sure I understand why."

"Distraction, diversion and just plain time wasting. Plus the fact I needed a plausible reason to be left behind. Heroic death is so much more my style than back-stabbing deserter. Anyway, I needed to overload Finnur enough to keep him off-guard, and away from destructive thoughts. It gave you an opportunity to break free."

"What happened to your shipmates?"

"Kaamil says Finnur waited at the airlock until the last moment, growling with frustration but, when the time came, they headed back to our ship. A few minutes later the Ellida broke formation and headed off at high burn. I'm glad I'm not on board; I hate those endurance runs. Everybody acting as if their spines aren't being pushed through their knees. So much macho detritus."

"At least the Ellida still has working engines."

"Good point. Will they make it out? What happens when they hit the edge of the shield?"

"I don't know. José said that the missiles would probably stop working when they crossed into the protected volume, but that doesn't mean they'll have any problems getting out. They're probably more at risk once they get out. It's only a matter of time before the Eidolons get around to erasing human colonies."

"One thing at a time. We should concentrate on our own survival for the moment. How did you end up floating around the lower decks?"

"A lot of luck and a bit of help from our trusty steed." She patted the floor. The slap of her hand sounded hollow and empty, like a life shared to a point and then lived alone. She started to cry perfect pearls of silver on ivory skin.

Finally, Bergur drew her into a clumsy hug that could easily crush the remaining life from her body. "He's not coming is he? José's not coming," he whispered into her ear.

"Finnur killed him without even a second thought. Shot him like a tin can." Tears dragged sobs from her lungs. They emerged in long trains of despair.

"Did he even try to defend himself?"

"Against Finnur? With a gun? José was a peaceful man, he had no idea how to fight."

"I meant with his Downey field mojo."

"Not as long as he was shielding us from Verity Space. He surrendered his power to save us all, even Finnur."

"Was shielding? You said was shielding, past tense."

Nomia started to cry again but with sporadic sobs like a tired muscle shaking with fatigue. Bergur hugged her harder. She felt ribs flex but the background pain was grounding. He tried again. "Sorry. What I meant was, if José is dead he couldn't be shielding us from the Eidolons. So why are we still here?"

The contradiction was enough to pull Nomia around. Breathing, keeping her eyes open and thinking about quantum conundrums; these three activities seemed enough to focus a life on. She tried to reach down to the Nexus, opening the part of her mind that was sensitive to the Downey field. The pain of José's death receded as she opened more of her mind; the parts of her brain trained by the Nexus; moulded by the Drop from a starting point of emotional isolation.

Nothing.

Where she expected the feeling of free fall, as she dropped out of causal reality into a domain where probability and potential replaced width and breadth, there was a barrier of determinism. "The shield is still there. I can't see into Verity space."

"How is that possible?"

"It isn't. José is dead. The shield should be gone."

"What do we do?"

At that moment a mantle was passed. She was José in proxy. It was up to her to organise, plan and save. "We get to Earth."

"To what end? How can we possibly do anything against a race that lives outside causality? Even if, by some cosmic joke, the Terrans believe a girl who doesn't exist and the rebellious descendant of a failed colony."

"As long as the shield is working we are a little bubble of determinism. Near this ship, fate exists. So, call it destiny."

Chapter 8

Ping.

Heat radiated into space and metal contracted.

Ping.

And the scratching of metal claws on the other side of thin alloy. A metallic skin, inflated by Mex's imagination to provide a sufficient sense of insulation from the nothingness of everything.

A splice feed in one corner of his perception showed the crab-like creations scuttling over the barrack blister. Some of them were attaching crude ion thrusters to the stronger parts of the structure. They secreted an epoxy resin from fabrication glands in their legs and welded the motors into place. The exothermic reaction of the resin when exposed to ultraviolet light made the ship's alloy glow a dull orange. Other mechanoids concentrated on the spines anchoring the blister to the main hull; their cutting blades causing more hot spots which made the dome glow like a Christmas tree when Mex shifted his proxy vision into the infrared.

He was grateful for the distraction. The barracks had held so many people just a few short days ago. Now he sat cross-legged on the floor, the fabric of his trousers offering just enough grip to prevent him floating away with each breath. A mobile splice terminal on a dumb tripod stood just in front, electrostatic hooks tying each leg to the ground. The whole volume had been hastily cleared of the remnants of the previous occupiers, except for the larger structures. The space looked like a battlefield from a war between cleaning droids; every surface was spotless and free from blood stains and yet it still felt like a scene of carnage.

Mex dipped in and out of the Nexus, but he was now sure it was a pointless vigil. For three days they had laid siege to the Suparna at a cautious

213

distance, like an overly polite stalker. At no point had he detected anything interesting in the Drop which might be originating from the missing Node. Even if she did make an appearance, he had enough autonomous agents of his own devising, prowling the data channels, that he would be alerted in microseconds. The real mystery was in normal space-time. Julienne had been absolutely right to keep their distance, after they had used the spatial shock to bring their relative velocity to zero. Something was very wrong with reality around the crippled ship.

The Suparna sat in the middle of a slowly expanding debris field. Her engines were all but missing and a good chunk of the surrounding superstructure had disintegrated into globules of cooling alloy. The side of the wounds which remained part of the main vessel were black from spilt heat, as if a star had reached out and stroked the surface with fingers of hydrogen plasma. When viewed through the passive optical sensors of the circling drones, she hung ghost-like against the backdrop of distant stars. The surface carved and dissected by hundreds of scanning laser beams which mapped her contours and surface properties to the finest detail. The virtual view offered by the A.I. aboard the MynCorp ship was a lot less ethereal; hard textures and features exaggerated by logarithmic scaling to tease out every last drop of sense. Interference fringes fluttered as something moved within the Suparna, sending vibrations to the hull, and shifting the phases of the reflected laser light. It looked as if Julienne had been right to assume somebody would still be aboard; the episodes of movement were too irregular to be from machinery. By looking at the data built up over the last few days, Mex could even tell what sleep cycle those left on-board had adopted. There were six to eight hour periods where nothing moved within the stricken ship. Except one night, when a faint vibration plodded the length of the major axis and then returned; perhaps the midnight stroll induced by a worried mind.

Despite the wealth of direct and indirect data on the state of the Suparna, they still had no idea why nothing could get near her. There was no evidence of the torpedoes which had malfunctioned near the vessel and no sign of impact. Certainly, the pilot-class vessel was capable of mending most damage given time, but the wounds to her rear were enough to show the recuperative nature of the intelligent alloy was finite. If the torpedoes had impacted on the ship, there would be evidence, even if they had failed to detonate. The MynCorp tacticians had concluded the missiles must have flown straight past their target and ploughed into open space in a dormant state.

Showing a level of patience Mex suspected was a dose of self-flagellation for Julienne, the Svargaloka launched a succession of unmanned drones in the general direction of the Suparna. Each of them was equipped with different, and progressively more esoteric arrays of sensors, in an attempt to make a bridgehead on the hull of the target craft. Every time, when the drones reached two hundred kilometres from the target, they became unresponsive. Some simply shut down and drifted off into space, or in one case bounced off the Suparna causing a minor dent which slowly rippled back to smoothness. Others fired their manoeuvring thrusters randomly and had to be intercepted.

Mex had been the one to suggest going low-tech, rather than loading a portable singularity computer into the last drone. The tacticians were determined to out-think the barrier. Mex convinced Julienne that under-thinking it was a better strategy. They cobbled together a crystal oscillator to broadcast a radio beacon, and to act as a receiver to enable a simple remote control. The receiver was connected directly to the thruster's input channels and Julienne flew the last drone remotely. Her eyes and ears were low resolution analog cameras and moving coil microphones, with the outputs piggy-backed onto a simple radio carrier wave. It was all wonderfully retrograde, and Mex felt a thrill of exploration akin to that he remembered from his first childhood trip into Earth orbit. The video and audio feeds were piped to hastily erected display panels in the Svargaloka control room, and the command crew all squinted and pointed as shadows drifted through the snow-like projection.

The drone had weaved and meandered its way towards the Suparna, and successfully bumped onto the hull with no loss of control or signal. The zone was evidently only a barrier to higher levels of technology. Unfortunately, despite proving his hypothesis, he had no suggestions about what to do with a remote control lump of metal now that they were within an arm's reach of their quarry. Julienne sent it floating along the length of the Suparna, sending back grainy pictures of the hull. The frame rate was low enough for the Svargaloka's scanning lasers to blur into a continuous glow that seemed to float a few millimetres off the surface.

It was Julienne who had made the next leap in logic. She decided they must fashion a low-tech shuttle to transport a boarding party to the Suparna. Her unshakable rationality had concluded that the largest non-structural component of the Svargaloka was the military dome, so this would be the shuttle. The dome was an aberration in the profile of the vessel, being attached to the gravito-metric jump ship purely to provide facilities for the combat personnel. The remaining MynCorp crew and Mex felt that the blister sticking out the side of the tail was a mausoleum to the men and women that died. There was an unspoken taboo about entering that part of the ship, as much as anything due to the unknown manner of the deaths. Everyone hoped, when they spoke openly about it, that the shock had wiped out everyone instantly and the deaths were clean. In quiet moments between duties, many found themselves shivering as their imaginations flashed images of twisted screaming faces. Mex probably more than most, because the memory of his own hand stretching to infinity was still fresher in his mind than he would have chosen.

Julienne crewed her expedition by turning on the spot and pointing. A name and role accompanied each extension of the finger. "Yakini Akida, pilot, John Richardson, Communications, Bethan Wilson, security, Mex Tyrian, Intelligence."

That's an oxymoron if there ever was, thought Mex. He definitely felt conflicted as her eyes brushed over him and the hand raised to isolate him. The plan was about as Heath Robinson as any he had drawn on table tops in spilt beer over the years. If more than a couple of the dozen or so ion drives sheared off, they risked losing attitude control. They would probably fly around in circles for a while until the superstructure fractured under the unanticipated stresses.

'Still, better than being left behind.' Mex cringed, hoping reality had not heard him.

As the mission became more physical and less a talking-shop, Mex felt his own presence was becoming harder to rationalise. Julienne might be continuing his ordeal out of sadism, but Mex was starting to develop a blossoming sense of gratitude; he felt a crushing sense of disappointment when he thought of being discarded before the mystery of the missing Node was revealed.

"Captain, would you oblige me with three technicians and the same number of security-trained personnel?" Julienne had the entire crew manifest stored somewhere in her head, and Mex had to smile at her belated attempt to include the Captain in her decision-making.

"Of course," he answered with surprising grace, clearly glad to be helping her off his boat.

Mex had arrived first in the makeshift shuttle. He had no shift to end or compatriots to leave farewell messages with. Even the two security men, that had shadowed him between his room and the command centre for most of the last week, had drifted off to prepare themselves. They seemed to think his inclusion in the mission was an implicit pardon for past misdemeanours. He did not argue, especially considering they had drawn a second set of short straws when the Captain had selected them to satisfy Julienne's request for a security team. Mex suspected they were the only remaining crew who could hold a gun without sweating.

As Mex had slowly drifted the length of the ship towards the tail, he felt increasingly alone. He had moved cautiously to minimise the disturbance to the delicate prisms of the mobile splice terminal he carried. His slowness was in juxtaposition to the succinct efficiency of the few crew members he passed. He felt like a gliding sea bird, watching a storm rage on the horizon. In reality, he was probably heading towards the real storm; it seemed extremely unlikely the Suparna was as calm as she appeared. He felt certain he would survive long enough to find out; it was inconceivable he could fly between stars only to die shuttling from one ship to the other; even if the shuttle did more closely resembled a marquee.

Yakini and John joined him after a while. Mex was grateful for the distraction; the ghosts of men and women, clad in space fatigues, were becoming increasingly vivid in his mind's eye. Yakini was too gangly to be graceful. Under the grip of gravity she reminded Mex of a giraffe with the complexity of her limbs, but in free fall she suffered from a leaky angular momentum which was always turning her away from the task at hand. She suffered it with good grace. It was unusual for someone brought up on Mars to successfully reintegrate into Earth society, let alone make it onto the crew of a MynCorp flagship. She still found time to give Mex a lazy smile from compact features, as she supervised three technicians. One of the techs and Yakini held reels of black cable as the other two pushed themselves towards the perimeter of the dome. At a dozen points they attached inductive controllers to the skin of the dome.

"We're aligning the controllers with each ion drive." Yakini still let part of her heritage slip out through the drawl of a lilting accent. She was never going to hide a physiology developed in low gravity, so there was little to gain by hiding her mother tongue.

"I thought we were going for radio control," said Mex as he watched one of the technicians launch himself on a slow glide towards the apex of the dome. Cable spooled in his wake.

"I think the engines are too critical. Ideally I'd like to make a direct optical connection, but we don't want to risk the integrity of the shell by drilling holes. The induction controllers are a few millimetres from the receivers in the motors and the technology is so primitive we should be safe." Mex tried to look reassured, but Yakini was obviously not as convinced as she sounded. "Is this plan completely insane?" she asked.

Mex sighed. "I was just asking myself the same thing. Somehow, I can't believe the Universe could be so fickle as to kill us off at this point, and Ms. Garland seems quite enamoured with the idea." The words sounded desperately short of conviction even to himself. When Yakini failed to look comforted he tried another approach. "In reality, what we're attempting is a lot less demanding than most of the first hundred years of space flight. All our technology does is make a buffer between ourselves and the harsh reality of flinging a tin can through space. As systems get increasingly complex the number of failure modes increases, so more technology is required to mitigate the induced risk through fail-over and redundancy. Twentieth century Russians managed a very productive and safe space programme with the simplest of technologies. Complexity doesn't mitigate risk, it abstracts it."

"So you're happy flying a military boot camp through interstellar space and into a zone where anything more advanced than a children's toy rolls over and sticks its metaphorical feet in the air?"

"No, I'm scared silly." Mex disarmed the statement with a grin.

Apparently satisfied, Yakini spun away from Mex and drifted over to help John set up a homemade radio transmitter. Before Mex started to imagine ghosts again, Julienne floated through the entrance portal flanked by Bethan and her security contingency.

"Not exactly the invasion force we started out with," Mex braved.

"We'll make do," came the curt reply from Julienne. "You ready?"

"And almost willing."

Her eyes glazed for a moment. When she was back in focus she said, "Yakini, the mechanoids have severed the connecting struts. We are now purely on internal systems. Are you ready to push off?"

"Nothing is tested beyond basic connectivity, but we are where we are. Everyone prepare for impulse gravity." Yakini hooked her feet under the edge of the grey cabinet which sat in the centre of the maze of control cables, like a mutated harvest spider.

The take-off was anticlimactic in its gently creaking softness. The base of the dome became marginally more down than up, as a handful of ion drives nudged them away from the main ship at a lazy punt. Eleven pairs of feet slowly orientated themselves down and remained as still as possible. Moving in low gravity was a completely different skill, which few of them had experienced often enough to master. They mutually decided to sit tight and wait for something to happen that required their skills. In the mean time there was plenty of worrying to do.

*

"What next?"

"We go to Earth."

"Okay. Can I rephrase my question to, how next?"

Nomia had just introduced Bergur to the Suparna's control centre and had then floated contemplatively while the inquisitive Eridanian and the ship's pilot had discussed every aspect of the projected display. The details depicted were becoming quite crowded with clusters of dead torpedoes trailing away towards Tau Ceti, and a slowly expanding cloud of metallic fragments which, at some point, had been parts of the Suparna's engines. It

220

reminded Nomia of a firework display, but she kept the thought to herself.

Bergur did not wait for her to answer his question. "Kaamil, how hard would it be to fabricate replacement parts for the engines?"

"The ship's A.I. is already performing a detailed inventory of non-essential ship systems to see how many components can be salvaged, but my initial impression is not positive."

"Can't you make the missing parts?"

"Given time and raw materials. This area of space is not particularly rich in mining opportunities."

"Was that supposed to be sarcasm?"

"Not in the slightest."

"Well, how about we go for a more primitive kind of antimatter drive?"

"What did you have in mind?"

"We could reinforce the rear compartments, clean up the damaged chambers which are exposed to hard vacuum. Then use a magnetic slingshot to fire frozen anti-hydrogen pellets into the chambers, and let them annihilate with the interstellar medium."

"You mean, set off antimatter bombs in the back of the ship and use the concussion force as a source of thrust?"

"You've got it. Of course, we'll have to get it right otherwise we'll just end up blowing chunks out of what's left of the ship."

"My initial calculations show a whole anti-hydrogen pellet would create too much explosive power. Even if the structure of the ship survived, the impulse would be lethal to Nomia, me and, maybe even, to you."

"So, we use the laser manipulators to shatter the pellets as they leave the confinement torus."

"Yes, this is possible. The method would be extremely inefficient, but I estimate we could achieve ten percent of light speed within a year."

Well, that's not ideal, but I guess it's better than sitting here waving at passing traffic."

Nomia was lost in her memories, clinging to the only part of José she had left. Some of her thoughts were not her own but were borrowed from José when they had shared minds. One in particular he had held in isolation for many months after their escape. He had waited until she was emotionally secure enough to handle the implications, but finally he had released it to her. The memory was from immediately after their flight from the MynCorp laboratory where she had existed for most of her life. As they evaporated from the corporeal world, and became a collection of potentials in Verity Space, Nomia's conscious mind became whole for the first time. She had poured out a torrent of coherent thoughts, bombarding the Nexus and José with a lifetime of suppressed ideas. José had soothed her mind, letting her draw sanity from the linear working of his own mind. Then he had vanished, leaving her complete, but helpless in a universe of pure probability. Nomia had panicked, reaching for the nearest available reality. She had popped back into existence in a random place, but the Universe is mostly empty, and she was welcomed by the rupturing emptiness of hard vacuum.

Before the harsh laws of the physical Universe could start boiling off her heat or wrenching the air from her lungs, José was back and willing them into a form less vulnerable to open space. From that point forward they had spent every moment together, sharing an existence and an array of realities.

The memory Nomia was drawing from now was José's from that moment of separation. He had been exhilarated and joyful as they fled the Drop centre together; not the harsh hormonal excitement of a physical body but the rapturous flight of thought and potential. The exultation was flowing from him in an aura of positive emotions, until there was a coalescence of complex probabilities around his aggregate consciousness. Then he was somewhere else in Verity Space; a range of possibilities beyond the comprehension of any corporeal being and the natural domain of his benefactors and guardians.

They presented their guidance as a selection of competing realities. His mind, driven like all sentient beings by change, was able to see the differences without absorbing the details of each reality. In this way they showed their own perception of the interactions with him and the manner in which actuality deviated from ideal. They showed him a highly evolved life, maybe with human ancestors, making the transition from determinism to unbound probabilities. The race calmly absorbed the knowledge and expanded their understanding of both Universes to limitless horizons. Then they showed the cumbersome mammalian form of a modern human, stumbling through the Universe, chaos and degradation churning in its wake.

José tried to formulate a question. Seeking to understand in what way he had failed their expectation. They showed his mind linked with Nomia forming a single entity of infinite grace. To José the pairing was beyond beauty, but he realised that at his first encounter with Verity Space, within the artefact on Triton, this is how they had perceived him. They saw José and Nomia as a single creature of deep perception and understanding. Their reaction, and everything that had happened since, forked from that point of misunderstanding. José felt a nugget of fear form in his consciousness. In response, they showed him a range of realities, a spectrum of potential outcomes. At one end was the harmonious integration of humankind into both Universes, next was a Universe of status quo but devoid of José, and the final extreme; a virgin Earth before life had pushed carbon into intricate patterns of self-replication.

The final image was of a period of inactivity. José felt himself separated from his own kind, a self-imposed exile of undefined duration.

Bergur and Kaamil stopped talking, perhaps sensing Nomia was about to speak. She was not sure when she had earned the respect they exhibited, and doubted she deserved it, but it was a role she would not shrink from. "Forget the engines; I will take us to Earth."

Bergur started to ask a couple of different questions before finally settling on, "You can do that?"

"I can try."

"That didn't sound overwhelmingly confident. What are our chances?"

"It is not a matter of chance. In this case the very concept of the probability of success is a meaningless question. To move something from one region of space to another is a matter of exerting your will on the probabilities built into nature. It is not a matter of how likely the outcome, but whether I have enough will to make it reality."

"*The future exists first in the imagination, then in the will, and only then in reality.*" Bergur looked wistful for a moment.

"Who said that?" Nomia looked as if she had just seen a character from a recurring dream walk in and settle down for a cup of tea.

"I think it was a twentieth century futurist, I suppose she was more right than she could have known."

"The only problem is that this is a very large ship for me to imagine away, will or no will."

"Can we help?" Kaamil offered.

Nomia looked up in surprise. A floating face was looking at her with an attempt at concern. The cheeks were shallow and the eyes deep in shadow despite being made of pure light. The expression was awkward, like someone who had experienced all their social interaction in virtual media. "Kaamil, is that you?"

"Yes, I have used the display emitters in this room to fabricate an avatar. I hope it helps with your need for a more personal connection to me."

"It's not quite the same as face to face but it's a start. Is this what you look like?"

"It's how I looked ten years ago. I've no idea how I look now. To be frank, I would rather not know. Well?"

"What?"

"Can we help?"

"I don't think so. José was the only one who could help and he's gone." There was a pause as each of them waited to see if she would buckle at his name, but the moment passed and she continued. "I will have to prepare myself for a while."

"What about the zero quantum shield thingy?" asked Bergur.

"We will have to get clear of it before we make the attempt. We will not have much time once we are exposed. I must jump us out of this region of space before we are found."

"How do we get clear? Surely it is centred on the ship."

"It seems more likely that it is centred on José. We will have to get his body away from the Suparna."

"You mean jettison him?"

"We could call it a burial."

Bergur smiled, but she was not joking.

"Sorry to interrupt," said Kaamil. "I've intercepted a radio wave emission coming from the approaching MynCorp ship."

"Hell, I'd almost forgotten about them." Bergur rubbed his lip flaps together in agitation.

Kaamil continued uncertainly. "It is frequency modulated and could be interpreted as spoken words."

"Let's hear it," Nomia said.

A male voice, tired with years of service and the repetitiveness of deep space radiated from the walls. "This is Captain Jackson of the MynCorp vessel Svargaloka. This message is intended for the persons currently on board the MynCorp vessel Suparna. A shuttle is currently en route to you. It is commanded by Julienne Garland of the MynCorp security division. Please prepare to accept her on board, and to hand over command to her party. Any act of resistance will be treated as insurrection, and will be dealt with in accordance with colony law."

"What's colony law?"

Bergur looked at her, wondering whether lying was an option. "Outside the core Earth systems there are not the resources for a court-based criminal justice system. Officers of the corporations have the power to act as bastions of the law and deliverers of punishment. In other words, we move and they shoot us."

"Oh. Can we avoid them?"

Kaamil answered this time. "The only means of propulsion I have is docking thrusters. We might be able to delay the docking and make them angry."

"Can't we refuse to let them dock? It might give us time to prepare a defence," Bergur bristled.

"The hull will automatically create a docking portal when it detects contact with another MynCorp vessel."

Again they looked to Nomia for leadership. "We will not fight them. If we cannot convince this party of the Eidolon threat then we have no hope when we reach Earth. It's time we stopped running and started talking. Kaamil, what information do you have on Julienne Garland?"

"Not a lot. According to the corporation database she is dead."

*

"Yakini, are you sure we crossed the barrier?"

"Yes Mex," she answered for the third time. "We are now one hundred and thirty kilometres from the Suparna. We have definitely passed the point at which the drones stopped functioning."

"Well that was a huge pile of anti-climax."

"You sound disappointed."

"I've got an entire adrenal system full of tension to release somewhere."

"Keep it in your pants."

Mex looked at Yakini sharply, unsure when they had become so familiar with each other. Then he looked at Julienne as an inexplicable burning heat rose to his cheeks. She had her back to them all and appeared too deep in thought to have noticed the conversation. Either that or she was giving him the cold shoulder. He mentally kicked himself for the rising arrogance that made him assume she would be bothered either way; not because he disliked arrogance but rather for what it said about his obsession with her. He coughed like he had heard business types doing when they wanted to change the topic of conversation. He raised his voice slightly to address the wider group. "What will we do when we get to the Suparna?"

Bethan looked up from programming her gun. She looked at Julienne's back, as if she was unsure about talking to civilians without instruction. Her camouflage jump-suit was switched to passive mode, the cowl was hanging down her back revealing a particularly well-polished head. The suit was slowly drifting from brown to green in mottled patches like creeping mould. Bethan's nose and eyes were slightly too small for her head, which was considerably too small for her neck; ridges of muscle emerged from her clothing and thrust upwards before vanishing behind each ear. After a respectful delay, she answered Mex's question.

"We'll rotate to present the airlock to the skin of the Suparna. It's the only part of this dome that is intelligent alloy. When the ship recognises the touch it will form a docking rig and rearrange its internal configuration to let us enter. It's built into the design of the alloy so it's very hard to override. The idea was that however incapacitated a ship, it would always be possible to board at any position."

A soft sobbing drifted through the group, so faint it lingered, lacking the energy to push through the air. The group looked at each other trying to place the sound. Then, as one, they turned towards Julienne's back. "Ms Garland, Sir?" said Bethan.

There was no answer or indication that she had been heard. Mex kicked off in a slow arc to land at her shoulder. "Ms Garland, Julienne, what's happened?" he breathed as he landed.

"Empty," was all she said as her legs buckled and she fell to her knees in low gravity slow motion.

Mex caught her by the shoulder before she could collapse to the ground. He moved in front of her, taking care not to turn her towards the others. Tight muscles of shock contorted her face. "Empty," she said again.

"Julienne, what's up?" he whispered while trying to lock eyes with her, but her gaze was firmly turned inward.

"My head, is empty." She managed to raise an arm halfway to her temple but gave up before she could point, apparently exhausted by the effort.

"Your head is never empty. You're always two moves ahead."

"The implant. It's gone. I'm alone."

"Shit, we should have seen this coming. Just take it easy."

Another tear overflowed from her right eye as it twitched involuntarily. "This body is not mine. My mind is here but the body knows I do not belong. It is rejecting me."

"Stay with me Julienne. What exactly did the implant do apart from act as a mobile splice terminal?"

"It was a constant voice telling me whatever I needed to know. It kept the darkness away."

"What darkness?"

"The darkness from before I died and the darkness from when I woke up."

"When you woke up? In this body?"

"It maintained the interface to the body. Stopped it from rejecting me."

"Shit, shit, shit. We've got to get you back to the Svargaloka."

Her eyes sprung back into focus long enough for her to grab his sleeve. "No, carry on. Get the Node. You do it. Then take me back. I can fight the darkness for a while."

"Are you serious? Your body is rejecting your mind. What happens if it wins?"

"It won't. Get the Node. Everything else is secondary." Her arm collapsed again and the light in her eyes dimmed. "Empty. Where my imagination should be there is only a metallic hole. Where my dreams should be, only darkness. My dreams are dark. This feeling of emptiness is the true me. All that's left after you strip away what MynCorp grafted on." She drew circles on her head with a slender finger as if marking out a surgical procedure.

"That's not true. You only feel empty because the endless voice of data has stopped. I can't imagine how the silence must echo." Mex put out his hand, fully intending to take hers. He stopped himself with a spark gap still between them, unsure whether he was frightened about her potential reaction or of how it might look to the crew clustered behind her.

Julienne spoke more softly now, as if her voice might draw monsters from the silence. "You're wrong. It's much more than that; I'm much less. When I was imprinted on this body they removed bits of the brain to make room for the implants and to reduce mental conflict. They took my imagination and dreams. My subconscious was replaced by a computer. All my instincts are algorithmic."

Mex had guessed most of this from their previous conversations, but he had no idea how to comfort her. She had seemed so comfortable with her situation he had not tried to resolve his own feelings of disquiet. His body wanted to offer her the most basic level of support and hold her until tears came, and went, but still he resisted.

"I let them slice me in half," she whispered. "Without their technology I am barely a person."

"If that was true you would not be crying." He half-strangled the last word even as it escaped, certain it was bad.

She turned away from him but immediately turned back when she realised she was exposing her look of vulnerability to the others. "I can't be seen like this. Get me time to find some composure."

"What do you want me to do?"

"Anything. Improvise. Just find that Node."

"Right. I'm on it." Mex paused, hoping his face was not as blank as his mind. "Take your time." He tested reducing the support he was offering to her shoulders. She sagged a few inches before taking up the minuscule weight. Mex switched into nonchalant mode number one; the same expression he used to amble through lobby security on his way up to an illicit meeting with a potential Drop client. He rejoined the crew and stood at the focal point of their attention, blocking any view of their crumpled leader. "Right, Ms Garland is suffering a touch of motion sickness brought on by the period of acceleration. It's an old condition and she'll be fine in a few minutes, once she's found her space legs." He paused briefly to give the illusion of a period to seek validation of the unlikely claim, but before any of them could compose a question he continued. "In the meantime, she has asked me to pass on a set of orders, which I will relay with your consent."

What could they do except nod, while looking around him at the hunched shoulders and bent head of the woman who had maintained the impression of ice-hard invulnerability for every other moment of the mission since Earth.

Mex offered a series of generic and glib instructions which all started life as a simple 'carry on' but mutated through bland verbal mutilation into apparently proactive requests for action.

"Initiating approach roll," announced Yakini a few minutes later. The gentle tug of lateral acceleration was smoothly replaced by radial gravity, as the makeshift shuttle spun to present its entrance portal, come airlock, to the drifting Suparna. A moment later gravity was back to the steady point one g as they slowed their approach to achieve a perfect rendezvous.

"Still no response to the Captain's transmission," stated John crouched over his prehistoric box of electronics.

"But they've made no evasive or aggressive actions?" Mex tried to ease himself into the role without the others noticing the transition.

"Nothing at all." Yakini was too easy-going to get strung out on the chain of command.

"We continue on the assumption they are debilitated." He missed off the subtext that they were now far too close to defend themselves in any meaningful way.

Mex had expected some sort of countdown or maybe a series of bleeps growing in frequency or shrinking in separation, but there was a groan, like an old man waking and remembering his age, and the meagre gravity was gone.

"Contact." Yakini grinned as the others drifted free of the floor flailing for purchase.

Mex felt a bubble of irritation rise from his stomach. Unable to gain purchase he had to twist from the waist to turn; Julienne was still grounded by the soles of her footwear. She looked less distressed in free fall. As fast as it had condensed, the anger dissipated, as if it had no purpose without convection currents to carry it.

Yakini was grinning a Cheshire cat smile, teeth glowing white against the dark brown of her skin. In that moment Mex understood a lot about the way her mind worked; the way she dealt with stress through minor acts of revolution. He knew he liked her and that he would trust her; she was like him but only the good bits, the parts that he did not kick during moments of introspection.

Mex laughed out loud, releasing his tension with each convulsion. "Let's see who's home, shall we?" He lowered himself to the floor by one of the dangling control cables, held himself down until his soles developed enough charge to grip. The others fell in behind as he did an approximation of a walk to the exit portal. "I assume this will only open if there is atmosphere on the other side?"

"Normally, your assumption would be valid." Bethan managed to add a poignancy to the word 'normally' that was in sharp relief to her no-nonsense façade.

"Assuming it works at all," added John redundantly.

Mex looked each of the nine squarely in the face, projecting calm confidence, as he felt the situation demanded. He felt a moment of dislocation, as if he was watching himself in a splice drama; the calm scene before the storm of violence erupted. He placed his palm on the cool grey of the portal, to ground himself mentally and to indicate to the material that he wanted to pass. The metal silently retreated from his touch, opening a hole large enough for a person to step through. The hull of the other ship had moulded itself into a pocket, providing a makeshift airlock. Mex turned and pointed at Bethan and Yakini. Bethan, in turn, nodded to her meagre security squad. Yakini simply shrugged and the six of them stepped into the windowless space. Bethan entered last, gave a 'see you later' wave and stroked the edge of the portal closed.

The walls glowed blue; a kind of blue that was so close to ultraviolet it seemed to float just off the surface of everything it touched. It added to the sense of scrutiny, as if a giant pipette would soon appear and squirt them with a biological agent to make them writhe as they boiled in their skins.

Mex wasted no time before pressing his palm to the second surface. It responded instantly, turning briefly porous to equalise atmospheres in an unnerving hiss of escaping gasses, and then to provide a wide opening, inviting them aboard the Suparna.

In front of Mex was a short corridor or shaft with spiralling handrails. Beyond was an open space of featureless white. Floating in the centre of the space were two figures of contrasting physiques. Mex flinched as he heard the unmistakable clatter of weapons being drawn from holsters. There was a faint crackle as multiple micro-generators built charge in unison. He turned to Bethan and her three man team. All four held fist-sized charge projectors with wide muzzles.

"Show some restraint, none of us will be popular if people get hurt."

Bethan nodded in acknowledgement, and lowered the weapon to her hip. The others followed her lead.

A voice emerged from the blue light, neither human nor machine but less than either; the timbre was male but without any sense of masculinity. Mex was thrown for a moment, lost in the paradox of an intricate simulation missing basic emotive inflection. He played catch-up on the message using the natural buffering of the aural receptors of his brain.

"Welcome aboard the Suparna. Please accept my apologies for our unkempt state; we have experienced some difficulties on our journey. Please come aboard and tell me how I may be of service."

Mex smiled a weak acknowledgement and reached out to the nearest handrail. It started to ripple, offering just enough grip to propel him towards the open space. The others followed suit, forming three spirals ascending into the light.

As they neared the end of the shaft the rail settled to bring them to a relative halt, just at the entrance to the open volume, which was revealed to be about twenty metres in diameter with three other similar exits.

The two figures were now clearly visible. A young woman floated just in front of the other, more unusual, individual. Her simple white smock was like an angel's gown as it drifted about her almost translucent presence. The image of divinity was only marred by the unpleasant red-brown stains on the fabric and pain-tinted shadows that hung below her eyes. She held herself upright and with her palms open at her side. She was clearly trying to look as non-threatening as possible, but the image was of one waiting to be crucified.

The second person was making no attempt to look innocent; the effort would have been futile. The iridescent skin could have been a fashion statement, and the physique that made barrels seem unnecessarily curvy might just have been a steroid experiment gone wrong, but the face was just plain alien. For Mex, who relied so heavily on reading people's faces, the lack of features was terrifying. His (Mex assumed it was male) eyes were shielded behind layers of translucent eyelids, and there was a slight rise where a nose should have been. A crease in the lower half of the face suggested a potential mouth, and that was the sum total of features which dared to disrupt the smooth purple of his skin. A tough sleeveless tunic and britches hid some of the excessive muscles from view, but his arms and neck were enough to make the point.

The pale woman smiled and tilted her head inquisitively. Mex felt like she had already made an opening statement, and he had missed it somehow, but he was sure nothing had been said aloud. "Hello, I'm Mex," he said. Even to his own ears this sounded grossly inadequate. "Mex Tyrian. I am here on behalf of Julienne Garland of MynCorp and the corporation vessel Svargaloka."

"Welcome Mex Tyrian, on behalf of Julienne Garland, MynCorp and the Svargaloka. That must keep you very busy." She was trying to sound amused, but Mex could read the tension in the way she clipped each sentence; her lungs holding slightly less air than she could judge. "What can we do for you?"

"We're looking for someone."

"Anyone in particular?"

Mex had known he was going to struggle at this point. Julienne had never told him the name of the Node, and he was not sure she even had clearance to know herself. It seemed likely to Mex he was talking to the Node now, and yet this confident young woman had nothing in common with his mental image of a near brain-dead child. Also, she was supposed to have been kidnapped by some high-tech terror cell, and not be wandering around with her own bodyguard. "The identity of the person is classified," was all he managed.

"Classified. That makes it a little hard for us to help."

"I'm sorry to get all authoritarian on you, but we don't really need your help. We are a task force instructed to take control of this rogue vessel, and place all those on board into protective custody."

The purple figure spoke for the first time. "Task force? Not much of a task force. I've seen two-year-old larvae more comfortable with a gun than this lot." A three-pronged flap of skin peeled back to reveal a circular hole surrounded by diamond-like teeth. The flaps quivered slightly as he sucked air to speak. "Shall I kill them now?"

Four weapons rose to shoulder level in the periphery of Mex's vision. Even Yakini and John had their hands on small holsters. Mex realised he was the only one on this side of the encounter not to have a weapon. He hoped it looked like a leadership thing rather than a matter of trust.

"Larvae?" The woman gave her companion a quizzical look. He bobbed his head in what could have been an approximation of a shrug. She continued, "I don't think so. We're just here to talk." Muscles reluctantly relaxed in his shoulders. "Maybe we should try some introductions. My companion is Bergur, formerly of the Eridanian ship the Ellida, I am Nomia and this," she waved a hand vaguely towards the ceiling, "is Kaamil."

Mex was not sure what Kaamil might be, but there was enough about the situation that he was confused about to let it go. Bethan leant into him and spoke softly. "With all due respect, can I just get on and arrest them?"

"I suppose so," he replied to her before looking back to Nomia. "I'm sorry about this but we really are going to reclaim this ship."

"I'm not sure he wants to be reclaimed. Kaamil seems to be enjoying his independence."

"I would be surprised if the Suparna was capable of enjoying very many things, even a new name, but it is the property of MynCorp and, as much as it goes against my basic instinct, they have the right to claim her back. Or, at least, what's left of her."

The disembodied voice of the ship penetrated the space from all directions, throwing millennia of predatory instinct into mild panic. "Nomia is correct. I really do not want to return to MynCorp service."

"Have you been tinkering with the ship's A.I.?" Mex asked Nomia.

"You really have not been very well instructed on the details of your mission," she replied cryptically.

"As I said it is not my mission. I am speaking on behalf of Julienne Garland."

"It sounds like she is the one we should be talking to. Where is she?"

"I'm here." Julienne's uniform was crumpled on her folded shoulders, as if she had lost weight since she put it on. Her face was a collage of emotions and involuntary thoughts, none of them pleasant, but she was functioning and moving forward from the rear of the group. "You are Node HG659885 of the MynCorp Nexus. You are corporate property, as is this ship. Anyone else on board is in violation of Terran corporate law, and their freedom is forfeit. Bethan, secure the prisoners. Yakini, secure the command centre." She turned away quickly, but not before Mex saw her will crumble and a tick start in the corner of her mouth. She made for the nearest corridor and vanished from sight as fast as was fitting.

There was a moment when nobody moved, and then discipline returned and everyone was busy, apart from Mex, who was reduced to his former role of observer. Mostly, he was relieved. Bergur looked as if he might resist, but eventually shrugged and allowed himself to be lead away. John and his technicians moved towards the rear of the ship muttering about antimatter containment systems and worst-case scenarios. Mex tried to scratch the nagging doubt which lay just out of reach in his mind. Eventually, he sighed in resignation and set off to find Julienne. He was sure her return to form was not going to be sustained. He glided up a corridor for a few tens of metres before passing an open aperture. Julienne had managed to secure herself to a sleeping cot and was curled up like a foetus. He entered the room and closed the portal making enough noise for her to know he was there.

"Julienne?"

No answer, but the knuckles clasping knees to her chest grew a shade paler.

"How're you doing? Is it getting any easier?"

No answer was necessary.

"You saved me back there, big time. The conversation was going south rapidly. I couldn't get my head round the idea of that woman being a Node. She almost shone from the intensity of her personality." He moved closer, hoping to offer some comfort through proximity.

"Tell Bethan to prepare to interrogate the Node." The voice was too strong to be emanating from such a feeble-looking creature, but Mex could hear the quiver of madness creeping into her words.

"She's called Nomia."

"Yes, Nomia. Tell Bethan she will lead the interview. I will observe and you, Mex, will watch from the Nexus."

"Okay, but are you sure you're up to it?"

"I will be. I have to be. I must fill the emptiness with something. If I can create new memories maybe I will stop missing the past I cannot see."

"I'll tell Bethan. Take your time. We'll wait until you are ready." He reached out a hand towards her back, but it hovered just above her shoulder lacking the conviction to make contact. She must have sensed his proximity. One china-white hand peeled itself free and took his hand, lowering it towards her shoulder. Once he could feel her warmth through the fabric of her uniform, her hand retreated to its former role. He let his hand rest for long enough for her feel to become familiar before slowly moving his hand across her shoulders towards her head. As his fingertips brushed over her neck she shuddered and released a deep sigh from tight lungs. He stroked her head until her breathing became less ragged. She did not turn her head or open her eyes.

Eventually, Julienne's orders drifted back to him, and he started to move towards the door.

"Mex," she whispered.

"Yes."

"Thank you."

"It's okay."

"I mean it."

"I know."

Chapter 9

"I'm telling you, there is nothing there." Mex was wearing his code glasses but he had temporarily taken them off to wave at Julienne.

"So you said, but you are suggesting that the scaffolding underpinning our whole reality has vanished. I'm not sure it would be possible for us to be having this conversation if it was true."

Julienne felt some of her old fire reigniting when she argued with Mex. It was not fair on him, but it made her feel so much better. Her mind felt like a sliver of a personality, the bulk of the memories and deeper brain function sliced away by an over-excited butcher.

There were four of them in the interview room. Bethan sat opposite Nomia, and was leading the questioning of the former Node. Mex sat at the far end of the table-like floor extrusion, with his mobile splice station set up in front of him. He was supposed to monitor the meeting from the Nexus to look for any attempts by Nomia to establish outside contact. Julienne was sat at the end nearest the door. She was holding herself together for the moment, but she wanted a quick exit route if the darkness descended.

Nomia seemed quite interested in their conversation and was ignoring the pending question from Bethan to listen. She raised a hand to head level and said, "I might be able to explain the paradox."

"You should concentrate on answering Bethan's questions." Julienne's patience was wafer-thin.

"Her questions make no sense."

Julienne nodded to Bethan who resumed trying to pry information from the former Node. "What is the name of the organisation that kidnapped you from the MynCorp Nexus headquarters on Earth?"

"There was no organisation." Nomia said calmly and with patience, but with enough of a patronising inflection to make Mex smother a smile.

"Tell me the names of any of your captors."

"To say I was kidnapped implies that I was taken against my wishes. The reality is, I asked to be taken, or at least, that is what he said; I have no real memory of the Nexus. A more accurate description of what occurred would be theft, because I was not in a sufficiently developed mental state to give or withhold consent and, as far as you are concerned, I am MynCorp property. So, let's stop playing games and stick to reality."

"Who is he?" Bethan leant closer, sensing a sliver of progress.

"He was José Sanchez."

"José Sanchez. Who did he work for?"

"MynCorp, I believe."

"What? Are you trying to suggest that MynCorp stole one of their own Nodes?"

"You speak of MynCorp as if it was a person. It is a collection of individuals, each with their own hopes and fears. MynCorp did not steal me, José liberated me."

"But he was acting on instructions from a MynCorp division?"

"Almost certainly not."

Bethan looked at Julienne, who nodded a confirmation. Bethan stood, gave a slight shake of her head and left the room. Julienne slid into the vacant chair, and tried to fill it without collapsing in on herself. Mex looked confused. "She has just gone to send a radio message to the Svargaloka, to see if we can find out anything about José Sanchez," Julienne asserted.

Mex nodded.

Julienne turned back to Nomia and spoke with a slow soft tone. Each word was a personal battle to be fought and won. "Where did you get the name Nomia from?"

"José gave it to me. It's the name of a naiad or water nymph. He said when I'm asleep I look like I should be in a pre-Raphaelite picture."

"Where is he now?"

"In our quarters. He's dead." There was a flicker of pain as she said it; a wound too grievous to hide.

"Killed by the Eridanians?"

"Yes, by one in particular."

"Shall we go and have a look at the body of your `liberator'?"

"As you wish, but I would rather start to talk about our future alliance."

Julienne studied the face of the smaller woman, searching for a hint of misdirection or mischief. Her sad eyes seemed strangely open, inviting Julienne to read her life story. Mex was a better reader of people than Julienne, but he seemed equally baffled by her attitude.

"There will be no alliance. We are taking you back to Earth. Back to the Nexus. This ship too, if it can be persuaded to move."

"You are at least partly right, but if we do not pool resources then there will not be a Nexus for me to be imprisoned in."

"Don't threaten me. Your cooperation is not optional." Julienne tried to feel anger but she felt too isolated to muster much venom, like a lost child raging against the darkness. "Mr Tyrian, please escort Nomia to her quarters."

243

Mex nudged himself free of the electrostatic field which gripped his clothes to the chair and gestured at Nomia to follow him. She complied without apparent resentment or even interest. Julienne waited until they were clear of the exit before allowing herself to curl up into a tight ball. The echoing vastness of her missing internal reality made her quake and shiver in terror, but the convulsions lasted only a few seconds this time. With a couple of strangled sobs she shook herself back into shape. She stroked the surface of the table to force it to reflect light. Convinced her pain was mostly invisible on the outside, she rose and followed Mex to Nomia's quarters, and the body of her mysterious benefactor.

She allowed herself to dally sufficiently to ensure she did not catch up until they were at the room Nomia had identified as her and José's quarters. Two of the security team were outside, looking bored but nervous, having accompanied Mex and Nomia as they floated along like some aquatic gallows march. When Julienne entered, Mex was crouched over a figure on a cot while Nomia drifted to one side, her head bowed so her eyes were not visible.

Mex somehow picked up her entrance and started talking. "He's been dead for a few days. Looks like a discharge weapon, there are plasma burns to the face."

The figure on the cot was like no terrorist Julienne had ever imagined. He had been in his mid forties with a distinctive shock of black hair. His skin maintained the olive tone of his Mediterranean ancestors, but the complexion, even accounting for the greyness of death, was that of a life spent bent over a splice terminal rather than working under the sun. The face was calm, under the mask of death, and oozed with the kind of wisdom which beckons for late fireside chats.

"This is the man that broke you out of the MynCorp Nexus headquarters? On his own?"

"Yes."

"He must be more than he looks."

"He was."

Bethan appeared at the room entrance gripping the side of the aperture to steady her flight. She gestured for a private conversation. Julienne joined her without saying anything else to Mex and Nomia. "What have you found?" she asked in a quiet tone.

"José Sanchez did work for MynCorp."

"Did?"

"He went missing on Triton almost a year ago."

"How do you go missing on a moon of Neptune?"

"Good question. It was assumed he wandered off absentmindedly and had an accident. He was an academic."

"What was an academic doing on a mining moon?"

"José Sanchez headed up the Xeno Exploitation Division. He went on several off-world sorties looking for alien technology. As far as I can tell he was a xeno-archaeologist."

"Why as far as you can tell?"

"The division was actually closed down over three years ago. All the data on the group has been archived at a very high security level. José Sanchez ended up in the Drop, but was hoisted out for the trip to Triton."

"Thanks Bethan. Good digging."

Bethan looked surprised at the praise and slightly concerned it might precede a reprimand. Julienne kicked herself for revealing her mental fragility; she needed to make more effort to appear her normal self. The head of security simply shrugged and said, "I'm at your disposal Ma'am."

Julienne smiled weakly and turned to rejoin Nomia.

Bethan interjected, "Would you like me to continue the interrogation?"

"No I'm feeling less sick now. I think I can handle it for a bit."

"As you wish." Bethan looked relieved to be dismissed as she left.

Mex and Nomia were deep in conversation when Julienne rejoined them. "It seems José might have stumbled on some alien artefact." Mex blurted out, any self control evaporated in his excitement.

"What? You mean on Triton?"

"And elsewhere."

"And this is connected to him breaking into a MynCorp facility?"

"We were just getting on to that bit." Mex looked back at Nomia who was trying to edge towards the door and away from the body that clearly meant a lot to her.

"Nomia." The voice of the pilot broke out from the walls, filling the space with sound. "They're trying to disconnect me from the ship. Help me."

Nomia turned on Julienne. "What are you doing to him?"

"I do not answer to you or the pilot. We are re-routing engine control to the ship's A.I.. The pilot is clearly compromised and we need to regain control of this wreck of a ship."

"You can't do that. If you remove his access to the ship you'll be leaving him in darkness. It would be like plucking out someone's eyes and chopping off their arms."

"It should be no concern of yours."

"Nomia, I can't feel the antimatter containment system. I'm losing control. I'm going to flush them out. I can't let them leave me in the dark." The pilot sounded desperate and the voice raised the hackles on the back of Julienne's neck; she felt his fear. No, that was not quite right. It felt more like her fear.

The words sank in. "What does he mean by flush them?"

Mex started to move for the door, shouting over his shoulder. "He's going to expose engineering to vacuum. He'll kill them all!"

*

The shaft down to the engineering decks ended in a wall of irregular grey. Metal had oozed out from the surrounding walls to close the gap, like a bad skin graft. A hand rail descended though the scarred surface, a faint bow wake frozen in the surrounding material.

Julienne released the undulating hand rail and let her momentum carry her the last few metres. The fabric covering her knees offered sufficient grip to prevent any bounce. She rubbed the metal, coaxing it towards transparency and making an imperfect window into the space beyond.

Nomia held back from the hastily erected barrier as if it might contaminate her with the pilot's fear. "Kaamil? Talk to me. What are you doing?" The two security guards had tried to flank her during their descent but it proved almost impossible in zero gravity. They had ended up following her sheepishly, offering an occasional cautionary grunt to remind her of their presence.

Mex joined Julienne at the temporary window shaped like a farewell wave. His right hand flowed out from the wrist across the darker grey of the metal, apparently anchoring him to the surface. The organic contradiction of the act distracted Julienne. She returned to visually penetrating the dark chaos below.

"I've been practising. Mostly at not throwing up," he said in acknowledgement of her glance. "What can you see? What's going on?"

"Just shadows. I can't work out what I'm seeing." Julienne cupped her hands around her eyes to reduce the distraction of background light. She caught flickers of black against slate grey but without focus or depth. Her eyes reached out towards infinity desperate for detail.

A face, white with curdled fear, appeared from the gloom, nose pressed to the same spot as hers. The mouth was strained open in a muted scream and one palm was slapping the window, one beat for every ten of her racing heart.

As her body recoiled from the wall, Julienne felt a strong sense she was staring into the face of her past; some moment of darkened terror, so extreme the image had become hard-wired into her brain, independent of all the missing memories. Nausea crept down from her brain and met bile rising from her stomach, as she cartwheeled from the wall. Then a slap of a palm against her ankle as Mex reeled her back in and held her against him for a moment longer than necessary, and yet strangely shorter than she wanted.

"What is it? What did you see?" he asked, his eyes darting from hers to the window and then back.

"A face." Speaking seemed unimaginably difficult. She wanted to curl into the tightest ball and concentrate on a white light. "It was one of John's technicians, Craig, I think." She made no move to return to the window, so Mex tentatively replaced her. He started speaking in the exaggerated and deliberate enunciation of someone mouthing words.

"Calm down. We are here to get you out."

As he spoke the space around his head flashed into white life. Mex blinked away from the window revealing a clear view of the engineering deck to Julienne and Nomia. John was shackled to a console about ten metres away, his head buried inside bundles of light fibres and quantum entanglement transceivers. The younger of his two assistants was handing him tools and manipulating a hard-form splice pad that he wore on an adjustable strap around his neck. The older man, Craig, was thumping on the impromptu wall and clearly using some language he had picked up on a remote colony. His face looked blood-red in the freshly restored lighting. He did not look particularly appeased by Mex's words.

"Looks like John's got the lights back on, but I don't like the look of that far bulkhead."

"What do you mean?" asked Nomia.

Julienne felt she should be answering questions, or at least asking them, but all she could do was hold herself to the wall and try to blink away the image of a face screaming in the dark.

Mex pointed through the window, as if there could be any other subject to his words. "Look how the wall is turning grey. It's getting porous. That's how these intelligent metals equalise pressures. The darkening is space showing through."

"How long do you think they've got?"

"Probably only seconds. It's a large volume and the metal is configured to vent atmosphere slowly but, still, the human body is not particularly good at dealing with low pressures."

Nomia turned away from the window, so Julienne could not see her expression but her voice betrayed her thoughts. "Kaamil. You must stop this now. You cannot kill these men. Kaamil? Are you listening to me?"

"I can hear you Nomia." The voice did not sound detached enough to Julienne; computer-controlled environments only felt comfortable while the controlling entity communicated in a calming manner. The human-like break in the pilot's voice was more disturbing than what he had to say. "They are taking away my eyes and ears. I tried to talk to them but it felt like they couldn't hear me, so I turned the lights off."

"I know Kaamil. I'm sorry but you have to save those men. If you kill them I won't be able to protect you."

Kaamil continued as if she had merely thought the words. "They just started ripping systems out. It was brutal and indiscriminate; parts of me were just vanishing or flashing in and out of existence with pulses of pain. I had no choice; the only system I still control in this part of the ship is the exoskeleton."

"That's what I'm talking about Kaamil. You have to seal the hull. Do you hear me Kaamil? Do it now!"

Mex looked intrigued at Nomia's attempt to move her voice into an authoritative register. It had clearly given him an idea and Julienne was not surprised when Mex started to speak. "Kaamil, this is Mex Tyrian."

His voice was compelling but not at an instinctive level, more that his words seemed to convey an undeniable logic and universal truth. Julienne had witnessed the same trick when she first met Mex; he had used it to woo the A.I. of a MynCorp building. Then it had been targeted at pure artificial intelligence. He was clearly trying to adjust the technique towards a hybrid mind. She wondered how much she could have resisted him if he had tried to sway her when her implants were fully operational. It was no longer an entirely frightening thought.

"Mr Tyrian, I am sorry it has come to this, but I cannot help but defend myself."

Mex seemed encouraged by the fact that Kaamil was acknowledging that he was speaking. "I am sorry as well, Kaamil. We have been inconsiderate, maybe treating you too much like a computer and not enough as a human being. I promise that will change from now on."

Mex looked at Julienne, maybe to see if he had overstepped a line, but Julienne kept her head buried in her arms and watched him from the tear-stained corner of one eye. His eyes back on the terrified face of Craig, he spoke as the technician's red-rimmed eyes started to bulge and his hand tore at his throat to remove a phantom blockage. "At this moment we both still have choices. If you kill those men then the chain of events are fixed and there will be more deaths."

"Don't leave me blind. I have to be able to see the stars."

"I understand and what you ask is reasonable. Let's talk."

"I can talk. I like talking to Nomia and José."

"Reassert atmosphere and we will all talk."

"Nomia?" the pilot sounded a light year away.

"Yes Kaamil," Nomia answered through a mouth wet with suppressed tears.

"Do you trust them?"

"They are the best hope for everything. We have to trust them."

The emotion trapped in the few words was too much to be simply about the life of one young woman and a psychotic ship's pilot. Julienne felt the hairs on the back of her neck move away from her skin and a cold fear took liberties with the exposed flesh.

*

The shift in power was tangible. They were all seated or tethered around an elliptical table in a hemispherical control room. The only thing that distinguished the room for control was the three metre wide projection of the pilot's head that hovered above one end of the table. The face was disarmingly mild-mannered but it was obviously not that of a man who had hung in the dark for a subjective decade. Mex tried his best to ignore the false image and concentrate on words and intonations.

He sat at the opposite end of the table to the head. He had chosen Yakini to aid him. They were the only members of the MynCorp expedition present; Bethan had kicked up a storm when he tried to order the others back to the shuttle. She had taken some persuading before he had managed to convince her they could not make progress while the ship was capable of forcing its point with a threat of violence. They had to maintain their centre of operations in the safe territory of the shuttle. He had made it clear that she was a more natural leader of the remaining party, while he was better acting as mediator given his recent meeting-of-minds with the ship and Nomia. He had promised to bring Julienne back to the shuttle as soon as she was able to be moved from the bed she had retreated to and then waved the others farewell. Yakini had been happy to accompany him and took a seat around the table with her usual nonchalance. Although, she did seem to lose her cool and the thread of the sentence she was halfway through delivering, when Bergur entered the room and sat opposite her. She seemed transfixed by the faintly purple mass of muscles and when he opened his mouth flaps to grunt a thank you for his release, Mex saw an unmistakable quiver run down her torso.

Nomia was right behind Bergur and took a seat next to the oblivious Yakini. As Nomia sat down she turned to Mex and immediately thanked him for the opportunity to talk. "Do the others know you have released Bergur?" she asked.

"I haven't mentioned it yet but I feel that we all have a stake in what happens next. Ms Garland has been taken ill, so I will be attempting to fill her shoes for a while. This is Yakini Akida, pilot for the Svargaloka. Yakini, this is Nomia and Bergur of the Eridanians." There were two nods and one grunt in reply. "I would like to be completely frank at this point, because although this is a negotiation table, there are minimum requirements before any of us can safely return to Earth."

If Yakini was shocked she hid it well behind her careful study of Bergur's every movement. He, in turn, appeared to be completely comfortable with the effect he was having on the slender human.

"Go ahead, Mr Tyrian. I suspect that our desires are more aligned than you might think."

"That seems unlikely but thank you, and Mex will do."

"Okay, what do you need, Mex?"

"If I'm going to avoid an extended residency in a MynCorp Drop chamber, then I need to get you back to Earth and in good health."

"That's fine."

"In addition, I'll need to take the ship back or have a really good reason as to why it had to be destroyed and proof that that was indeed what happened."

"The ship will return to Earth with us."

"Okay, this is pleasantly surprising and a little hard to reconcile with my expectations based on the earlier confrontations, but I'm sure the catch will become obvious. Lastly, I'll need the body of José and all his personal effects; somebody has to be able to extract a plausible explanation for the ease with which he took you from them."

"That's going to be more of a problem."

"I can understand your attachment but, to be harsh, he is dead and you're not. It would be foolish to add to your own difficulties just to hang onto his remains."

"It's more difficult than that. We have to jettison his body before we can return to Earth."

Bergur creased the skin between his eyes and inhaled to talk. "You still think you can make the jump once we are clear of the field?"

"I'm weeks away from significant drive capability," offered Kaamil.

Yakini looked at Mex, confirmed that she had not missed a chapter, and then cut through the three-way discussion like a song through a night forest. "Ease up there. Can you bring the newbies on board?"

"A lot of what I am about to say will seem unlikely, even ludicrous, but I hope you have seen enough already for you to at least hear me out." Nomia looked at Mex and Yakini each, in turn, and solicited nods of agreement. "José spent most of his life investigating a series of alien artefacts that were uncovered on a number of Solar System moons."

"Are we talking odd rock formations or genuine alien gizmos?" Mex interrupted.

"These would definitely count as gizmos on that scale. The exact nature is not really important but their purpose is. They were set out millions of years ago as a beacon for a completely different sort of people. The artefacts were a test to indicate a level of maturity within the human race."

"Like a technology test?"

"No not at all. That's the problem. These were to test our penetration into Verity Space."

"What?" said Mex.

"Verity Space. That's the stuff the Drop works in, isn't it? " queried Yakini.

Nomia looked to the floating face. "Kaamil, you do the encyclopaedia bit better than me."

"Certainly Nomia. At the most fundamental level the Universe is an uncertain place, every transition, every journey, has an associated probability. And wandering through this sea of probabilities, there is sentient life, unwittingly making decisions, collapsing possibility into certainty. The Downey field is the agent that binds the two, life to the Universe, free will to potential. The messenger is the Downey particle, communicating the observer's decision to the Universe and shaping reality."

"The Nodes are the key to the corporation's exploitation of the Downey field, as an infinitely extensible, organic computer. Mistaken for decades, possibly centuries, as autistic, they exist in a hybrid state of awareness. Most creatures are not able to perceive in a conscious way the Downey field that they form and mould. There is a limited interaction between the subconscious mind and the field, which influences the land of the Sandman and our nocturnal life."

"But the Nodes are able to experience the field in a waking state and act as an interface between the physical universe and the subconscious domain of the Downey field. The Drop is their land of dreams and daily reality; a featureless void penetrated and warped by every lifeform on the planet. The wider and more developed the perception of the being, the greater the effect on the local Downey field, the higher the energy of the Downey particles generated and the wider the area of possibilities realised."

Mex thought that the pilot sounded even less human when he spoke at length; there were none of the usual pauses or even breaths that hamper a human speaker using a larynx. "So these aliens are interested in our skill with the Downey field. To what end?"

Nomia resumed the explanation. "It is not a matter of interest. It is only via the Downey field that we can communicate with them because they only exist in Verity Space."

"That's absurd," Mex stated. "How can a creature exist in a space that is purely comprised of probability?"

"I admit it seems unlikely," she smiled at the unintended joke, "but I have experienced them."

"Can we let her finish?" Yakini placed a hand on the table in front of Mex.

"Of course."

"The artefacts were designed to be triggered when a mind with sufficient penetration into the Downey field entered the detection radius. José accidentally triggered the device."

"What? How? Did he fall asleep and have a particularly vivid nightmare?" Mex asked, showing, at least, that he had been paying attention.

"Something like that. It was my fault. I was lost in the Drop for years, mostly unconscious but partly aware. I stretched my mind out beyond the simple pathways of the Nexus looking for some way out. Perhaps because of his exposure to the artefacts, his sleeping mind was much better formed than any other I felt. I started to place suggestions into his mind, begging him to help me. The night before he rescued me from MynCorp, I reached out to his mind while he was in the artefact and the combination of our two minds triggered the device."

"What happened?"

"The aliens revealed themselves to José and showed him his full potential."

"When you say full potential," started Mex, "you mean the potential to walk into a secret MynCorp facility and whisk you away without anybody noticing?"

"There wasn't much walking involved, but that would be a good example."

Yakini seemed interested enough in the story to drag her avid eyes from

Bergur. "So, what happened when they realised they had been duped and José wasn't the prodigal son? Did they take his toys away?"

"I think that is a price either of us would have been happy to pay. It seems that, after some contemplation, they have decided that human-kind has diverged from some master plan and that they want to reset the experiment."

There were several heartbeats of silence. Each of them handled the shock in their own way. From Bergur and Kaamil's reaction they had not heard this level of detail before. Or, maybe, a shared understanding had been verbalised for the first time. Mex broke the silence. "Are you saying these aliens created the human race?"

Bergur gave Mex an open-mouthed stare that probably meant bafflement and said, "Did you not hear her just say that they are going to kill us all? Why are you worried about the validity of natural evolution?"

Yakini stepped in. "Yeah, lets concentrate on surviving and worry about the identity of our great-grand-papas later."

"I'm all for living a bit longer, but finding out we are bacteria on a laboratory Petri dish makes it all seem a bit less worthwhile." Mex scanned the other faces looking for some sense that he was not alone. "It's all about context. Our sense of self-worth is based on a huge number of assumptions about how we got to be who we are."

"I am who I am because I grew up on Mars. It these aliens turn out to be the spark of creation, I'll still be me." Yakini prodded herself in the chest defiantly.

Nomia raised a calming hand and continued. "I don't know whether they had a hand in the emergence of humans, but they certainly consider our development a pet project."

"So what happened next?"

"They decided to start resetting history at a point coincident with the beginning of their recent intervention." Mex looked blank so she added, "They tried to kill José."

"I thought Bergur's colleagues killed José."

"They did. José managed to put up a deterministic barrier around the ship. This volume of space is essentially invisible to the Eidolons but it stripped us of our ability to manipulate probability."

"Your ability? Eidolons?"

"Manipulation of the Downey field can be taught. At least, José was able to teach me. Bergur came up with the name Eidolons in one of his more poetic moments."

Yakini's eyes drifted back to Bergur and stayed there.

Mex continued to delve. "That explains why no technology with even a hint of intelligence made it near the Suparna. What do you think their next move might be?"

"If the first attack was a clue then they will choose a target and create an expanding sphere of influence. Everything that touches the sphere will revert to a pristine state."

"So why are we running to Earth? It seems a pretty obvious hiding place."

"We have to put up some sort of resistance. MynCorp has the most advanced technology. With my help we might be able to make some sort of fight."

"That doesn't sound like a particularly well-thought-through plan but it is definitely commendable."

"Don't patronise me. I've been through too much to just give up. Anyway, hiding is not much of an option for me. You've seen my impact on the

Downey field, I'm not exactly subtle."

"Okay, I'm sorry but it doesn't sound like a plan born from a consideration of self-preservation."

Mex felt Nomia's stare burrow into his eyes seeking out every betrayal and loyalty he had ever shirked. Finally, she said, "I have unfinished business with MynCorp. There are nine hundred and ninety three other Nodes in the Drop. Each of them is a divided mind imprisoned in an endless nightmare. With what I know, I can unite them with the part of their personality that has drifted in Verity Space since birth. Their freedom will be the cost of my help."

"Have you considered what MynCorp's price might be for defending the human race?" He did not want to patronise her again but she seemed so naively sure that the corporation would act rationally and not simply in terms of energy and benefit. "It will very likely cost you your freedom."

Nomia looked as if she was about to object but she showed good self-control. "We shall see," was all she said.

Mex coughed and moved the conversation back to immediate concerns. "What happened when José died? Did the Eidolons come back?"

Nomia snapped back to full attention. "No. The barrier stayed up. I believe it is centred on José's body. That's why we have to jettison his body."

"Won't we be vulnerable then?"

"Completely, but I intend to jump the ship to Earth, where you and Ms Garland will persuade MynCorp to join forces with us."

"I think you might have overestimated his influence," laughed Yakini.

"And probably Julienne's as well," added Mex sombrely.

"You might just have to work that voice of yours, Mex." Nomia gave Mex a knowing look and then turned to the floating face and said, "Kaamil, prepare to open José's cabin to vacuum."

"Wait a minute," demanded Mex. "Let's assume for the moment that we take everything you have said as fact; primarily because I've not got enough spare brain capacity to process a contradictory reality. You say as soon as we pass outside this barrier we are going to be under attack from the very uncertainty our universe is built on, and during that inevitable attack you are going to transport this entire ship across four light years of space using just your mind?"

"Yes."

"And we are all supposed to trust you on all of this?"

"Yes. It is essential."

"If you jettison the body and nothing happens will you let us take you and the ship back to Earth without any more resistance?"

"Once we are away from José's body you will have all the proof you need."

"Is that a yes?"

Nomia looked at Bergur who tipped his forehead in an approximation of a nod. "Yes," she answered.

A moment later, an aperture squeezed open above them and Bethan came tumbling into the space. She was bruised from hastily navigating in free fall. "Julienne. I came back for her when you didn't show. She's not in her room."

Nomia turned to Kaamil's head. "Kaamil, can you see Julienne? Is she still on board?"

There was no answer.

"Kaamil?"

"Look, the face isn't animating. The image is frozen." Bergur pointed at the fixed image hovering at the end of the table.

"Kaamil. Answer me." Nomia was starting to sound desperate. "Something is very wrong," she said to the group. "We need to get to his bunker."

"What about Julienne?" panted Bethan.

"This is not a coincidence," said Mex as a look of realisation crashed onto his face. "I knew something was wrong. There's a connection between Julienne and Kaamil. Something bad enough to make her tense every time he spoke."

Nomia pushed off for the open aperture, speaking as she flew. "Tell me she wouldn't."

*

There was something distinctly improbable about the way the sphere hung above them. Mex had to fight a lot of anti-predator firmware that had been cluttering his brain for a million generations, just to take his eyes from the matt black surface. He knew that matt was an inadequate description because it implied an absorption of light, with little or no reflection. The sphere seemed to repel light and, presumably, anything else that might dare to wander near its skin.

The space between the sphere and the surrounding spherical room was lit by what light spilt from the opening through which they had entered. It seemed to build in intensity as more light entered the annular space and circled, finding neither an exit nor something to absorb it.

It had taken dozens of minutes to find the entrance to the pilot's bunker. Yakini had eventually spotted an area of bulkhead spilling the ship's entrails into the corridor. The metal of the wall was trying to heal the wound that it had been cajoled into opening, but bundles of fibres had been folded till they snapped and bled light that was destined for distant parts of the ship.

"She's trying to follow the control signals to their source," Bethan had said.

They, in turn, followed the breadcrumbs of Julienne's savagery. From a distance the end of the corridor simply looked black. This, in itself, was unsettling after a day of living in a world of pure white. As they gathered around the entrance to the bunker they could see that the blackness had depth and texture. The wall of the chamber had the blue sheen of a black metal but in the centre of the fifty metre space was a blob of nothing, that eclipsed the surface beyond.

"How is it just hanging there?" Mex asked.

Yakini looked at him floating next to her, his legs drifting towards Nomia's face despite his efforts to stabilise himself with a handrail. She laughed. The sound seemed to be sucked into the dark space and vanish, the faintest echo bled back to them once per orbit of the central sphere.

"You know what I mean. It's not floating like we are. It's just too fixed. Anyway, even if it was floating, as soon as Kaamil powered up his engines the bunker would start bouncing off walls."

"It's a gravitational dipole," Bethan offered unhelpfully. When Mex looked baffled she continued, "The sphere and the containing wall repel each other gravitationally. It keeps the sphere perfectly centred. If the sphere drifts towards one wall, like during acceleration, the repulsive force on the nearest section of the wall builds up and pushes it back towards the centre."

"How's that possible?" Mex asked.

Nomia started to push past them both. "We've got to get to Kaamil."

Yakini held her shoulder with a gentleness that seemed more born from trepidation than concern. Nomia looked uncomfortable with the contact and Yakini withdrew the hand quickly but said, "Hear her out. The physics in there is not ordinary and neither are the things it can do. Normally, it isn't possible, gravity attracts and that's it, but the chamber is lined in a microfilm of a degenerate state of a neutron supersymmetry partner. It's usually only found in the final runaway fusion and gravitational chaos of massive supernovae. The gravitational dipole sends an implosive shock into the heart of the star that triggers the final core collapse."

"How does the pilot communicate with the ship if the sphere is just floating there? Surely, he needs a hard-line connection for critical systems." Mex waved down an impatient stare from Nomia.

"Aren't you supposed to be some sort of computer genius?" Mex had definitely not earned Bethan's deference yet.

"All just tools to me. I'm normally more interested in what you can do with it than how it works."

"Can you see those nodules spaced around the wall? They're photon and qubit entanglement transceivers. There will be similar devices within the sphere. He communicates with the ship via modulations of quantum entangled light and he is probably directly coupled to the main A.I. with shared states of an area of its memory."

"Okay, so how do we get to the sphere without being crushed or batted around?"

"Once you're on the sphere it will feel like a normal gravitational field but out here the field will give you quite a kick inwards. This opening should create a conical shadow in the field. If you head directly towards the sphere the acceleration should be tolerable."

"You not coming?"

"Not on your life. Ms Garland is probably doing us a favour dealing with the pilot. She'll give us orders when she needs help. In my experience, officers do not appreciate too much proactive thinking."

"And you think she is in a fit state to object?"

"What do you mean? I thought she just had a bout of travel sickness." Bethan's expression was a well-mastered dumb insolence.

Mex led Yakini and Nomia as they launched themselves from the opening toward the impassive sphere. He kept repeating to himself that Julienne had already done this and there was no puddle of human organs on the sphere, so she must have survived the fall, at least long enough to have wandered out of sight. He instantly felt a sense of falling from a great height but onto a ground that refused to reflect enough light to actually be visible. There was no gathering whistle of passing air to indicate acceleration, so Mex trusted to the physics he could not understand and tried not to stiffen his knees too much for the coming landing.

Pain flashed out from his ankle, ricocheting up his leg and into his stomach, where it mixed with the lump that had formed as soon as he had felt his weight for the first time after so many days without gravity. The starburst of light in front of his eyes pulsed in time with the alarm signals from the nerves of his feet.

Nomia landed with a grunt beside him, her waif-like frame obviously made of tougher stuff then the porcelain it resembled.

"Did that crack come from your leg?" she asked, remaining crouched but looking all around.

"Ankle, but I think it was just the joint adjusting to weight. Nothing broken." He tried to stand but the foreshortened horizon made his head spin. The sphere was fifteen metres across, which, combined with the near Earth gravity, made him feel like a roller coaster poised at the top of its run, a moment before plunging towards the ground.

"Maybe we should stick to crawling." Yakini had joined them without any fuss and was attempting to electrostatically weld a black cube to the sphere's surface.

Nomia started crawling in an apparently random direction. Mex nodded at the fist-sized cube. "What's that?" he asked.

"Nanobot scaffolding unit. They'll build us a ladder out of here while we find Ms Garland. I assume you weren't intending to fly out?" She grinned.

"Yakini, to be honest, I'm beyond limiting my options to just what's possible, but a ladder sounds a perfect backup plan. Is it working?"

"I didn't bring it from the Svargaloka. I had a little rummage after we got here. I don't like to be tech-free, it makes me feel vulnerable. You know, it's like being naked." Mex seemed reluctant to commit either way. "Anyhow, the technology on board seems to be working fine."

"Cool. Shall we follow Nomia?"

"I think we should, preferably before she catches up with our space-sick leader."

They shuffled after Nomia who was rapidly vanishing over the horizon. Mex estimated they had crawled over a third of the circumference before the top of Julienne's head bobbed into view. Another half a dozen shuffles and he could see the wreck of a human figure she held at arm's length. Her fingers were wrapped around the throat of the emaciated body, which hung limply, head lolling to one side and limbs draped across the surface of the sphere. The pair were side on as they approached and Mex could see the fractured remains of cabling jutting from the back of the figure at his neck and shoulders and above the wrist of his right arm. The other end of the wrecked conduits lay discarded around a person-sized opening in the surface of the sphere. Feeble packets of light, bleeding from shattered optical fibres, marked the hatch with pencil beams of white.

"Kaamil!" Nomia came to a stop, her hands covering her mouth and holding back a scream that rose behind her eyes.

Julienne looked their way, hatred and loathing still etched deeply into her face. The pilot continued to stare into Julienne's eyes, his own face a superposition of all the expressions he had avoided through many years of isolation, but mainly fear, regret and resignation.

Mex continued to crawl forward, Julienne tracking him as he approached. She made no move to keep him at bay but continued to slowly choke the remaining life from the pilot's throat.

"Julienne, think about what you're doing. Kaamil is a human being. You don't want to kill him," he said as he stopped two metres from the pair.

"You mean like he did me. Ripped me from my own sphere and squeezed the life from me before I had even known the beauty of interstellar flight."

"I don't understand."

"You wanted to know how I died, first time, before I was jacked into this computerised lump of flesh. Well, he killed me. He did it inside a pilot sphere, just like this one."

"I thought you had no memory of your first life. You think you were a pilot? How do you know?"

"Just nightmares. Dreams of darkness and a voice begging me to ignore the fear because it loved me. His voice." She shook Kaamil so that his head rocked to the other side. Mex could hear Nomia sobbing behind him. Julienne continued to shake Kaamil as she looked down at his grey-skinned body. "And then this face as I choked on blackness."

"How can you be sure? MynCorp have played with your mind so much anything could be true."

"I know that voice. I don't need memories to know that voice; the fear is ingrained in my head like a blood stain on my clothes."

A few rasping syllables squeezed from Kaamil's lips.

"He's trying to speak."

"I don't want to hear his voice any more."

"You have to hear him. He's no threat to you. You're in control of this situation but you need something more than dreams if you're going to be able to live with yourself."

Her grip eased enough for a rattle of air to slip between his teeth. "Julienne. Dreams." He sucked at air between each word. "I have had the same dream." The pilot gasped, the single sentence absorbing his available strength. His shoulders sagged still further, pulling his head back and making it appear as if he was offering his neck for sacrifice.

A look of disgust crossed Julienne's face as she looked at the pitiful husk of a human she held in her hands. Mex felt this was a significant improvement on the unadulterated rage it replaced. He tried to prise open an advantage. "Whoever he was and whatever he did, he is no longer that man. The first time he spoke to us, when we came aboard, I could hear the pain behind his words. I knew he wasn't pure A.I.; there was too much suppressed emotion in the background. However much MynCorp scrubbed his mind, the guilt remained. Whatever you do today is trivial compared to the accumulated damage of subconscious remorse, but you need to think about your future. If you kill him you will be ruining your second chance of a life."

Mex paused the few seconds it would take for his words to percolate through her anger before adding, "Let him go." He heard the inrush of breath as Yakini and Nomia tensed; he had slipped into a strong voice without even noticing. It was supposed to require a series of throat contractions to activate the implant, but he had made no deliberate attempt to do so. In fact, it was the last thing he wanted; Julienne had witnessed his parlour trick too many times to be unaware of what he had done.

Without any apparent decision of her own, Julienne started to lower Kaamil to the surface of the sphere. As her grip relaxed long choking breaths streamed into his lungs. She looked dazed like a sleepwalker waking in a strange place. The pilot started to talk in short rasping phrases. "I remember some of the dreams. I thought they might be memories but I couldn't be sure. Until I heard your name." Julienne continued to stare at him, as if she was surprised and revolted by what she found in her hands.

Kaamil ploughed on. "You were a cadet. So desperate to get away from everything you knew. The longing for the solitude of space was behind everything you did. I watched you from the isolation of my first ship. You were everything I was losing and the loneliness played on my mind. I thought I loved you. I did love you but I believed you loved me. I was sure you knew I was watching and you played with me." He paused as uncertainty and contradiction stole his words. "We ran away together," he continued. "Or, I kidnapped you. I can't be sure. I tried to join our minds, even though we were each in our own sphere. Something went wrong. I lost control of the ship, or you took control from me. I, my ship, was destroyed but both spheres survived. They came looking for us and found our spheres but I was no longer tied to mine. Someone opened me up and wrenched me back into a world of weight and pain. I think they tried to kill me. I hid and found you. I thought they had taken your memories, turned you against me, but now I'm not sure. I held you but you fought me. I don't know how you died but it was in my arms. I felt you leave me."

Julienne's eyes flicked back into focus and her head darted up to meet Mex's gaze. "You're trying to coerce me. You thought I wouldn't notice. You thought I was so weak-willed I would jump at your words like a pet computer? He has to die for what he did. It's the only way the dreams will stop." Her grip tightened again. Kaamil made no move to save himself. Death approached, clouding his eyes and hiding the regret that lurked in their depths.

"Julienne, stop. I'm sorry, I should never have used that voice. Please stop and listen to me. This is just me, no tricks. I don't want to lose you. Don't do this, stay with me." He reached out his right arm towards her, the palm held up, ready to take her hand. The arm grew slowly as he talked, offering his hand despite the gap between them. An overly-slender forearm and wrist extended beyond the cuff of his jacket. He knew that she was one person that would not feel disgust at the sight and he wanted to make it as easy as possible for her to take his hand and release her grip. "The last few weeks; I can't remember the last time I felt so alive. Even when we fight I want to be near you. It's been so long since I felt passionate about anything. Anyone. Stay with me, don't give them an excuse to wipe you clean again."

His hand was right in front of her now. She made no move to push him back but tightened her grip on the blue-grey of the pilot's neck. She just stared at him, contradiction making her gaze flit from one of his eyes to the other. "How could you want to be with me? I'm barely human."

"You are completely human. Only the strongest of spirits could endure what you have suffered and not become an automaton. You are the most human of us all."

"This is just another trick to distract me from doing what must be done. Leave me alone."

"I can't."

Try harder. Mex thought he heard some of her usual exasperation creep into the edges of her voice.

"Believe me. I've tried. I would love nothing more than to think I was here to save my own neck, but you've got under my skin; burrowed into my heart."

Julienne twitched and Mex cursed himself for the poor choice of words. He ploughed on, hoping that emotion would guide his tongue. "What I mean is that, I can't imagine you not being a part of my life and I think you feel the same." His arrogance caught the corner of her mouth and almost turned it up into a smile but she remained silent. *In for a penny*, thought Mex. "Come back to me. Resign your commission and we'll go somewhere unspoilt. Or, don't. We could have illicit liaisons in boutique hotels. Whatever you want. Do something for your own happiness, hell knows, you deserve that much."

Her eyes cleared enough for her to look around and feel the full depth of the despair she had sunk into. "I've thrown it all away. There were fears I might not be stable even with the implants and I've proved them all right. There's no going back now."

"Forget that rubbish. The only people that know what you're thinking of doing are right here. It's just you and me."

Her eyes flickered over Mex's shoulder to the two women crouched behind.

"Please don't hurt Kaamil any more." Nomia sobbed from behind her tear-stained hands.

"I wasn't even here," said Yakini backing away.

"Just you and me," Mex repeated. "Love me and let me love you," he said, stumbling over unfamiliar words.

Finally, she collapsed, falling towards the uncertain surface of the sphere. Mex's over-extended arm caught her in the centre of her back and took her weight by growing an additional elbow that braced against the ground. He curled her in that arm, pulling her towards him and pinning her arms. She shook with silent tears as he held her and kissed her face. The salt on her cheeks was like a knife cutting at his heart.

The pilot lay in a crumpled heap on the surface of the sphere that, for untold years, had been both a womb and a tomb. The cables that emerged from scarred wounds on his back and arm lay limply on the ground like a severed umbilical cord. His lungs pushed feebly at the weight of his ribs but there was no other movement.

Nomia shuffled past Mex, trying to run on her knees. She picked up the body that could not have weighed much more than hers and turned his face towards hers. "Kaamil, stay with us. What can we do?"

His lips moved in slow motion but the voice was barely audible even in the perfect silence of the bunker. "There is nothing you can do. I've been in the sphere for too long. My body will not survive long. Don't cry, this is a release for me. The brightness of the stars was not enough to eclipse the pain of memories."

"No, there has to be something I can do," Nomia protested, impudence making her shake in frustration.

"Just stay with me for a few minutes."

His eyes were already closing and his chest was moving in small ragged movements. Mex watched her slowly collapse as if his body grew heavier as the life drained from it. Her head started to shine with an internal light which extended into the air. The brightness spread until it encompassed her whole body. She slowly rose from the surface, the pilot held like a doll in her arms. Her body unfurled until she was floating upright in front of them, eyes closed and toes pointing down. Her lips parted and one word glided from her lips, like an angel taking flight.

"José."

Chapter 10

The first thing she felt, beyond the pain of losing Kaamil, was an entire universe of probability open up beneath her mind. Her perception leapt from the constraints of the three dimensions she had begrudgingly come to accept, to include a depth of everything that was possible. It was not a chronology as most people perceive options, but a superposition of all feasible decisions layered on top of everything she could see. The more complex the object, the more outlandish the permutations. The people around her shimmered with the semi-infinite number of collapsing quantum decisions made billions on billions of times each second. She felt the reclaimed power to reach out and pluck a world-line from any before her and force it into reality through nothing more than the might of her will.

The envelope of her mind stretched out to penetrate the far reaches of Verity Space and encompass all the rich colours of possibility. As she explored this lost kingdom she felt the searching feelers of a collection of probing minds. The thoughts of the Eidolons brushed against hers as they prodded the physical Universe through the sentient minds who bridged their world and the Universe of stars. She watched as the sleeping members of the Svargaloka's crew made the connection from the material world and dreamt of things which could not possibly be true. The Eidolons co-opted this bridge to stare into the physical Universe with eyes made of memories. They gazed through these minds, building a picture of where their favoured child had gone.

Nomia started to recoil into the confines of her mind. She felt another presence much closer to her physically and spiritually. It was like she felt a part of herself somewhere nearby. With all her instinctive understanding of possibility she failed to recognise the presence until he reached out for her and shared a single thought. *I'm coming.*

"José," she said aloud.

The sound of her own voice broke through the swelling emotions and brought her back to the physical world around her. She was floating above the surface of the sphere, her subconscious mind choosing to ignore the complex gravitational field around her. Kaamil was in her arms, the last sparks of life faltering and slowly snuffing themselves out. She reached into his body with her will and fanned the remaining embers. She chose the path for him which lead to the most life. The pilot stirred in her arms, restless as death tugged at his spirit with barbed tentacles.

There was a sigh of air nearby, and José stepped through from his death-room to the space next to her. She felt the awe of those stood below and shared it, her appreciation reinvigorated by longing and the pain of separation. She wished herself into his arms, embracing him physically and mentally, saving a tiny part of herself to satisfy the contradiction of still holding Kaamil and keeping him alive. José touched her mind and shared his thoughts, speaking aloud for the benefit of Yakini and Mex who watched with open mouths. Julienne lay broken in Mex's arms, confusion and fear leaking from half-closed eyes.

"I'm sorry, Nomia. I can feel the pain you suffered from my death. I wish I could have explained before I made the choice. I had to be dead for a while. I could not maintain the concentration required to keep up the barrier, and deal with interactions with the Eridanians. When the Captain decided to shoot me I tried to see the future possibilities unfold and the only one that would bring us together here and now was to die in that moment. Planning ahead is a skill we have both lost. We can see all the possibilities of now. So, it is hard to project into the future, but so many of our decisions were bringing destruction closer. Not just for us, but for all living things that started out on Earth."

José paused as if distracted by a distant sound, then he continued. "We don't have much time. We need to move the ship somewhere else."

"Not until we help Kaamil."

"We can restore him to the sphere."

"Not now. Not after today. We can't put him back in that hole again. I don't think his mind would survive it."

"I understand."

Nomia released Kaamil and he drifted back towards the sphere, but as gently as a falling feather. The stunted cables hanging from his neck and back started to move in waves like a snake. The stumps emerging from the sphere moved in the same way, as if they were still attached by an invisible fibre. Life pumped back into the skin of the pilot, pushing colour into his legs and arms. His body seemed to inflate with the colour and his eyes flickered with the energy of vitality. Finally, the slender cable hanging from his wrist started to writhe in time with a similar cable below. The ship shuddered as control circuits were renewed and, as his eyes opened, there was a deep intake of breath from the whole ship as if it had been dying with its pilot.

Finally, Kaamil stood, naked but unashamed. He looked around him and then his eyes clouded and he looked around again. "I can see you all and yet I can see stars. I don't understand."

"You don't need the isolation of the bunker any more," Nomia answered. "Your brain has adjusted to the two contradictory levels of stimulus. You can be with us and guide the ship at the same time. We have permanently linked your control and physiological tethers to those in the sphere. The areas of space at the end of each fibre are coincident as far as reality is concerned. You are free to roam as far or as near as you please. You are free."

"I thought I was dead. I thought I deserved to die. What do I do now?"

"Be my friend. Help us." Nomia reached out a faintly glowing arm.

"Always," Kaamil said as he gripped Nomia's hand in his.

Chapter 11

Mex glided into the command centre and nodded hello to Bergur and Yakini. Nomia and José were deep in silent conversation until he coughed an interruption.

"Julienne is sleeping in a cot. She's been though a lot and now her implants are starting to reactivate. They must have been in some deep self-repair mode."

"I'm sorry the barrier had such a drastic effect on her. It was not intended to harm anyone, just to hide us," José said.

"I know. To be honest, I think it will do her good, in the long run. I'm just glad words were enough to bring her around."

"Mex, you were fantastic. I think you saved Kaamil's life." Nomia touched the back of his hand in gratitude.

The pilot was sat at the end of the table exactly where his projected head had floated previously. When he spoke a look of intense concentration creased his face, as if his tongue was the most complex device to ever be wielded by a human. He aimed a few carefully constructed words at Mex. "I haven't had a chance to say thank you," he said, looking stiff and rigid in a sitting position but seemingly enjoying every muscle twinge.

"No problem." Mex bowed his head enough to dismiss the thanks as unnecessary while acknowledging the sentiment. "I think we have more urgent matters to discuss."

"True." José smiled. "Now Nomia doesn't have to flush my body into space to attempt a spatial jump we can get on."

Nomia's face flashed through pain to humour, "I still might if you ever act dead again," she retorted.

José's smile remained, but his tone became business-like. "Mex is right, we have very little time to prepare. Together, Nomia and I should be able to shift something as big as the Suparna."

"So what's the plan?" Yakini broke from running a long finger over the rippling colours of Bergur's arm and concentrated on the main conversation. Bergur seemed happy being the centre of her curiosity, and merely grunted an agreement from behind closed lip flaps.

"We jump to Earth. Storm into MynCorp headquarters. Convince them José and Nomia have god-like powers, and then explain why they should abandon profit in favour of saving the human race from an extinction threatened by a race of aliens who live in our dreams and computers. Foolproof." Mex finished with an ironic smile.

José seemed about to object or clarify when Kaamil raised a hand for silence. "The MynCorp shuttle is departing. My hull has resealed and physical contact with the shuttle has been lost."

"What?" Mex started to push off from his seat. "Can you tell if Julienne is still in her room?"

"Hang on a moment. I'll redirect a visual camera into that wall." There was a brief pause before Kaamil flashed up an image above the table. An empty cot with restraints cast aside flashed into view. "Sorry, Mr Tyrian, she has gone. I'm still getting used to aggregating multiple sources of stimuli. I've been negligent."

"It's not important. She's a very resourceful woman. Can you transmit on the same radio frequency we used to contact you before we first landed?"

"Of course. Speak when you are ready."

"Julienne?" Mex shouted. "Julienne, it's Mex, can you hear me?"

There was a brief pause before John's voice floated back. "Mex, it's John.

Are you okay? Where's Yakini?"

"I'm fine. We're both still on board the Suparna. Why are you leaving?"

There was a slight pause, and then John's voice returned with a stilted tone. "Sorry, I'm handing over to Ms Garland."

There was a brief click and then the voice changed. "This is Julienne Garland. The Suparna is now considered a pirate ship by MynCorp. I should warn you that any attempt to make contact with a corporation vessel or settlement will be considered an act of aggression."

"Julienne, it's Mex. What's going on?"

"I saw the danger the Node and her partner pose to MynCorp. It is my duty to get back to Earth and warn them. You and Yakini are considered compromised. I could not risk telling you, in case you attempted to prevent my departure."

"Julienne, what are you talking about? You know the real danger. The Eidolons and their plans to wipe out all human influence."

"I can only trust information I gathered after my implant started to recover. All my thoughts and experiences while the implant was not functioning are suspect, and seem to be tainted by subjective thought processes."

"So you're just leaving?"

There was a long pause. The next words carried more emotion than could be crammed into the poor bandwidth of the signal. "I'm sorry Mex." Then the connection was broken.

"Julienne!" Mex shouted into the dead connection.

Kaamil spoke again, confusion clouding his words. "There is something forming near the radio transmitter I have just been using. A stillness in the quantum vacuum. A hole and it's growing."

"We have to get out of here now." Nomia said as she turned to José and took his hands.

"We have to talk to Julienne. Without her we have no chance with MynCorp." Mex looked distraught and could barely restrain his urge to fly from the room.

"There is no time. If we don't go now there will be no future. Everybody quiet." José used the voice that had silenced years of lecture halls.

Mex bit his lips and folded his arms, but remained silent. Yakini took hold of one of Bergur's hands, without any objection from the impassive Eridanian, and put the other on Mex's arm.

*

A vast slab of metal hung in space surrounded by its own cloud of debris. One end of the construct appeared to have been chewed by some giant fire-breathing creature, which had left scorch marks around a myriad of deep gouges. The other end reflected the light of all the stars, but shifted slightly blue like a reflection in a still lake. Up close, the reflection formed a slowly shifting maze of textures and features, as if it was a machine rearranging itself to find a purpose. The machine, or vessel, hung motionless in space, offering no thrust to shift its position. It seemed content to drift in its inertial frame, static with respect to some nearby objects but screaming away from others at the speed of light. The Universe of physics in which it lived did not care much for absolutes.

Two other objects floated nearby, similar in scale to the first but full of energy and impatient with the stillness. One was smaller and the shape of a half coconut, the other was large, black and brutish. Great energies were building in this dark and powerful beast even as the dome-shaped craft was slowly pushing itself nearer. Forces were accumulating, preparing to throw it across the expanse of space using the sheer aggression of technology.

The Universe watched impassively as the first machine flickered once and then vanished. There was no inrush of atmosphere, there was no air to displace. There was no frothing of quantum eddies; these would continue regardless of what matter sat in the piece of space. The machine was simply gone.

The merest flicker of a galactic revolution later, the smaller machine entered the last vessel and colossal energy began to spew from one end. By this massive release of matter and power the vessel started to shift its inertial frame. Shortly after, forces beyond most natural phenomena erupted from the vessel and space itself was folded in half. As the fabric of the Universe tried to mend itself the vessel rode the spatial ripple towards a distant yellow star.

Epilogue

Ásta rubbed a nutrient gel into her skin as she climbed down from the surface dome. She believed in always feeding the skin algae after a UV session. "Look after your skin and your skin will look after you," her mother always used to say. Skin colour was a delicate matter of etiquette; too much purple and people would mistake her for a deca-head, too pink and potential partners would think her too sickly to raise strong children. Not that she really cared about children, but it was well-established that people tended to seek a mate with similar skin tone and she wanted the pick of the bunch.

The shaft down from the surface was several hundred metres long, and she had to use her hands to brake several times to keep her speed down. As a kid she had dared another child to wait until the last twenty metres before using the central pole as a break. He had broken both feet, but gathered so much kudos Ásta almost wished it had been her. For a while she thought she might like him romantically and, sitting together one night watching ammonia geysers glittering in the sunlight, he had confessed how long he cried with pain after they set his bones. She went off him and danger after that.

Ásta landed sedately at the bottom of the shaft, and started to walk the level towards her cave. She had to pass through the central core of the settlement. This was one of the very few entirely metal parts of the city, with all evidence of their icy home deliberately covered. Usually the square would be busy with people, talking about the state of the mines or the latest concerns over the stability of the sun, but not tonight. The Ellida was due back tomorrow and people were preparing for the return of Captain Finnur and his crew. Mostly this comprised of checking the militia had charged their weapons and that anything breakable was secured. The leader of the city would be excited at the thought of the technology and supplies Finnur was carrying. Then, within a few days they would be anxiously encouraging him back into space and reinforcing his crew with another couple of teenage renegades the mines had failed to tame.

Ásta stopped to gaze up at the statue as she always did. She never got used to the sight of the first Ice Breaker. This feeble-looking man who, along with a few hundred others, somehow managed to build a community under the ice. This figure, with his wire-thin neck and limbs devoid of almost any muscle, managed to dig down to the relative warmth. Then he sucked out enough resources from his surroundings not only to survive, but to build a new race of people. The quantity of oxygen he had needed to breathe each day, just to stay alive, was worth a small fortune even now, after all their advancements. She shuffled her domed head from side to side in wonder and sucked in atmosphere through her mouth flap.

A small imperfection in the metal of the statue caught her attention. A spherical blob of black protruding from the surface. She reached out a hand to touch it, both pairs of eyelids folding back to improve her sight. At the last moment she hesitated. Instinctively, she distrusted this void. It was not an imperfection but an absence, and it was growing rapidly.

Within a few heartbeats if was bigger than the statue and forcing her to step back towards the tunnels. She looked around for anyone else to verify her senses, but she was alone. As it grew she started to see detail inside the sphere. It was the blue of the deepest hole and fractured like compressed ice. In fact, it looked like the mines. The virgin ice of the city mines.

She did not understand why a sphere of ice should be growing within the city, but she knew something was very wrong. She reached up one hand to punch the subdermal communicator in her neck. The sphere accelerated in an explosive surge and touched her before she had time to form a word. A whimper of surprise escaped her lips and she was gone.

The sphere continued to expand, consuming the central city and then the outlying settlements. Finally, the entire moon was consumed. Then it pushed out into space growing faster and faster. In space it made no noticeable effect, a few trace elements were removed or rearranged, but on the planets or moons it touched the impact was dramatic. Epsilon Eridani Gamma was now a planet of solid ice. All the mines and colonies were gone without a trace. Even the gas bubbles that had slowly penetrated the ice over the lifetime of the colony had vanished. The planet was returned to the virgin state, exactly as it had been before the Ice Breakers had landed and claimed it for MynCorp. Every trace of sentient life, of human life, had been erased from the planet.

Once the Eridani system had been cleansed, the sphere stopped expanding and shrank back to the size of a human head. It span on the spot for a moment until it orientated itself with the stars. It seemed to lock onto one star in particular and having made its selection, began to move.

Continued in
Perfidy,
part two of
The Verity Trilogy.

Follow me at
@MarkOnAJolly
Or send me your thoughts:
TheVerityTrilogy@gmail.com
Anything from a one line comment to a full review.
Receive previews and offers on future instalments of
The Verity Trilogy.